WELCOME TO A

RICH PUBLICATIONS

PRESENTATION

FEATURING RICH GILMORE

Real Book Series
Chapter I

Punaney Galore

The sexiest story ever told...

RICH GILMORE

RICH PUBLICATIONS LLC

Published by
RICH PUBLICATIONS LLC
P.O.Box 118
Lyndhurst, NJ 07071

www.RichPublications.com

This is a work of fiction. Names, characters, places, and incidents either are the product of the author's imagination or used fictitously. Any remsemblance to actual persons, living or dead, events or locals are intended to give the fiction a sense of reality and authenticity. All are fictious events and incidents that did not occur or are set in the future.

Special book excerpts or customized printing can also be created to fit specific needs. For details write to RICH PUBLICATIONS LLC P.O. Box 118 Lyndhurst, NJ 07071

ISBN: 0-9746834-0-X
TXu1- 142 - 468

Written by Rich Gilmore
Edited by Tanisha Gilmore
Cover design by Rich Gilmore and Roland Hall

Printed in the United States of America

Special Thanks

I thank God for the Spirit, the Gift, and the Assignment,

Thanks to my wife and life partner Tanisha for holding your man down like a real Diva. Thanks for being a good thing for me and to me...Luv Ya Lil Mama,

To my right hand Tom a.k.a "T- Boogz" thanks for being in the pit and working the grind like a soldier... Let's get it my nucker.....

To my mother Adrienne, my sisters Kenya and Niya, my nieces Keniya, Meadow, and Raven...luv y'all

I would like to send a special thanks to every African American writer, artist, thinker, business great, and publisher past and present, for paving the way and for opening the doors that I run through. I will continue to move us forward raising the bar as I go.

Thank You: Terry McMillian, Richard Wright, Bishop T.D. Jakes, Federick K. Price, Carl Weber, Earl Graves, John Johnson, Iyanla Vanzant, Toni Morrison, Jesse Jackson, Omar Tyree, Eric Jerome Dickey, Zane, Walter Moscly, Iccberg Slim, Donald Goines, Shannon Holmes, Terri Woods, E. Lynn Harris, Mary Monroe, Vickie Stringer, Nikki Turner, Bishop Eddie E. Long, Oprah Winfrey, Bob Johnson, Malcom X, Russell Simmons, Martin Luther King JR, Michael Baisden...And to all my fellow authors, publishers, positive people, and business greats in the "game". Keep doing the thing and continued success.

SPECIAL BIG THANKS

TO YOU

THE READER....

Other Hot Books by Rich Gilmore

Punaney Galore

INTRODUCTION

DENALI

How much ass is enough for one nigga? How many women does a man have to unfaithfully lay down with before he can faithfully stand with one? I'm saying, how much fire can a man play with before his balls catch on fire? Well as of today I'm still trying to figure that shit out.

I'm a thirty one year old, tall dark and handsome single brother, with enough money to buy a Third World country. I stand six feet three inches tall and have a slender but muscular one hundred and eighty five pound frame. I got that sleek Michael Jordan look happening to perfection and the ladies love it. I always keep my head freshly shaved, with my pencil thin goatee shaped up. I also rock a five carat platinum stud in my left ear.

I get money in a variety of ways but all of my money is legal and clean. Shh..it, there are too many niggas dead and beating their dick behind bars because they got caught chasing dirty gold. Besides, I learned early on that money is the easiest thing to have in this country once you create value for other people. This is "America America", the land of long paper, right? So I gotta get it and be about it.

I own seven walk up apartment buildings in Harlem and in the Bronx. I also own several neighborhood businesses and I have a stock portfolio that would make Warren Buffet jealous which my man Yes manages for me. But of all my business enterprises my nightclubs are my golden goose. I own two of the hottest spots in New York City. The Kingdome and the Boom Boom Room are mine and they keep money rolling in faster than I can spend it. I have to be one of the hottest niggas in the city next to Donald

Trump, Jay Z, and Puffy. I guess that explains why chicks are always chasing my cars down and offering to do me sexual favors. So you better believe that my nights are always full of soft lips, thick hips, pretty legs, and stimulated clits...

AKIL

They call me "sexual chocolate" and I hate that damn name. I can't help the fact that my skin is smoother than a newborn's ass and I have that good ole dark African skin tone. They used to call me "A-Black", but I out grew that name growing up.

My dreads are now shoulder length and my beard is always diced up to perfection. I have that Afro-Centric Eric Benet and Maxwell vibe going on but I'm as gutter as DMX. My good looks are always getting me into trouble with the ladies. Unlike my peoples Denali and Yes, I'm a married man.

I have been married to my college sweetheart Sole`, for the last eight years. We married young because she got pregnant our senior year in college. She went to Morgan State out in Baltimore while I remained here in the city and went to Hunter College. At the time she was pregnant Denali and Yes tried to convince my simple ass that the baby wasn't mine. They said that I shouldn't get married because of a baby anyway. At the time I was too stubborn to listen. I was also raised to think differently about the situation. My father said if I was man enough to sleep with Sole` and get her pregnant, then I should be man enough to commit to her and be a father.

Boy how I wish I would've listened to my stupid ass friends and not my father on that call. One month after I said, "I do" and married Sole` she had a miscarriage and lost the baby. So at twenty two years old, I was married, a college graduate, but crazy hot in the ass. I was legally married to Sole` according to the marriage license and ceremony we had at the church but I was still a single man at heart. Shit, I figured no piece of paper or ring was gonna stop me from doing my thing. Nothing was gonna stop me from doing me.

At twenty two, I was the world's ultimate married bachelor. And don't you even fix your mouth to ask that stupid ass question people always ask a cheating married man. Of course I love my wife...

YES

I'm the beige brother of our crew. I don't know how many times someone has approached me on the street asking for my autograph mistaking me for Christopher Williams. Growing up when light skinned brothers were the shit, I'm telling y'all I was the man. I milked that silly phase for all it was and definitely had more than my fair share of women. I had mothers, sisters, daughters, aunts, shit I even ran through my share of wives. I figured if poppa wasn't home, a nigga was coming over for more than just a little dinner. I always said that if a nigga couldn't satisfy his woman he had a problem on his hands that I could solve for him.

I'm actually the one who introduced Denali and Akil to the "game". Even though they would never admit it, I was the one who got them their first piece of ass. It was me who cut them their first piece of pie. I remember it all just like it was yesterday. It was the summer of '83, I was fifteen, Denali was fourteen, and Akil's scared ass was only thirteen at the time.

My uncle Sugar, who was a pimp at the time when 42nd street was the original "sin city", had invited us to a party at his luxurious brownstone. My uncle Sugar had this brownstone on 117th between Lenox and Eighth Ave that he had converted into a whorehouse. When we arrived the place was packed with neatly but flamboyantly dressed men, all wearing loud flavored suits.

Some of the men there were wearing curls, some were sporting thick finger waves in their hair, but the majority of them were still rocking the seventies afro looking like Doctor J in his ABA days.

They were all handsome men that possessed a mesmerizing quality and presence about themselves. Somehow, even in a room full of the city's elite my uncle Sugar stood tall above them all. Sugar was still "the man" among "the men". The party was packed with women in every room, out numbering the men at least five to one. Oh, and when I say women, I mean some fine ass women. I had never seen so much beauty and booty before in all my young horny years.

The place was cloudy with reefer smoke and that Teddy P was playing loudly in the background as the red and blue lights lit up every room. My uncle Sugar who at the time couldn't have been more than twenty five was the wealthiest, smoothest, and the most charismatic man I had ever known. He had a way with words and was a math whiz. Instead of using what he had in a positive way, like going on to college and becoming an engineer or something, Sugar decided to pimp women and be a hustler.

My uncle Sugar was the man on the streets and everybody knew it. He had the baddest bitches, slickest wheels, and the most money in his deep pockets. Sugar was legendary on the streets of Harlem, right along with Pee Wee Kirkland and Nicky Barnes. My uncle lived by the fast streets and died by the streets at the tender age of twenty eight.

Sugar died at the hands of an angry hustler who wasn't mad because of business reasons, but personal ones. My uncle Sugar had slept with this man's wife and then turned dude's nineteen year old sister out. Sugar put his "pimp" on her and had shorty turning tricks for him out on the track. What can I say? Sugar possessed a magic with the ladies.

When word got back to homeboy that Sugar fucked his wife and had his sister on the track turning tricks, dude just lost it. Homeboy hunted my uncle down like a bloodhound and put seven hot ones into Sugar's head, once he caught Sugar slippin'. To add insult to injury, the nigga then cut Sugar's dick off and buried it in his mouth. Homeboy definitely sent a message for the police and streets to see.

Hearing about that should have scared me straight, but it didn't. I still wanted to be like my uncle Sugar. I just didn't want to end up in an abandoned building dead with eight inches of my dick in my mouth. My uncle taught me everything I knew about women. So I was way more advanced than Denali and Akil when

Sugar invited us into his special room, to be entertained by six of his baddest bitches. Sunshine, Almond, and Tasty, along with three more of his top moneymakers, were the entertainment.

When we got to the room the ladies immediately started dancing, undressing, and caressing us like we were Big Willy's. They made sure that it was two of them to one of us as we started doing our thing. I will never forget the look on Akil's innocent face. Dude looked like he was gonna shit in his pants, as Tasty took her clothes off and invited him to have a taste.

Denali has always had a laid back nature about his, but son was happier than a kid in a candy store as Almond undressed him exposing his bird chest to the room. There we were three horny but inexperienced teens in a room with six full figured, mature ass women. Sunshine, Almond, and Tasty along with their three sexy ass friends taught us more about sex in one night than my uncle and his friends could teach us over a lifetime.

We kissed, licked, sucked, and penetrated every hole the ladies offered us as we exchanged partners and positions, for five freaky hours. What a way to get initiated into the "game", an orgy with six bad ass prostitutes. From that day on me, Denali, and Akil would never look at women or sex in a loving way. Shit how could we...

CHAPTER 1

DENALI

Being raised by my wise grandmother taught me a lot about old school values and living principles. My grandmother was forced to raise me because my parents were tragically killed in a plane crash on their way home from a vacation trip. My parents were taken away from me at the tender age of six years old. The lost of my parents really broke my heart. It just shut me down emotionally.

At the time, I was mad at the world and especially mad with God. I couldn't comprehend, why God would take my perfect parents away from me, like I thought he did. My parents were the best parents in the world before they died. They were wise enough to leave me a trust fund worth one hundred thousand dollars. But by the time the life insurance monies and the twelve years of interest were added on, the fund ballooned to three hundred and twenty two thousand dollars. I actually used that money to pay for college, before I dropped out of school to build my business empire.

As a kid, I loved to party, dance, and play basketball. I was always well dressed and the center of attention. So I never had a problem with popularity or getting girls. I was well known and respected in the five boroughs, way before I started stuntin`and buying up the city.

Growing up, my grandmother would always talk to me about two things: Women and money.

My grandmother would say, "There are two things that money and women can do for a man. They can give him confidence or drive him crazy." Grandma was always on point with her advice, especially

14

about money and women. It seems like the more money I make the more I see housewives turn ho. It's like the more money I make, the more I see people trip all over themselves, trying to get on my good side.

At times the whole scene is disgusting. Especially, when the same muthafuckas, who wouldn't whip my ass as a baby, now want to kiss it for a "few dollars". It never ceases to amaze me the things women will do for a nigga with paper. If I really wanted to, I can get my dick sucked in the middle of a church service on Easter Sunday. I'm telling y'all, some broads are just that thirsty for the paper. Trust me, I ain't trying to glorify my shit, but it's that serious for a nigga.

Before my grandmother passed she would always talk to me about self-determination, and never allowing someone's ignorance or foolishness to stop me from being successful. It's funny because at the time my grandmother used to burn a hole in my damn head with all of her "black man/white man" psychology. I now appreciate and apply everything she ever taught me to my business operations. Grandma was right, "They can't stop you if you control yourself".

Before my parents died they were the owners of two soul food restaurants in Harlem. They were also very active in the community. They say, my parents were always feeding the homeless and helping out those who didn't have. My parents believed in family and community so they did whatever they could to make Black America a better place.

The entrepreneurial spirit has always been in my family. My grandfather owned a pool hall and liquor store in his day. My grandfather was a self taught and well read Black man, who believed every man should control his destiny in this life. He taught my father that the key to freedom, is education and control over ones money flow.

They say the Casanova spirit must've also been in the male genes. Rumor has it that my grandfather and father were known to have stepped out late, many a night, on my grandmother and mother. They say my father was a great man, who did a lot to improve the community, but word is, my father was also extra sweet on the ladies.

15

I guess like father like son because I can also make a dollar out of fifteen cents. And I too have a sweet tooth and special craving for the honeys...

AKIL

Growing up, writing has always been my niche. In school I won just about every poetry and writing contest I entered. So it was only natural that I became a writer later on in life. I'm now an entertainment writer for Brother Magazine. I also do some freelance work for the New Yorker, the Village Voice, and for the Amsterdam News. Not to mention, I authored two best selling books. So I always see a fat check, every first and fifteen of the month.

Growing up, I knew I would always be successful at whatever I did. My parents left me no choice. My parents taught me that failure is a word for losers. So I never ever conceived of not accomplishing my goals. My parents also showed me how to believe in God and taught me the value of hard work. My parents have been together since forever. As a result, I've always had a healthy image of what a loving relationship "should" look like. Although my parent's marriage isn't perfect by any standard, I never recall them being abusive, whether physically or emotionally towards one another. Well at least not in front of my ass. They didn't do any of that shit in front of me.

I've been blessed, to have grown up in a nurturing environment with my younger brother Jalil. Jalil is eighteen months younger than I am. He is now a film producer out in LA. Jalil is one of those first class "Hollywood" niggas. He's one of those niggas, all into the interracial "Los Angeles" relationship thing. I don't have anything against who he dates. I really don't care who he marries. Especially since a few of my jumpoffs have been bunnies.

I don't fuck with Jalil anymore because he completely lost his swagger. By the way Jalil acts now, you would never know the rabbit grew up in the "hood". Niggas piss me off when they move out of the hood and get light in the ass. I don't care if Jalil is my brother or not. Until he gets his soul back, I'm finished with the dude.

My father worked as a police officer and my mother as a high school English teacher, so I've always been around "real" models. Growing up, I never wanted to become an athlete or entertainer, like so many other kids on the block. Well, there was that phase I went through when the Sugar Hill Gang and Melly Mel hit, and I wanted to become a rapper. But other than that, my parents have always taught me to "stay out of the box."

Denali and Yes have been my best friends since pre K. We are more like brothers than friends. I know that they would die for me if they had to, and I would do the same for them. Growing up, I wasn't as wild and crazy as Denali and Yes. Those two niggas would fuck anything soft, with a sexy motion. Unlike Denali and Yes, I always wanted a relationship with a female before I had sex with her. I was taught to respect the young lady before we "lay in between the sheets". But that shit completely changed the more I hung around Denali and Yes' horny asses. Now that I think about it, those dudes brought the playa out of me...

YES

Growing up, I was the man of our household. It was only me, my twin sisters Keisha and Iesha, and my mother, but we wanted for nothing. My mother was a young extremely attractive administrative assistant at Charles Schwab. She knew and taught us all about personal finance and economics. My moms did such a good job that I went on to become a stockbroker after college. Meanwhile, my sister Iesha is an investment banker and Keisha is a bank manager out in Detroit.

My mother made it her business to instill in us discipline and perseverance. I guess that's why I'm such a good stockbroker today. I won't take "no" for an answer and I will work until I drop. My moms always dated men that had lots of money. The type of men that were eager to trick it lavishly on her and her kids. I think my moms made a conscious effort to only bring professional black men around me and my sisters. I guess moms knew how much I craved for male attention. My moms knew how much I admired my uncle Sugar, before he was murdered.

My mother never wanted me hanging around my uncle Sugar. Moms didn't approve of Sugar's lifestyle or of how he treated women. But Sugar was still her little brother and my uncle. So she cut me some slack. My mother always said, "A man can make and live with his own decisions." That's why, she allowed me to do my own thing and make my own calls growing up.

I was never a one women man. I always thought that was for "squares". My motto was "why only have one if you want to have fun." That explains why I always needed at least four or five freaks to juggle. My uncle Sugar said, "A man should always have at least four thoroughbreds in his stable. One woman to love him, one woman that freaks him, another that makes him look good, and then one to pay him for his services." I guess that explains why Sugar always had a church going woman, a prostitute, some red bone on his arm, and some young thang that he was preparing for the track.

Sugar's philosophy must've rubbed off on me. To this day I always keep at least five bitches in rotation...

CHAPTER 2

New Years Eve 2000

DENALI

Every night my clubs are packed with a bunch of "pretenders". I always get a club full of broke ass, no benefits having, best friend's clothes wearing, niggas. That be frontin' hard for some freak ass, two to three kids, four to five baby father having, chicken headed females. But tonight is New Years Eve. We are hours away from a new millennium. Everybody and their mother's mother must have rented something for show, or the true playas have really come out tonight.

It's definitely a car show outside and more limos lined up than prom night. Every Benz from the C to G classes are parked out front, or looking for a parking spot on these crowded city streets. There are enough Lexus' outside to run a car dealership and enough big boy trucks to go to war in Iraq with. Even though Jack Frost is outside touching niggas, the ladies are still out showing off their thick asses, in the tennis skirts underneath their furs. Even though its Eskimo weather outside, the ladies are still wearing the tight fitted DKNY, Chanel, and all of that other designer shit, people put on their back to have an identity.

One of my bouncers Tyrone, who we call T-Boogie told me that Veronica, my first baby's mother wants VIP treatment tonight for her and the five platinum digging ho's she brought in here with her. Now Veronica is drama central all the way. I'm talking "ghetto fabulous" with a capital "G". Veronica is the mother of my son Donte`. Veronica's mind isn't right so she fails to realize that although we have a baby together, that I'm not fuckin` with her like that. I didn't want her ass yesterday, don't want her ass today, and don't plan on wanting her tomorrow.

Veronica is the only chick that played her cards right and won big on a nigga. Veronica likes to smoke that purple too, so we would always be lifted when we would bang out. So on one night, I fuck around and gave Veronica a little too much loving.

So now she can proudly strut around the city like she's the shit because she caught the biggest fish in the pond. Now, that would be me and my money.

Veronica is my baby mama drama to the tenth power. I think any nigga that is really getting it out here, has at least one Veronica to deal with. To this day, Veronica is the only piece of ass that I ever regret having.

Me and Veronica only got up about three times. But one time is all it takes to get caught up. So one night I got caught slippin' and gave Veronica a son. Veronica now uses our son as bait to get what she wants from me and out of life. But I'm nobody's fool. I take good care of my little man. My son wants for nothing materially. I want to be more involved in Donte's life emotionally, but Veronica moved them way out to Connecticut to inconvenience my ass. I guess if I really wanted to I would be more involved. It's Veronica's mind games and bullshit that I don't want to deal with.

I now just deposit five grand a month into her bank account to take care of Donte` and for their household expenses. Plus, I bought Veronica that new 2000 Chevy Tahoe she drives around town. But with Veronica it's never enough. She comes from a family of gold diggers. A bunch of model looking bitches that know exactly how to go deep into a nigga's pocket. I can't front, Veronica is a beautiful looking girl. She's half black and half Brazilian, so physically she is awesome. But all that Veronica is physically goes out the window once you really get to know her and watch how she moves.

Veronica is a manipulator who trapped me into getting her

pregnant. I say that because to my recollection, I always had the jimmy on extra tight. I never lay down with a broad without strapping up. But then again I was probably lifted off of the hydro and forgot to tie it on that night. Oh, and if you need to know, I rock magnums baby. Shit ain't nothing little or average about my dealings, *YOU KNOW*...

AKIL

I love my wife Sole` dearly. But there is so much ass to lust out here that I'm always being broken down. My man Rich from work, always used to tell me that lust is never satisfied. He also said, "A man that lust will lose what he loves because of it." Rich is a real good brother. He's one of the few younger men I admire and look up to.

Even though he is younger than I am, I respect the cat a great deal. My man Rich, has really got his mind right and appears to have the family thing in order. He is married to a lovely sister named Anya und has a little girl named Joy. Me and Sole` use to spend a lot of time with Rich and Anya, but they moved down to Atlanta last year. Now we just talk on the phone.

Tonight, I plan on giving Sole` a new wedding ring to replace that one carat on her finger now. When we married I was only twenty two and my money was shorter than a fat baby's dick at the time. Today, my days are brighter. I'm now in a position to buy Sole` damn near anything she wants. Shit, I'm no fool. I know I have to do something to save our marriage. Especially as much as I have been fuckin` up lately...

SOLE`

I'm really growing tired of Akil's broken promises, inconsistency, and questionable behavior. He knows that he is my first and only everything. And I think his ass takes full advantage of that. I've forgiven Akil more than I probably should have at this point. I guess that's why he continues to ruin our marriage with his bullshit. I know the average woman would have left his black ass by now. But

21

I meant what I said at that altar. I know that if I wanted to I could have any man that I choose to have.

I'm five feet five inches tall, with jet black long straight hair that comes down to the middle of my back. I have soft hazel eyes, flawless caramel colored skin, with two little girl dimples on my cheeks. Men are always tripping over themselves whenever they see me because I can also fill out a pair of jeans with the best of them. And I do mean with the *best of them*. I've also been told that my walk is one of my best assets. Men say that I show them what heaven looks like, with my walk. I can't lie, I have hips for days.

I'm always being propositioned by some man, asking to buy me this or saying he can do that for me. It's so bad, even the women are checking for me on a regular basis. So if you're wondering, doing better for myself isn't the issue. I'm intelligent, sexy, and a successful business owner. But none of that means anything because I love my husband Akil.

I do know one thing, I'm not about to love a man more than I love my damn self. I don't care who that man might be, father or husband. I'm not about to do it. Lately I've been hanging out with my sorority sisters Michelle and Dana. We all go way back and we still enjoy each other's company like we all just met yesterday. We do all types of things from comedy clubs to doing community service together.

We even took a "ladies only" trip, out to Jamaica a few months ago. I met some fine ass brothers out there. The only thing is, I already have a fine ass man at home. There isn't much that another man can do for me physically. Even though Akil gets on my last nerve from time to time, I still look at that man and get moist and hot all over. In Jamaica, we met all types of men that had it going on. One of the guys I met was actually from New York. He said he lived in Brooklyn, but I forget dude's name.

I know one thing, I could never forget that body and the pearly white smile that made my kitty cat happy, as we talked. I've never ever cheated on Akil, but lately I've been tempted like Jesus in the wilderness. The sex with Akil is still spine tingling. I mean, he can still take me there, but the emotional intimacy is gone. I don't know what to expect for the New Year. But if shit don't change around here, I'll be making some changes ASAP. I'm not about to go through another half ass year of marriage with Akil. It's either all or nothing this year. I ain't going for the bullshit anymore...

YES

As I pull up in front of the Kingdome in my new chromed out CL500 Benz, I see more women with their asses out than a rap video shoot. Bitches always lose their cool on club night baring it all. But a nigga ain't mad at nobody.

After I parked my car, I walk through the clubs door. I then see Akil and Sole`, looking like new money, strolling through the crowd. They were making their way to the dance floor, as DJ Kid Capri was playing that Frankie Beverly and Maze "Before I let go", driving the dance floor crazy.

Damn, it's jumping off up in here tonight, I thought. The Kingdome is one of the few clubs in the city where people actually come to dance and not to floss. But tonight it's off the hook up in here.

I don't know how long I'll be doing the VIP thing tonight. I want to mingle with the common folk. I want to get my party on with my nine to five, twenty to fifty five thousand dollars a year people.

I've worked hard myself this year and have finally joined the seven figure a year broker's club. So I plan on celebrating like it's not only New Years Eve but my birthday as well.

"Happy New Years babyboy. Good to see your pretty ass showed up tonight. I called your plantation earlier and they said you were already gone for the evening." Denali said jokingly, as he greeted me smiling from ear to ear. "Shut up nigga. I've done told you about the plantation shit." I said as I gave Denali a brotherly embrace.

Me, Denali, and Akil are always crackin` on each other like we did as kids. It doesn't matter that we are now rich, successful, and powerful men in our fields. All of that means nothing because we were friends and brothers before the money and lifestyle. I always

23

said that Denali could be a stand up comedian if he wanted to. Lee is very sharp and witty. Denali can put a funny spin on anything. I guess with all that he has gone through, you learn to laugh at life or cry and die.

"You know I'm just fuckin` wit you nigga." Lee said as we looked at the crowded dance floor from his bird's eye office view.

"Man I've been at work with my sleeves up trying to catch up with you money bucks." I said to Denali teasing him for having so much damn money. We then just stood there for a few minutes, watching the sexy ladies on the dance floor. "White man got you working hard, you're a good slave dawg. I suppose you're a house nigga because you all light skinned and everything." Denali added, this time laughing harder than before. "Whatever chump." I responded smiling at the joke myself.

Denali and Akil make it their business to remind me that I have some of that Pilgrim's heritage in my blood. I can't help the fact that those two niggas are as black as shit. I always say that when I stand in between them we look like some piano keys or an Oreo cookie.

"Have you seen Akil and Sole`?" Lee asked as he looked at himself in his office mirror. "Yea, they're downstairs on the R&B dance floor getting their boogie on." I answered as I spotted one of my many freaks in the club.

"I need to send for them, the ball is about to drop in twenty minutes. Let me go tell Shawn to get them. Wait right here I have to go check on something. Veronica is in here being disrespectful again, acting fabulous as usual." Lee said as we stood outside of his office making our way to the VIP. " Oh go do your thing pimp, I'm cool. Just don't hurt anybody." I said knowing Denali's temper.

As Denali turned and signaled for Shawn to go get Akil and Sole`, I had a very emotional moment. I was so proud of the men and friends Denali and Akil had become to me. I've seen them grow from confused little boys into confident and successful men. It always trips me out to see Denali calling the shots like the big dog he has now become. I remember the days when he was so skinny the nigga could hula hoop through a cheerio...now look at him.

Growing up we would always see who could get the most girls and back then it was no contest. For every girl Lee had, I had three of her friends, sometimes I even had a sister or aunt. Akil's little romantic ass never wanted to participate, so it was just me and Denali "trying to sex all the girls in the world", like we used to say it. Now it's a different story. Everybody knows Denali and every woman wants to give him some. I'm no slouch myself, but Lee is on some unbelievable shit with the ladies.

I've seen the dude leave his club with four to five different sexy ass females, every night for two months straight, when he really wants to "play". I don't know what type of pills he takes or what type of magic he drinks, but the niggas balls are incredible.

Just as I'm reminiscing and laughing to myself, I was interrupted by a soft voice,

"How are you doing handsome?" The voice called out from my right side. As I slowly turned my head tracing the voice that had spoken to me, I would have never thought in a million years that it would go down like this. I had just laid eyes on the prettiest woman I had ever seen. And... and...and I was speechless. Baby was looking so good that she had taken my breath away. Never before had I stood in awe of a woman, looking like a chump. But that was then and this is now.

She stood five seven, with a curvaceous and voluptuous frame. A frame she displayed perfectly in her tight Versace dress. She had a dark mocha chocolate complexion with honey blond braids. Honey had that supermodel's appeal happening. She looked like Naomi Campbell, but much, much better. "I'm fine Ms. Lady and thank you for the compliment. May I ask you your name, by the way my name is Yes." I said extending my hand for her to shake also displaying my bling bling.

"It's a pleasure to meet you Yes. My name is Amerie. Is Yes your real or club name?" She asked revealing that heavenly smile, as her eyes sparkled under the club's dim lights. "It's what mama had them put on the birth certificate." I responded as I stepped into her space a little bit more. "Oh, is that right. I just had to come over here and introduce myself to a fine brother like yourself. I hope I'm not stepping on anyone's toes but I think you and I need to become friends." Amerie said while giving me a seductive look.

Chicks are always stepping to me in a club but honey is different, I can just feel it. "Nah there are no toes to step on but mine and I don't think you're trying to do that. Especially since you're trying to be my friend." I said as I started to lean into her a little bit more. As me and Amerie were standing there talking on the balcony, Denali returned...

DENALI

"Veronica what's going on? You know tonight is the most hectic night of the year for me. I'm expecting a lot of athletes and high profile figures tonight, more than usual. So I can't afford to have you and your loud ass girlfriends in VIP unless someone invites y'all." I said to Veronica's pretty ass while trying to remain cool, calm, and collected. "I don't care who you are expecting tonight. I bet that bitch India is in here. If she is, it would be wise of you to send her home or just keep her locked away. I'm warning you Denali, if I see her it's gonna be on." Veronica said as she paced back and forth like she was ready to hurt something.

India is my second baby's mother. She is the mother of our daughter Imani. India is probably the only woman that I've ever loved, besides my mother and grandmother. Everyone knows how I feel about India and Veronica has a major problem with that. India is a wonderful soul and a virtuous woman. We were together for three good years but life took us in different directions. India is now a gospel singer and is all into the church thing. So my lifestyle isn't in her best interest anymore.

If I was to ever settle down and get married, it would be to India and Veronica knows what time it is. "Now you know India wouldn't be caught dead in a nightclub. So stop trippin' off the bullshit already." I said to Veronica as I started walking her further and further away from the VIP.

26

Veronica is a very materialistic and into the wrong things type of girl. So the fact that I bought India a cranberry red 430CLK drop top Benz and dress her with furs and diamonds, drives Veronica's shallow ass crazy.

With me and India, it ain't about the money, or about what I can do for her. When she looks at me, I see hearts in her eyes and not dollar signs. With all the other women I deal with, it's always about two things: My money… and my money. "Veronica, the ball is about to drop in about ten minutes. Which means it's about to be a new year and I don't have time for you and your old bullshit. So please be civil or I'm gonna have you and your girlfriends, with their weaves and diamonds thrown the fuck out of here. You know I'm too grown to be playin` games so don't take me there." I said, looking at her like I was a second away from blowing her spot up. I knew that would solve the problem and calm her crazy ass down….

AKIL

It feels good to be spending the evening with my wife. I almost forgot just how special and sexy Sole` is. "Baby you know that I've never stopped loving you, right? You are the only thing in my life that I feel brings me closer to God." I whispered into Sole's ear as I held her waist on the dance floor. "Yea I know that daddy, I know that baby." She responded giving me that pretty dimpled smile.

"I couldn't be happier than being here with you tonight baby. You are the sexiest woman in here, and I'm not just saying that because I'm trying to take you home tonight to get some." I said figuring I'll add some spice to our marriage, so I started the role playing game.

"I don't think my husband would approve of you trying to take me home tonight." Sole` responded, playing along with me. "Oh, so you're doing the married thing. Okay, okay?" I said looking down at her, giving her a sexy smile.

"Yea, I'm doing the married thing partner." She responded looking back up at me with a sassy look on her face. "Well if your husband ain't here tonight, he can't catch us. We grown, so I won't tell if you don't tell…

SOLE`

I have to give Akil his props for making an effort to be creative and not just in the bedroom. I'm glad we're spending quality time together like this again. Because ever since the last time we went out dancing together and he ran into five different women that had him acting real suspicious and nervous, he avoids taking me with him to the club.

Damn my man is fine. Akil is looking and smelling so good tonight, and by the way these bitches are in here staring at my husband, I'm not the only one who thinks so. Men have no idea just how insecure women can be when they have a good looking, rich, and successful man. Although Akil is more than my man, there are those moments when I feel very insecure about our situation. Especially when he comes home late at night and rushes to the shower…

AKIL

I'm really gonna get my shit together, just look at how Sole` is responding to me. It's almost as if she's been patiently waiting for me to show her some special interest again. She's acting like that freshmen girl who has the biggest crush on the school's most popular guy, back in high school. Her hazel eyes are so bright and full of admiration, it looks like she is falling in love all over again. "Akil, Denali has asked that you and your date come on upstairs and celebrate with us." Shawn the clubs manager said as he looked Sole over like she was a piece of meat.

"Shawn this isn't my date. This is my wife Sole`. Baby this is Shawn the club's manager." I said introducing them for the very first time, and I've known Shawn for three years. Shawn then looked at Sole`, looked back over at me and gave me that, "yea I'd say she was my wife too nigga, if I was trying to get some" look. Sole` then turned to me and shot me a "he didn't know you were married, we'll talk about this later" look…

DENALI

"Damn nigga, I leave you alone for two seconds and you

28

already got your hands in the cookie jar." I said to Yes, as he was politicking with some gorgeous ass female "Denali this is Amerie. Amerie this is my brother Denali, but we call him Lee." Yes said introducing me to his new lady friend, with this silly ass look on his face. Damn this honey Amerie is finer than a muthafucka and has enough ass for everybody. She is definitely something me and Yes is gonna have to share, I thought privately to myself as I looked her over.

"It's a pleasure to meet you Amerie. Why don't you join us and celebrate the New Year with the rest of our family. Are you alone? If not, I'll send for whoever you're with. The ball will drop in about seven minutes so lets get upstairs…

AKIL

Once we finally got upstairs and into Denali's special conference room in the club, I started trippin`. I've been in this room millions of times and have had a million different women on this table alone. I've ran through Kiki, Tanya, Jackie, and Sadie, just to name a few of my jumpoffs. The worst part is they were all associates of Sole`. Don't you sit there shaking your head. I know that I'm a dirty dick ass nigga.

Damn this room, this table, and that sofa. The shit is making me sick to my stomach being here in front of all of this with Sole`. Especially, since she seems so happy to be by my side tonight. It always bothers me whenever my demons get close to my angel. I know deep down inside that I don't deserve to have a wife like Sole`. I know that sooner or later my shit is really gonna start to stink, and that scares the hell out of me…

SOLE`

"Denali, you are really doing it big this year. It feels good to see so many black people having such a good time, here in style." I said as Denali gave me and Akil loving hugs while he greeted us. "I'm probably the only black night club owner in New York City. I have to do things big to leave my mark. You know they think we don't know how to own and run shit." Lee said jokingly as he put a cigar in his mouth. "I know that's right." I added with a proud smile on my face.

I then turned to Akil who looked troubled and deep in thought. "What's on your mind daddy? Is there something troubling you?" I asked Akil knowing my husband. "Nah baby I'm good. I just can't believe it's about to be the year 2000, a new millennium...

YES

"Happy Kwanza my African people." I shouted as me and Amerie made our entrance into Denali's plush conference room. "Fool sit your loud Christopher Williams, Al B Sure looking, fake Afrocentric ass down and grab a bottle of Moet. The ball will drop in three minutes". Akil said as his eyes lit up when he saw me. I then embraced my brother Akil and hugged and kissed Sole`, who was looking awesome as usual.

We always make it our business to openly display the love we have for each other. We think more black families and friends need to be more loving and affectionate towards one another. That's why, it's nothing but love in our circle. "Who's the pretty lady?" Sole` asked without an ounce of intimidation in her vibe, which is common among women when there's another attractive woman in their space. "Sole` this pretty lady is Amerie. Amerie this is the rest of my family. This is my brother Akil and my sister Sole`...

DENALI

"I'd like to propose a toast, will everyone get a bottle. Shawn pass the ladies some glasses. May this year be a fulfilling experience. May we all move closer to what we love and live in health and abundance." I said as the whole club, city and country started counting down. Five, four, three, two one...Happy New Year!

AKIL

As we toasted, hugged, and drank some Moet I decided that now was the perfect time to do my thing. "I'd like to do something special, for a special person, but I'll need everyone's attention." I shouted calming the room down. "Do your thing playa." Yes said giving me his blessings as he puffed on his Cuban cigar.

"Baby we've been married for eight years now and my love for you is stronger today than I ever thought possible. When we married, we had nothing but our love, dreams, and goals. I stand here today happy to say that our dreams have come true. Our love is always tested but we pass consistently. Today we live a very blessed lifestyle and I want to give you something that I promised you ten years ago on our first date." I said as I dropped down to one knee.

"Baby, take this ring as a new commitment, a symbol of my greater love for you." I said as a tear rolled down my cheek and hit Denali's marble floor. I then opened up the Tiffany's box I had and put the new seven carat platinum and diamond studded wedding ring on Sole's ring finger, to replace the one carat she originally had. "Damn dawg you cashed in your retirement plan and sold the Jaguar?" Denali said in his attempt to fight off the tears I saw developing in his eyes.

The atmosphere was so emotionally intense that I saw Shawn let a tear go, and that niggas six seven, two hundred and a thousand pounds…

SOLE'

Akil is so unpredictable and mysterious. I had no idea he would pull off something like this. I said something had to change and what a good start. I'm so touched by this. I sure do love this man, especially when he acts right. Wait until Dana and Michelle see this…

DENALI

My man Akil is a funny nigga. He has to be the slickest cat in the world. It's amazing that he always knows what to do and when to do it, in order to save his ass. In school he was always good at cramming and charming the pants off of a female professor for a higher grade. That's my man Kil, Mr. Houdini. He always knows how to get his dick out of some quicksand…

YES

It's good to see Akil doing something right with his marriage. Sole` is such a beautiful woman. In fact, she was almost my wife but Akil beat me to the punch. I remember it like it was last week. Me, Akil, and Denali were at the Garden watching the Knicks and Nets play. As we were taking our seats, we saw Sole` and her family at the game. Kenny Anderson is her cousin, so her family was there at the game to support their "star".

At halftime, I noticed Sole` at the concession stand buying a hot dog. She was looking so good wearing some tight Guess jeans with a soft pink Calvin Klein top that matched her pink Reebok fifty four elevens. So when I went to tap Akil who was originally on my left side, I was surprised when I noticed that he had somehow already beat me to the punch. Akil was all in Sole's ear whispering sweet nothings, as she glowed brightly. They both looked so happy and good together that I couldn't hate, not even for a second.

I could see that there was something special happening between them as they talked. From that moment, nearly ten years ago, I knew there was a magic between them that couldn't be denied…

AKIL

"Well family, me and my beautiful wife are going back downstairs to get our boogie on. My man Kid Capri is doing the damn thing tonight." I said doing my infamous two step. "Come on baby lets go. Lee, Yes, and everyone else, Happy New Year, and God Bless. If I don't see y'all again tonight enjoy yourselves and be safe…

DENALI

"Okay, y'all go do the thing." I said to Akil and Sole` as they walked out of the door looking like kids in love.

"Yes, let me holla at you for a second playboy." I said as I put my arm around Yes' muscular shoulder. "What's up dawg?" Yes responded. "Babygirl is finer than a muthafucka. And I know you're in a giving mood, because I don't remember getting anything for Christmas nigga." I said as I tightened my hold around his neck.

"You're a funny guy Lee. Yea babygirl is fine but I don't know how she gets down. I can't seem to read this one. Even though shorty stepped to me I feel like I'm chasing her. The shit feels crazy." Yes said with that stupid look on his face again. The nigga looked like he was losing it. "Come on now you know it doesn't make a difference, all females have a little freak in them. A true playboy knows how to bring it out." I said to Yes in a fatherly way.

"Nigga don't hit me with that pimpology shit. I know the game and the rules. Remember I recruited your bitch ass. But all jokes aside I'm telling you babygirl has got something else happening." Yes said looking over at Amerie in amazement.

"Well find out what she's working with and get back at me catdaddy. If not with her, I know she has some girlfriends. So plug me in and stop acting scared." I said to Yes as I patted him on the ass in a "make it happen" kinda way....

YES

"So Amerie, what's your story married, boyfriend, kids, or all of the above?" I asked as we sat in Denali's special lounge area, sipping champagne. "I'm single. I just moved to the city a couple of months ago. I'm originally from Baltimore, but I went to school in Virginia. I lived out there for three years after graduate school and worked as an elementary school teacher. I decided to move to New York to pursue my acting career." Amerie said rather shyly, as if she was embarrassed by her dreams.

"That sounds great. That's a good thing. I can respect someone who pursues and lives their dream." I said to affirm her before I continued. "So you just woke up one day and decided that you wanted to make it happen? That's fly, it shows you have a lot of heart Ms. Lady." I said as we smiled at each other, both feeling the magnetic attraction between us.

"Well it wasn't that simple. My life started to get a little too hectic and out of control at the time. I was forced into a life or death situation and I chose to live, but not just any ordinary life. I decided to do the things I love to do. Now all I need is a love to share it with." She said as she touched my knee and gave me a warm smile. I knew honey had something extra going on. She's not like every other pretty face I meet. For starters, she is very charismatic and she is one of the loveliest things I have ever laid eyes on, besides Sole` of course.

What I like most about Amerie is that she has class. Her Versace dress and matching Marc Jacobs bag, lets me know she has taste and maybe a few dollars. But that doesn't seem to be all that she's about. She has a presence about herself that's hypnotic. She feels so good to be around. She also looks like she knows a secret about me that she's not telling. But most of the chicks I meet know something about me, that they usually keep a secret.

Me and Amerie talked, laughed, and danced for the next four hours that felt more like four minutes. She has definitely captured my attention, which isn't an easy thing to do. I'm not the easiest guy for a woman to impress. I've seen it all and experienced every element in the "game". It has been years since I chased some ass but Amerie has got me on the track like a race horse.

"I had a wonderful time with you tonight Amerie. I hope this is only the first night of many more together. Maybe the next time it will be a more intimate vibe than in a club." I said as I helped Amerie put her Chinchilla fur on. "Same here baby. So when will I hear from you again?" Amerie asked in a girlish way, gazing at me with those crystal clear eyes. "I'll give you a call sometime tomorrow, okay baby." I said as I soulfully hugged her wrapping my arms firmly across her body. I made sure that she understood she was someone that I wanted in my arms.

After letting her go, we locked eyes looking deeply into each another. At that moment, I saw something in a woman for the very first time. I can't really explain exactly what I saw, but it kind of looked like the other half of me. She must have felt and saw the same thing because we then kissed each other gently on the lips, trying to feel each other out.

After realizing that the sensual vibe was mutual between us, Amerie then opened up her winter fresh mouth and welcomed my tongue passionately into hers as we kissed deeply. It wasn't a sloppy spit everywhere type of kiss, but still a very wet one.

"Wow baby, that was nice. But I think you better go before we move too fast." I said as I tried to stop my boat from rocking. In all my days, I never kissed a female and lost my balance because of it. That kiss was some serious shit, I'm telling y'all. "I guess you're right sweety, I think I better leave. If I don't leave now who knows where this will end up." Amerie said as she gave me a soft luscious peck on the cheek before she walked away.

After me and Amerie departed, I decided that it was time for me to head on home and get some sleep. As I walked out of the Kingdome into the New Year's winter frost, I realized that I was hungrier than a prisoner of war. I needed to get something to eat ASAP. As I jumped into my Benz, I decided to stop by the Royal and grab something to eat. When I got to the Royal, it was more crowded than it usually is on a club night.

The Royal is this old school diner that everyone loves and knows about. It makes you feel like you're in Happy Days or something. As I'm placing my order, I realized that there were women everywhere in the place. At the table in the rear next to the kitchen, I noticed a table of four gorgeous ass females. They appeared to be a girls group or something. But as I'm checking them out I then noticed a familiar face in the midst of their clique. It was Sandy, this freak from Harlem.

I often bang Sandy out. She has some good pussy and her head game is only for the strong. But baby is an order of fries away from a happy meal. Sandy has one of those pretty faces that persuade many a nigga into doing stupid things. Shorty is a freak on the low, but a lot of young dudes are mesmerized by her. Niggas don't know how she really gets down. As a result, Sandy stays in the pockets of one of those fake ass Nino Brown niggas from uptown.

Sandy is a freaks freak, for real. She has tattoos all on her ass and down her back. Sandy is into all kinds of freaky shit. Her ass even tried to turn me on to some "crazy white boy" sex slave shit, but that ain't my thing. Don't get me wrong, I'm a freak. I'm just not about to let some freak blindfold and beat my ass with a whip. Sorry pal but I ain't the one.

When I realized that Sandy noticed me, it was only a matter of time before she made her presence known. "Hey sexy, Happy New Year." Sandy said with a devilish look on her face as she pushed up all on me. "Happy New Year to you baby. What are you getting into after this?" I asked, knowing that I didn't have to bullshit with her. Those other niggas might not be hipped to Sandy's game, but I am. "I'm not getting into anything. Why you trying to get up in me?" Sandy asked as she nibbled on my earlobe and very slyly grabbed my dick with her left hand.

Say no more to me about it. Shh..it, no woman has to threaten me with a good time, I thought to myself with a grin on my face. "So what about your girlfriends?" I asked as I caught serious eye contact with the light skinned honey, by the window, with the curly weave. "Well I know Tamara is a grown ass woman, if you know what I'm saying. The other two are coworkers from the office." Sandy said as she patted my chemical blowout.

I always keep my hair cut and mustache diced up. Denali's funny ass calls me Steve Harvey because I get a hair cut every two days. I'm one of those official fly Harlem niggas. Niggas are always hatin` on me. Everything from my hair, to my shoe and jewelry game, keep niggas on their toes. "So why don't you and Tamara follow my car to the house." I said to Sandy, with my hand on her ass. I then realized that I was about to get the two for one special.

So here I go again, another night, another episode. I know as soon as I finish with these birds they will be taking their freak asses' home. I don't care how cold it is outside or what time it is when we finish. I don't do the "spend the night thing" for no chick...

CHAPTER 3

DENALI

I'm always looking for ways to improve myself and my business enterprise. That's why I am always reading, going to a seminar, taking a class or something. I just picked up this book called "All Man" by some new writer Allen Mann. Homeboy is talking about some serious shit in this book about manhood. Some of this shit is disturbing, like when he says that, "A man's addictions are his Gods".

He says, "Whatever a man is addicted to will be the master of his destiny." Homeboy definitely has a unique perspective on what it is to be a man. I hope he's wrong about that addiction shit, if not, I'm serving and worshipping the pussy God. This book is definitely a page turner I'm gonna really get into this dudes work. Maybe I'll learn a thing or two...

SOLE`

"Akil, I have a surprise for you." I said as I scrambled the eggs, in our lavish state of the art kitchen. "What is it baby, can it wait? I'm already running late, as it is" Akil said as he kissed the back of my neck and headed for the door. "Is your stomach still hurting? Did you throw up? I think it was that Chinese take out from last night. That shit had me on the toilet until about three this morning." He said as he tied his gold Hugo Boss silk tie, while he stood tall looking at himself in our twelve by six foot mirror.

"I'm fine daddy and yes it can wait. In fact, meet me at Justin's tonight for dinner. I'll tell you about it then." I said realizing that I would be eating breakfast by myself this morning. "Okay baby, enjoy

37

your day and I'll see you later." Akil said as he walked out of the door leaving a trace of Burberry cologne behind.

Akil doesn't know that I've been throwing up every morning for the last two weeks. I also haven't seen Mary in about two months. That night after we left the Kingdome's New Years Eve party we came home and really got it on. We must have made love until four in the afternoon, the next day. I'm quite sure that somewhere in the middle of all of that loving we made it happen. So I have some news for Mr. Butler.

I know after my miscarriage the last time, the doctors said that I couldn't get pregnant again. I guess no man's opinion is greater than God's Will, because according to this stick... I'm pregnant...

YES

These nervous ass clients are beginning to drive me crazy. Everyone is calling in a panic because the market is coming down faster than a fat chick on a bungee jump.

"Tell Mr. Torro and any of my first A clients that call, I am arranging a way for them to recover some of what they lost. Also let them know that I will get back to them as soon as the arrangement is final." I said to my personal assistant Carmen.

Carmen is a recent graduate of Baruch College. She is a little lovely with a fat ass, but she has too much babyfather drama for me to take serious. During our Halloween party last year she came dressed as a devil and was looking real good in that red leather suit. So we messed around a bit during the party and before I knew what happened, I had Carmen in the bathroom, busting her ass down from the back.

As it was really getting good, maybe a little too good, I realized that the condom had popped on us. It immediately woke the both of us up and we decided that we weren't gonna get down like that. So since the party, we never took it there again. But me and Carmen flirt like crazy. "No problem Yes. I'll do just that, for you sweety." Carmen said giving me a flirtatious smile and wink.

I'm one of only a few brothers down on Wall St. that is

really getting money. Although more and more brothers are getting into the game, I don't think they come in to win. I was never satisfied with just making a hundred or two hundred grand a year. I always wanted to hold my own and step with the big dogs. I guess I get that from Denali. He is always talking about how important it is to have money if you want influence and control.

My man is right because ever since I became a million dollar broker the whole office is on my dick. It's funny because I come to work all dapper in my Brooks Brothers suits, designer shoes, silk ties, and "the powers that be", feel comfortable around me. They don't know that I come to hold it down for all the brothers from the hood who they said couldn't make it.

So in a very short while I'll be leaving this firm to do my own thing. I plan on setting up shop right in the hood too. I plan on taking Carmen with me. Carmen is more than my personal assistant. She is more like my business partner. That's why instead of the $45K she was contracted to be paid from the company, I personally doubled it. Being a stock broker is a demanding but exciting job. Being a million dollar broker means I have to work smarter than the average broker and be more disciplined.

That's why I love Carmen so much, she helps me to hold it down and represent our people well in this "white man's" game. These damn clients must've forgotten that I've already made them millions upon millions of dollars. Shit, they are acting like I'm personally responsible for the dive in the market. Investors always trip when things start balancing themselves out. I always tell my clients that they will lose sometimes but my job is to make sure they win far more than they lose. But ain't nobody trying to hear that shit right now. The dot.com phenomenon has investors spoiled.

"Yes, there is a Ms. Taylor on the phone for you." Carmen said with a little jealousy in her tone. "Okay good, I'll take the call." I said with a warm smile on my face. Since New Years Eve, me and Amerie have been kickin` it hard. Amerie really helps to calm my nerves. Dealing with this office and shit, I can get crazy at times but baby helps to relax me. She always has a word of encouragement and is a comedian on the low. I really enjoy spending my time with Amerie. She allows me to be me, which is the best feeling in the world for a man. When I'm with Amerie I don't have to perform or people please.

"What's up baby? How are you?" She said as I could hear her smile over the phone. "I'm stressed, these damn clients are on my ass about their money." I said exhaling out some frustration.

"Don't let it stress you baby. One day you are gonna realize it wasn't even that important." She said giving me a calmer perspective as usual. "Yea I know baby. It's just sometimes I feel like getting gully with some of these cocksuckers. They really don't know how I really do." I said causing the both of us to laugh.

"I know that's right. Look baby, I hope you didn't forget about our date tonight. I have something special I really, really want you to have. If you stand me up this time I'm gonna have to find someone else that wants what I have to give." Amerie said sparking my curiosity. "You know that I'm sorry about the other day. I got caught up, but I'll be there tonight." I said before we hung up.

Truth is, I had ran into Mocha the other night, this exotic dancer from Queens. Mocha really knows how to work her shit, so I figured I'd share a few nuts with her. Me and Amerie have been seeing a lot of each other over the last two months, but she still hasn't let me into her secret garden. She hasn't even invited me upstairs into her apartment, not even for a drink. Hopefully, tonight will be the night Amerie stops bullshittin' with herself and brings a nigga on in...

AKIL

I have an interview today with Mariah Carey for next month's ten year anniversary edition of the magazine. I hope she shows because we've been trying to get her to talk to us for the last two months. Working for Brother Magazine has introduced me to many celebrities and personalities. I've met and interviewed practically every athlete, actor, actress, and entertainer that I admire.

My favorite interview of all time had to be with Halle Berry. She was so relaxed, open minded, and down to earth. For a split second I kinda thought she was giving up some rhythm, like many of the other actresses I had interviewed. But I then realized that she just has a very warm personality and my imagination was getting the best of me. That whole day was crazy because when I got home it dawned on me. Why would I want Halle Berry, when I already have Sole`?

"Akil someone has sent you flowers, a bottle of champagne, and a package. I put it all in your office for you." Shelia the office receptionist said to me as I walked into the office twenty minutes after nine. "Thanks Shelia. How are you feeling this morning? You're looking good as always." I asked as I returned her smile.

"Oh I'm fine now that you have walked in." She replied. Shelia is a honey dip, with a sweet personality. She's about five three and keeps her tracks hidden well. Sheila is thick as hell. Not a Star Jones thick but more like a Trina thick. Sheila has ass for three days but she's happily married to some dude who works construction. She has one of those blue collar, dirty fingernail, hardworking brothers and I respect that. I even met the dude once and he seemed real cool. He wasn't on any of that egotistical bullshit. So I never went at his foundation When I stepped into my office it didn't look like the corporate setup that it was, but more like a flower shop.

Who in the hell is behind all of this? Immediately a few of my ladies crossed my mind. Could it be Leila? Nah, she's still mad with me. Maybe it was Rochelle? I thought.

I went straight for the gold package that looked like a birthday wrapping. When I opened the package there sat a pair of boxer briefs, my gold money clip, and the diamond stud earring that I thought I lost. There was also a note with an envelope attached to it. The note read:

" *I enjoyed what we had. Despite what you said, you will leave your wife. I want it all and will get what I want, one way or another. I*

41

want you but sense that is not an option right now, twenty five grand will do. If I don't get the money in two weeks, a copy of what's in the envelope will be sent to Fantasy Travel."

Fantasy Travel is Sole's travel agency, I quickly tore open the envelope, like it was a letter from a long lost love. And what I saw didn't surprise me one bit. I know that whatever is done in the dark will sooner or later be brought to light. So there it was, pictures of me getting head from Tracy, while I was asleep.

Now no one knows about Tracy. Yes doesn't know about Tracy, Denali doesn't know... no one knows. Tracy is unlike any other women I had an affair with. Tracy isn't like the women I meet in the club, through my work, or on the street. Tracy is a very special situation....

DENALI

India has been on my mind like crazy these last couple of weeks. I really miss having her by my side, but she's all in love with that Kirk Franklin ass nigga Paul right now. If I could get her attention again, I wouldn't lose it for the rest of her life. If she would get back with me, I'd come correct, no bullshit this time.

I really need to go see how India and my baby Imani are doing, I thought then headed out to their house. When I pulled up to India's house which is in Mount Vernon, NY I parked behind the cranberry red CLK Benz I had brought her two years ago, for her twenty fifth birthday.

India is everything I want in a woman, but didn't realize I had until she was gone. She is beautiful, half Cuban and half Black. Her father was a Marine who married her Cuban mother. They met and fell in love while her pops was stationed out in Cuba.

India is a statuesque five feet six inches of beauty. She has wavy long hair that is styled differently every two weeks. She has light brown eyes, which is odd because her skin tone is so dark. When I first saw India I thought she was Dominican. But within the first two minutes of talking to her, I knew she was a sister. India is beyond physical appeal. She is real, a rider, that woman I need in my life.

Ever since India gave her life to the Lord, which was right after Imani was born, she has changed. She is this new person now. She stopped smoking trees, which she did sparingly anyway mainly because of me. She stopped coming to the club and getting her party on, and India can dance her ass off. I respect and admire her relationship with the Lord but I miss her so much.

When I finally got to the door, I realized that in my heart I didn't want to be standing in front of the door as a visitor. I wanted to be coming home with my own set of keys, like the man of the house. I guess in my heart, I do want the marriage and family thing. But my body won't have any of that shit right now.

When India came to the door, she looked so beautiful. She had on a burgundy colored satin nightgown that had a split in the front, showing off the firmness of her thighs.

Now India has BODY. She is always at the gym doing aerobics, she eats right, and takes good care of herself. She is one of those image conscious females, so she takes extra good care of herself.

When she greeted me at the door her eyes lit up when she saw me standing there unexpectedly. "Hey baby." She said as she jumped into my arms and gave me the warmest embrace. I could still see the love she has for me all in her pretty eyes. "How are you doing Dinko? Why didn't you call? I would have made something to eat for you and would have put something sexy on, if I knew you were coming over?" India said, smiling as we held each other.

That's what I miss the most about India. She is one of the few people in my world who loves to give to me. "I'm so happy to see you baby. I've been thinking about and praying for you like crazy these last two weeks." India said. *That probably explains why every night for the last two weeks, I've been thinking about India before I go to sleep.*

"Where's daddy's little princess?" I asked India as we walked into the large family room that was furnished in contemporary Italian furniture. "Sleeping beauty is having sweet dreams. She's been a little under the weather. So please don't go and wake her, she just went to sleep." India said as we stood in the living room. "Okay, besides I also drove up here to see you babymother." I said as I grabbed her hand and smiled.

"Well let me take your coat. Do you want something to drink baby?" India asked so sweetly. "Water will be fine baby," I answered, thinking about how much I missed her supportive and nurturing ways.

As I sat there in the family room, looking at all of the pictures of India and Imani, I realized something was missing from that equation. I was missing from the equation.

When India returned, she handed me my tall glass of water as some Yolanda Adams played in the background.

"What were you reading?" I asked noticing a book underneath the cream cashmere pillow on the sofa. "I was reading the book of John." She answered as she took a seat right next to me, causing me to get a wift of her sweet smell. "How often do you read the Bible?" I asked trying to sound interested, but knowing that I really wasn't.

"I read everyday, it's like food to me. Why, are you thinking about reading the Bible?" She asked enthusiastically like she was receiving a breakthrough. "Nah, I'm straight." I answered realizing that I needed to stop bullshittin`. Because the last thing I'm trying to read is the Bible.

"You are really looking good India. I mean really looking good baby. I've been missing you so much." I said changing the subject as I looked at her bronze thighs, while she sat with her legs crossed. "I've missed you too Dinko." India said giving me an emotional look.

"Since New Years you've been on my mind, but these last two weeks it's been stronger than ever. It's like I can't get you out of my mind India. Now I know that Paul is a decent brother and I know you're into him right now, but we are made to be together. Me and you belong together. I don't know how I know this, but I know we are meant to be baby. I respect where you are right now in life, in fact I'm happy for you. I'm really not trying to bring conflict or confusion to your circumstances, but I really miss having you as my center. India I want you back in my life." I said looking her dead in the eyes with no compromise. I couldn't hold it in any longer.

"I know all of this might be coming as a surprise to you but if I could, I'd make you my wife baby." I said as I then kissed her on the forehead. "Dinko stop before you make me cry." India said as she stood up and shook her emotions off. She then walked to the window and stood there looking up into the sky, with her arms folded.

"I have wanted to tell you something that has been on my mind and in my heart for a long while now. Dinko, I've loved you since the moment you told me your name. From that day I knew that I wanted to spend the rest of my life with you. I was only a twenty two year old inexperienced young woman when we first met. And I have to admit, I was fascinated and in awe of who you were at the time. I was moved by the things you had.

"I'm now a mature twenty seven year old woman. And I'm still in love with and fascinated by you Denali, this time for different reasons than before. When I'm with you, I feel like I'm in a right place. It scares me to feel that way because you still belong to that crazy and chaotic world. That crazy world that I have been delivered from.

"I know that in order for me to be with you I would have to step back into my past and live in that twilight zone again. And I'm dead to that. No more smoking, drinking, and acting wild and out of control for me. I am a woman now and a mother of a little girl. How I carry myself now means the world to me baby. It's not only about me and my wants. I now have to set the example for Imani. I don't care how young she may be, kids are always watching.

"Right now, I have a peace beyond understanding and a joy above good times. The Lord has made me into a complete woman but I still yearn for a man. Not only do I desire a man physically but I also need a man spiritually and within my soul Denali.

"I thought Paul was that man, because he's born again, loves God, and works in the ministry. But my heart and soul tells me otherwise. I realize that it's not only a man that I desire. It's my man want. I desire the man that I'm a reflection of. That man who will become great because of us. That man God has purposed for me to be with. I know beyond doubt that you're my man Denali Shea Shaw…

YES

Amerie really has me diggin' her something tuff. She doesn't play any little girl games. She is truly a mature woman, and I'm loving that. It has been a while since someone has gotten to me like this. I don't know why she's got me open like a bag of smoke, but she does.

Maybe I'm open because Amerie is causing me to bring out qualities that I've never expressed to a woman. I'm patient, caring, and sensitive to her desires and feelings. For me, all of this is definitely a first. I have never ever let a woman into my emotional zone, but Amerie walked right in like she had a key.

For the first time I can remember, I'm considering featuring just one woman. I'm finally comfortable with the idea of having just one woman in my world. The shit is unbelievable to me, the more I think about it.

Tonight, me and Amerie are going to see this play at the Beacon Theatre, another "Lord why black men ain't shit", man hating theme.

When I picked Amerie up, she looked so elegant and pretty as always. She had on a light brown nicely fit Moschino dress with some tan, three inch Prada shoes, and a matching necklace and bracelet. Amerie always looks so good. I definitely like Amerie's style. She knows how to rock the professional attire but also looks good in a sweat suit, hat, and sneakers. Like she wore when we sat courtside at the Knicks game, a few weeks back.

"Hey baby, you are looking good as always." I said as I opened the door to my money green Lexus GS300 for her. "I see you are still trying to impress me. We'll have to see how long that lasts." Amerie said as we hugged and kissed before she sat down in the car. "Damn baby, what you have a different car for every day of the week? Amerie asked as Blackstreet's "Joy" was playing in my car. "Something like that. What can I say I like whips…

CHAPTER 4

AMERIE

This man is so fine. It's been killing me not to sleep with him already. Yes is different, so I have to treat our situation differently. Ever since I saw him so smoothly gliding through the club, I was intrigued by what he had going on. My girl Porche hipped me to his whole profile before I could even ask her. She told me that he was a seven figure man, single, and real tough on the ladies.

She said that his sex is great and added that he could suck a fart out an ass. She said a lot of women have tried to lock him down but to no avail. She knew all of this because she had sucked Denali's dick a few times, as she tried to get into his pockets. Her friend Toy fucked Yes a few times in the club but said that was as far as he would allow it to go.

She said Yes wasn't trying to take her out or do anything but fuck and get his dick sucked. After she told me all of that I made sure that I went at this alone and not off of a referral from some chick that he knows is a ho.

I did know all I needed to know about him before I even approached him. I'd figured I would move slowly, but my steps were methodical. I wanted what Yes had going on and knew exactly how to get it. He was everything I was looking for at the time. He was young, black, fly, sexy, and rich. I really didn't care if he was single or not. With a face, ass, and game like mine, a man's status was never my concern. I had already fucked and sucked a New Jersey Net, a Rocafella, and Tony, who's an investment banker way before I stepped to Yes.

47

I put it on Tony's weak ass so bad that he bought me my loft, and then gave me another thirty grand to furnish it. Tony is my official sugardaddy but I'm always in at least three niggas pockets. Shit, my lifestyle doesn't come cheap. Men are so damn lustful and predictable that it makes my job easy.

Didn't BVD warn them to never trust a big butt and smile? But niggas are always thinking with the wrong head anyway.

My whole world changed once I really got to know Yes. I would have never thought that my feelings would ever get involved in the "game". I came to New York to strike it rich, not to fall in love with some sucker. But Yes talks to me in a way that makes me feel feminine and precious. He doesn't come off like he wants something from me. He seems to be content in just getting to know me, and I mean the real me. We talk about everything. I've already told Yes things that not even Porche knows about me. Yes is my baby and I think I'm falling in love with him because I don't know what's going on anymore. What in the hell is going on with me? Am I slippin`...

AKIL

I don't know what I'm gonna do about Tracy. I know if I give this bitch the money, then I'll become a bank, and I ain't trying to do that. I already coughed up ten grand last fall, but greed is never content. So now I have to deal with this shit. I'll figure something out. But I need to hurry up and get my black ass to Justin's, before Sole` has a baby.

When I finally got to Justin's, I saw Sole` sitting alone sipping what appeared to be some wine. I couldn't tell what type of mood she was in but I did remember she said she had a surprise for me. When I got to the table, I crept up on Sole` from behind. "May I join you sweet lady?" I asked like I was Billy Dee Williams. "Good evening honey. How was your day?" Sole` asked me with excitement all in her eyes.

"It was hectic today. Mariah Carey was a no show, so I'll have to travel to LA in two weeks to do the interview." I said sounding disappointed because I hate traveling all over for a fifteen minute interview. "I'm sorry to hear that daddy, maybe you can spend some time with Jalil while you're out there." Sole` said to comfort me. "Well maybe I can." I said realizing that I haven't seen my brother in a few years. "Yea, I'm quite sure his fiancée would love to finally meet you honey." Sole` said as the waiter came to our table to take our orders

After we ate dinner, me and Sole` began to talk some more. As Sole` was talking, I started to zone out while her mouth was moving. I could see Sole's lips moving, but all I could think about was Tracy and the bullshit.

Tracy isn't a skeleton in my closet but a mummy. I stepped to Tracy correct, as a man's man, because what I saw was all woman. Tracy had the femininity and the looks of a beauty pageant winner. But as I got to know Tracy the truth came out. Tracy, was really T.R.A.C.E.Y. The woman I thought was all woman was actually a man. When I realized that Tracy was a Tracey, I was gonna whup his ass. But he wrote me a letter that said...

[*Within every man lies a woman. When God made me he mistakenly gave me the body of a man but the nature of a woman. I apologize for leading you on to believe I was a woman when I'm not but I'm more woman than you will ever know. I'm not trying to turn you out, or turn you onto any homosexual activities. I plan on having my operation completed in a couple of days. I don't want to penetrate you but I want you to penetrate me. In jail men do it all of the time and never once do they consider themselves to be gay. I don't want to take your manhood I just want you to accept the uniqueness of my womanhood. I know you feel something greater than the physical attraction with me. We have too much fun together and share too many things in common for you to throw that all away. So don't fight it, be free. Just think about what you felt when you thought I was a woman.*]

For like two weeks I battled with my feelings and the psychology of what Tracey was saying. I know that I am all man there is no doubt about it. Yet, I battled with the idea because all I could think about was the oral pleasure Tracey had hypnotized me with as we sat in my Yukon parked off of the West Side Highway. My body had never experienced the electric shock it did as Tracey put it on me. I mean, I never lost my hearing and sight because of a nut.

At that time, me and Sole` were going through the motions and Tracey brought a lot of newness and fun to my world. So with all of that going on inside of me, I gave in and continued to let Tracey blow my wood.

"I'm sorry baby, the whole Mariah Carey thing is on my mind. Did you say something?" I asked Sole` as I came back to life. "Yes I said something daddy. I said that I love you and I'm pregnant." She said with a big smile on her face. "I love you too baby… you're WHAT...

YES

After dinner and the show, I asked Amerie if she wanted to go out dancing but she said she was tired and it was getting late. She said she just wanted to go home and unwind for the night. I figured that was my cue that the night was a wrap. So I was just waiting for Amerie to hit me with the Russell Simmons, "Thanks for coming out God Bless you and good night." So when we pulled up to her building, I was surprised when she said, "Why don't you come on upstairs and unwind with me", as she kissed me softly on the neck.

I don't remember when was the last time I was so excited and nervous about a seductive suggestion from a woman. I had that I'm about to bust my first nut excitement going on. I just hoped that I would stay in the water longer than I did my first go round.

"That sounds good to me." I said in my Barry White tone. When we finally got to her place I was pleasantly surprised because from the outside her building kinda looked abandoned. Surprisingly, Amerie actually had a duplex loft with a picture perfect view of the city's skyline. The place was decked out. She had an African and Asian vibe going on. It felt like I was in a Buddhist temple in Johannesburg.

"Nice place baby, I'm impressed. It looks like Will Smith's

apartment in the movie Bad Boys." I said as I was looking at the exotic fish that were swimming in her large aquarium. "It's funny that you say that because that was the inspiration behind how I decorated and designed the set up." She responded. Just like with Will Smith in Bad Boys, I was wondering how she could afford a place like this. I figured her rent ran her three grand a month minimum and if she paid for it flat out it probably ran her a two hundred grand conservatively. Plus, she definitely has about fifteen grand of furnishing up in here.

I know her off Broadway gigs don't pay that much so what the fuck is really going on?

"Damn baby you hit the lottery and didn't want a brother to know about it...

AMERIE

Yes has turned out to be a different man than I assumed him to be. He is the first man I've been with that I don't want to manipulate. Yes is the first man whose money I don't want, nor do I care about. The fact that he drives a different car every day of the week means absolutely nothing to me.

When I first spotted Yes in the club, I noticed that he had a different swagger about his. When Porche put me on to who he was and how he gets down, I thought of him as a challenge. I figured, I would be the first chick to turn him out and go shopping up Fifth and Madison, with his money.

But now that I've really gotten to know him, I want to be upfront and real with him. I'm actually thinking about marriage, kids, and building a future with him. Maybe I've been on the wrong track this whole time. Using my looks and body to get what I wanted from men has gotten me a lot of things but nothing that means anything. I've gained alot of material things in my day but lost a part of my soul in the process.

My ability to feel life was numb until Yes came along and touched me. I'm a twenty nine year old woman and never once have I had a truly meaningful relationship with a man. Maybe being raped by my uncles and mother's boyfriends made me vindictive towards men? Maybe all that they put me through has caused me to subconsciously hate men and myself?

Never before have I felt this safe and secure about allowing my heart and soul to open up to a man. I'm not even sure if I know how to love a man. All I know is manipulating and using men to get whatever it is that I want. Now here I am trying to love a man for the first time.

I want Yes to have all that I have to give. Yes truly is such a sweetheart underneath that hard exterior, once you really get to know him. I think that we both have been afraid of love and commitment in the past, but we can't deny how we feel or ignore what's real between us right now.

"No, baby I didn't win the lottery." I responded to Yes' sarcastic question. "So do you have a rich uncle or something?" He asked as he walked around my place. "Something like that... something like that...

DENALI

Me and India have slowly been doing our thing again. This time I know things will be different, because she is not the same woman I was dealing with before. Since that night we made our confessions, we have been doing nothing but talking about family, God, love, and life. It feels like we have started all over again. Getting to know each other's worlds again is kind of romantic.

I have a new developed respect and appreciation for India as a woman. She has really grown and matured. When we first met she was easily impressed by what I could do for her. I bought India clothes, jewelry, kept two grand in her pocket daily, and took her everywhere from Jamaica to Paris, and that shit turned her on.

Now she isn't impressed by what I can do for her. India seems more interested in who I am as a man. Things like keeping my word, how I feel, and what I think, are now priorities to her. Since we've talked about God and spirituality, I've been questioning a lot of my beliefs about manhood, women, and love. Everything in my life is looking different to me. India has been asking me some serious questions. She is causing me to look at things in a new way.

India has invited me to church with her this Sunday. I told her that I would have to think about it. But she knows how I feel about those "hypocritical church going, using God to get rich assholes". I probably won't go, but I'll see how I'm feeling come Sunday morning. Hopefully, I won't wake up in a bed full of women from my usual crazy Saturday night..

CHAPTER 5

SOLE`

Since I told Akil that I was pregnant he has started acting real strange again. I just know that something is wrong, it's all in his eyes and on his face. He's been coming home all types of hours at night reeking of alcohol, looking like he lost something. Large sums of money have been missing from our bank account, and I see no evidence of where it's going.

I know that Akil loves cars, but I haven't seen any new toys in the garage where we store our four cars now. When I question him about his whereabouts and what's going on, he tells me he's working late or that he's hanging out with Denali and Yes. I understand that every man needs his space and time to hang out and do the things men do, but I'm almost certain something is going bad.

I had the same feeling when I found out he was messing around with some model named Solara. It wasn't the first time that I caught him out there, but I promised myself it would be the last. If Akil is fucking around this time he's better off with the bitch he's sleeping and creeping with. Shit, I'm done even worrying about it. But I'm still gonna give him the benefit of the doubt. He just better prove me wrong. He better be working late and hanging out with Denali and Yes for his sake…

AKIL

I gave in and sent Tracey the twenty five grand and now this muthafucka wants another twenty five thousand. For the last couple of months, I've been living in hell. I've been living with the fear of being caught and it's driving me crazy. I can hardly stand to be around

Sole`, because I can barely look her in the eyes. No amount of sex is worth jeopardizing my marriage, reputation, and livelihood over.

Of all my infidelities with women, I'm now being hunted and haunted by a fucking dude. A nigga that I thought was one hell of a woman…

DENALI

I decided to go to church with India on Sunday and it was a good experience. For a minute I was trippin` out because I saw at least twelve people in the church who are regulars at my clubs. Two of the chicks that were in the choir are the biggest freaks in the city, I can testify to that personally. But the shit that put the icing on the cake for me, was when I saw this married chick Talia, in there acting all "holy holy" with her husband and two kids.

Funny thing is, Talia is always just a phone call away from a beat down. We even got up a few weeks ago. She likes to do it in her house, in her bedroom, while her husband is at work. I really don't like getting down like that, but Talia gets extra horny at the idea of getting caught. She gets so horny that she allows me to put it anywhere. And Talia is a bitch that loves to pull the condom off and swallow my nut down her throat, whenever I feed it to her. So I give it to her just how she wants it.

I always make sure I'm holding my tooly whenever I take my ass over there though. Shh..it, a nigga ain't gonna catch me sleeping with my dick in my hand. That's a move for suckers.

When Talia's dirty ass noticed me, she didn't even panic like I thought she would. She just gave me a wink and continued to praise the Lord, right along side her naïve ass husband. See that's what I fear most about women. They are the best liars and manipulators in the world. I bet that her sucker ass husband has no idea those are my nut stains in his sheets, when he lays his head at night. I know that the shit is dirty, right? But that's how shit really goes down out here. It could be happening to your ass???

When the pastor finally came out and the service got going, a powerful Spirit came over the whole building. Once he started speaking it was almost as if he was talking directly to me.

"We weren't made by the hands of average. Our Creator God is perfect and extraordinary. When I walk the streets and look into the eyes and lifestyles of the men and women I see, it's clear to me that we don't know who we are. It's clear to me that we don't know where we've come from. As a result we have a false sense of self and erroneous beliefs about manhood, womanhood, success, and life.

"I often see black men following the paths of domination, destruction, and death set up for them by the "lustful and prideful" man and not God. Look at how we treat our women, abandon our children, die in the streets chasing ill-gotten gold, and murder one another like animals. Women, power, money, or any other false thing men chase, will never make you the extraordinary man you were created to be. We are the Glory of God." Pastor said in a smooth manner

As he preached, a very uncomfortable comfort came over me. It was like his words were stirring something up in me that has wanted to come alive. "He's pretty good." I turned and said to India as we held hands. "God is using him, that's all." She responded like it was nothing.

After the service was over, I was feeling real good and fresh. I felt like I had just taken a long hot shower and bubble bath. "I'm glad I decided to come along baby, thanks for the invite." I said as I hugged India and noticed that Kirk Franklin ass nigga Paul heading our way.

"Praise the Lord my brother." Paul said as he approached us. "What's going on my man?" I said refusing to play his verbal church politics.

"That was sure a good Word today. So India, how have you been? I haven't heard from you lately. Is everything okay?" Paul asked as he looked over at me, while I was holding Imani against my chest, as she slept. "Yea everything is good partner, couldn't be better." I said staring Paul down before India had a chance to say a word.

I had Paul by four inches and about twenty pounds. So if he

wanted to, I was ready to jump off. I didn't care if we were in front of a church or not. I'm always ready to pop off if need be. India, knowing my style and temper decided to step in. "Why don't you put the baby in the car and wait for me there." India gently suggested giving me a "calm yourself down look"...

INDIA

How awkward is this, standing here in front of the church with the man my heart desires and with the man I "should" be with on paper? After Denali took my advice and headed for the car, I figured I'd level with Paul about my situation. He at least deserves an explanation.

"What's his problem?" Paul asked as Denali was slowly walking away, staring Paul down in the process. Denali was definitely showing that he was still from the hood, with ghetto tendencies.

"I don't know, he gets like that from time to time. So how have you been Paul?" I asked trying to change the subject quickly. "I've been blessed. I can't complain, but I'm missing you. I guess I know why you haven't returned any of my calls. So you're now back with Imani's father. I thought you said it was over between you two. What happened to that "we grew apart" mess you told me?" Paul asked as he loosened his stylish red tie.

"If I could explain to you what is happening between me and Denali, I wouldn't be so confused about it myself Paul.

"I know that you are a good man and a blessing to me from God. But my heart isn't there with you and I. I don't want to lead you on sweety. I'm terribly sorry Paul, but I'm in love with my daughter's father. I believe that is where I belong with him raising our daughter together." I said to Paul trying to be considerate of his feelings. After all this man has been nothing but good to me and Imani.

"I just hope you know what you're doing. I just hope you're moving forward and not backwards. Just remember what was once good for you can also be bad for you when the season changes." Paul said looking over at Denali, as he sat in my truck. "What do you mean?" I asked knowing he always speaks in parables.

"I mean, your favorite summer swimsuit can make you sick if you wear it outside in the middle of a winter...

CHAPTER 6

YES

It's been over four months and Amerie still hasn't given me any of that pussy yet, but amazingly I'm not stressing it. We have really gotten close over this time. We talk about everything and I do mean everything. I was surprised to see just how much we have in common and how well we compliment one another. Amerie is a good fit for me. I feel like I can tell her anything and she'll just listen without judgment. She has the same "I've seen and heard it all before" personality that I have. And it makes her very understanding. With all that I've done and been through, it's important that I'm with a very understanding woman, who is also thick skinned.

In fact, let me give her a call to see what she's doing. "Hi baby." She answered immediately recognizing my voice over the phone. "What's up babygirl? What were you doing?" I asked as I turned the music down a bit in my Suburban truck. "I just finished exercising. I'm about to go over this script for tomorrows audition." She answered in her soft tone.

"Oh that's right, you do have an audition tomorrow. I know you're gonna get the part." I asked giving her a boost of confidence. "Yea I hope so. My agent told me a lot of well known actresses are auditioning as well. Just keep your fingers crossed for me baby. What are you doing for the evening? She asked. "I'm actually on my way to play pool with Lee and Kil. I was figuring after I finish up over there with them that I would swing by your place to see you. But I forgot that you have an audition tomorrow, so I guess I'll see you tomorrow night." I said not wanting to be a distraction to her.

"It won't be a problem seeing you tonight baby. I told you

that you're my good luck charm. So come on over right after you finish playing pool. I miss you anyway baby." She said causing me to smile.

"Alright then, I'll call when I'm on my way. I'll see you later baby." I said before hanging up with Amerie.

Tonight I'm supposed to meet up with Denali and Akil and play some pool. I miss hanging out with the fellas but we have all been so busy the last month and a half with our lives…

AKIL

"What's up babyboy?" I said to Denali, as I snuck up on him and lightly punched him in the stomach. "Damn nigga, you scared the shit out of me. What's up with your pretty ass?" Denali asked as he gave me a pound and hug. "Man shit is crazy right now in my world dawg." I responded getting ready to confess my sins. "Feel like talking about it? You know whatever it is you'll get through it. You are a strong dude Kil." Denali said to comfort me.

Denali has a special way of lifting someone's spirits when they are down. I think he got it from his grandmother. I've actually seen Denali hold a conversation with a bum on the street for hours like they were long lost friends. Then he'll go into his pocket and give them three or four hundred dollars.

I remember one time, Denali took a special liking to this one homeless dude and personally helped dude get his life in order. I think the guy actually works for Denali now. "Yea I know I'll get through it, I don't have a choice playboy. What are you drinking, the regular?" I asked as I was making my way to the bar.

"Yea, give me a shot of Jack and a Heineken." Denali responded as I walked off. The Galla is one of the coolest lay low spots in the city.

We come here because the average nigga would never think about spending what we pay to get in here to play pool. The Galla is for the athletes, entertainers, and big money spenders in the city. Jerry Seinfeld, Derek Jeter, and Allan Houston are all regulars here. When I returned to our table, Denali was eating some hot wings and was on his cell, as usual, handling business.

"Tony what the fuck do I pay you for to begin with? That's your mess now clean it up. And don't get back to me until then!" Denali said before hanging up the phone and shaking his bald head. "This nigga Tony has to be the laziest and softest nigga in the world. If he fucks this deal up for me he's gonna be frying fish with a dress on. That's my word." Denali added as he took a second to regroup.

Seeing Denali play hardball always inspires me. I think Denali is one hell of a real model for all of those knuckleheaded niggas that want to hustle to get money. I watch this dude "from the hood" make million dollar deals routinely. And Denali has never sold a drug in his life.

"I'm thinking about selling the clubs Kil." Denali surprisingly said to me as he swallowed his shot of Jack down. "Why would you want to do that? You have the hottest spots in the city." I asked looking at him as if he had lost his rational mind. "I'm growing tired Kil. Ever since I was sixteen, I have been involved in parties, promotion, or some element of the night life. I've made millions of dollars and slept with enough women to make Hugh Hefner proud. I don't know what's really going on with me but I'm going through some changes Kil." Denali said to me in a serious tone.

"Well, ever since I've known you, you have always been able to make a dollar out of fifteen cents. So if you sell the clubs what would be next, even though your rich ass don't need anymore money?" I asked causing Denali to smile. "Kil I don't know doggy, I don't know…

YES

"What's really good ladies?" I said to Denali and Akil as I joined them in the Galla, at our usual table. "What's up with you daddy, coming up in here glowing and everything? You look like you've done seen the light. Amerie must be putting it on that ass. Look at your man Kil, he's all light on his feet and everything." Denali said as him and Akil started laughing at me.

"Word up dawg, you're glowing. Oh shit, this nigga is glowing Lee." Akil added, laughing like he just heard the funniest joke. "Why don't y'all get off my dick. I'm glowing so what." I said as I gave them each a pound and hug.

"Baby is something special man. Never before have I felt like this about a woman. I don't now how all of this shit has happened, but I'm cool with it." I said smiling from ear to ear as I thought about Amerie. "Damn dawg you got bit wit that cupid shit, you're in love nigga. Kil just look at your man. The nigga is light in the ass now and everything." Denali said as he slapped Akil a high five and started laughing again.

"Nah seriously, I'm happy for you playa. Shit, there isn't anything better for a man than love, especially with a special woman." Denali said looking like he was talking to himself. "It's good to see that somebody is winning out here." Akil said with a troubling look on his face.

Denali has always been the motivator and comedian of the crew. I'm the older brother and Akil is the younger brother. On the surface, Akil looks like one of those poem writing, candle burning, sensitivity cats. Contrary to what his looks might lead one to assume, Akil is a fighter. I've seen Kil knock more than a few niggas to the ground when he's rubbed the wrong way. "Kil why are you looking like your dog died. Sole` has your ass in the dog house again?" I asked. "Word, you look like your balls hurt, or like you just shit on yourself." Denali added...

AKIL

I've known Denali and Yes far too long for me to try to bullshit with them, or to hide what's really going on with me. Besides, Denali has a gift for smelling someone's bullshit anyway. I guess that's why he is so good at negotiating and such a good judge of character. I always said he'd make a good detective, lawyer, or judge. If I am to tell anyone what my deal is, it would have to be my brothers. Right now these are the only two souls I can trust.

"I'm going through the storms right now and I don't have an umbrella." I said trying to be philosophical. "What the fuck are you talking about storms and umbrellas?" Denali asked looking at me like I was crazy. "Word son, is being a daddy getting to you?" Yes asked as he sipped his Corona. "It's not becoming a father that has me troubled. I've never been happier about something in my life" I responded still stalling. "So what is it nigga, spit it out?" Yes asked impatiently...

YES

How many times do I have to tell Akil's out of control ass to slow down? A married man has no business trying to keep up with or out do his single friends. When a relationship doesn't work out for me and Denali, it's no big loss. But Akil is married to a beautiful woman. I never understood why he couldn't do right by Sole`. Even I know that a married man will lose one hundred percent of the time competing against a man that has nothing to lose.

I tell Kil all of the time that he's playing the "game" with a whole lot more money than me and Lee. I always tell Kil, that he's gonna fuck around and lose his marriage and house playing the game like we do. But Kil has the hardest head in the world, so until he falls down he won't walk straight.

Akil's father once told us that a married man must divorce the single man in him if his marriage is gonna work. I guess Akil must've forgotten that and all of the other gems his pops passed on to us. I just hope if or when I get married, I make decisions like a married man and not as a bachelor...

AKIL

"I was messing around with this bitch and now she's black balling me. I'm talking some big time extortion shit. She took some pictures while I was sleep of her sucking my dick. Now she's threatening to send the pics to Sole's office if I don't continue to pay her off. She's already beat my ass for seventy grand. I'm not gonna be able to keep giving this bitch money like this. I've already dipped into me and Sole's joint account to pay this bitch off.

"This whole thing is stressing me out. I'm thinking about selling a property if shit really gets thick. I haven't made love to Sole` in a while and I know she thinks I'm not attracted to her anyone because she's pregnant and put on some extra weight. But she is even more beautiful now that she's pregnant. I'm loosing weight and my hair is falling out over this shit." I said pointing to the left side of my hairline, showing them the balding underneath my dreads.

DENALI

"Damn Kil, I don't know what to tell you, but you are in deep now babypaw. Sometimes a man has to find his own way out, especially when you willingly walked right into the situation. I just hope you don't lose your marriage behind this shit. You know Sole is on her last thread with you and this bullshit." I said being honest and upfront with Kil.

Everybody wants to do the crime but cries for help and forgiveness when it's time to do the time. I'm really not in a position to judge another man, but Akil needs to get his shit together pronto. But then again which one of us doesn't, as far as the ladies are concerned.

AMERIE

For the first time, I think I'm in love with a man and not his money. It's a miracle for me with all that I've been through with niggas. I would've never thought in a billion years that I would find myself feeling like this.

Growing up, my mother got involved into prostitution and she didn't know how to separate her dark side from her mother side. So I was molested and raped by many of the men my mother had coming in and out of the house, way too many times for me to remember. After running away from all of that, I ended up living with different men doing what I had to do to survive.

I made sure that I went to school during the day but at night I had to lay underneath some nigga that I really didn't want on top of me. I started stripping at the age of sixteen, so that I could support myself and wouldn't have to rely on some man's dollar. I danced for about two years until the older dancers taught me how to really get money, diva style. So at eighteen I was used to dealing with the rappers, athletes, and big Willy type.

I learned that a real woman comes to the table with her own situation. That's why I went on and graduated from college. I also have a salon in Virginia, so I know how to get money for myself. When I decided to move to New York, after my girl Porche convinced me that it was still big money out here and that all of the Willy's weren't dead or in jail, love was the last thing on my mind.

I came out here to pursue my acting career and to find money. Everything was going according to plan, until I met Yes. I know he is probably wondering why we haven't had sex by now. But I want to make love to this man and have him make love to me in return. I want Yes to have all of me and I want to give him something of value. I've given up my body so recklessly and for all the wrong reasons in the past that now I want to do it right.

"Hey baby, I just fell asleep." I said as I opened the door for Yes as he walked in wearing a butter soft brown leather jacket. "Oh I'm sorry to wake you baby. I forgot to call because I was talking to Akil and we got to arguing as usual. That nigga is off the hook with his shit." Yes said as he gave me a full kiss.

"Well come in here, I was just laying on the sofa listening to the radio." I said as I walked him into my living room that was lit with a red light bulb. "Damn baby you trying to seduce me? You know I'm easy?" Yes said as he took a seat on the sofa. "Shut up silly. I always put my red light on whenever I want to relax and think at night." I said realizing that Yes was looking rather tasty underneath the red light.

Being that me and Yes haven't sexed yet, all we do is talk and cuddle. For some strange reason, I have now become this very affectionate woman. "I love being in your arms at night baby." I said to Yes as we just laid there relaxing, listening to music.

"I love having you in my arms. Do you want to hear

something funny baby?" Yes asked with his smooth voice. "Yes I do." I said as I laid my head on his broad chest.

"I've never been the cuddling, holding a woman type. I was always on some stone cold, I don't give a fuck shit towards women. But with you it's different. I'm not afraid anymore to feel what I feel." Yes said as he dipped his head and started kissing me.

As we were kissing I started to feel the nature in Yes' pants rise as he caressed my hips and back. "Damn baby I didn't know you had it like that." I said as I really felt just how much Yes was working with. As we continued to kiss, I started to think, as much as I want Yes, it just didn't feel like the timing was right. "Hold on baby, I think we need to fall back a bit." Yes said as he pulled back off of me.

"What, you don't want to do this either?" I asked sounding like a little girl protecting her virginity. "Yea, I do want to do it, just not right now... not like this." Yes answered as he held my hand. So for the remainder of the night we just laid there underneath the sexy red light, telling jokes and talking about the life we want together. With Yes, I'm finally learning how to deal with a man without sex or money being the cause of the relationship...

CHAPTER 7

AKIL

There is definitely no peace in a lie. This whole situation is taking a toll on me. Everyone at work, to the people I run into in the street are all asking me if I'm alright; like I'm using drugs or something. Besides a little weed every now and then, I'm drug free. But from the way I've been looking lately, you can't tell.

I should just tell Sole` the truth because she did say "for better or for worst." Only thing is how many times am I gonna ask for her forgiveness. I have messed up so many times in the past that it's an act of God that she's still with my cheating ass. I'm no fool, I know niggas go at Sole` all day every day but somehow she sticks to me. The last time I fucked up, I swore to her before God that it would be my last time. But here I go again.

How would I approach her? What would I say? "Baby, I know that I promised to be faithful and true to you and our marriage, but I've been nothing but a liar, deceiver, and unfaithful husband to you. I have once again violated our union, but not only with women as before. This time I went one step further and messed around with a dude." Is that what I should say? Hell no, picture that shit...

SOLE`

This will be my last day at the office. I'm seven months pregnant and as big as a house. My ankles are swollen and I'm tired of the everyday hustle and bustle of running my own business. I know the doctors have confirmed that I'm having a baby, but a baby what? My ass has ballooned to a chunky one hundred and ninety five pounds and I feel, every extra forty five pounds that I've put on.

Men have no idea what women go through during pregnancy. I think if men knew, they would be more supportive during the pregnancy. Lately, Akil's behavior has been more erratic than usual and I'm disgusted with all of his shit. I'm so excited and humbled about being a new mommy that it helps me to overlook Akil's bullshit.

I have come a long way from living in that two bedroom apartment with my mother and two sisters. My mother raised us to be independent women, but never to be independent of love, receiving help, and sharing your life with a man. My mother sacrificed her own personal life early on. She wanted us to see that a black woman can stand alone. My mother made it her business to instill in us teamwork and the power of family. After me and my sisters were of age, my mother started dating again. That's when she met and married my stepfather James, who she has been married to for the last fifteen years.

My mother has always said that "Men and women are here to work together and to make each other better." I often call my mother when I need some good womanly advice and the last time we spoke, I told her all about me and Akil's situation. She said to me, "A man and a woman both have to battle to make a relationship work. A man battles on one level and a woman another, but they should never battle against each other. Never let your ego stop you from loving your husband. Only love can make a marriage work."

My mother is a very philosophical woman who takes the teachings of Jesus, Buddha, and every great spiritual leader to heart. My mother is the reason why I believed I would graduate from college and build a multimillion dollar business from scratch. She is the reason why I knew I would be successful in life. She is also the reason why I continue to fight and work to make my marriage work. I just hope mama is right about me and Akil…..

AKIL

My man Rich once told me that what we confront becomes weaker and what we run from grows stronger. He also said something about the important things we avoid doing now, will be forced upon us later. Rich always had a slick way with words and a very objective perspective about life. I should give his ass a call.

"Yo Rich its Akil, what it is catdaddy?" I spoke into the phone. "I'm living and winning Kil. What's up with you?" Rich said sounding happy to hear from me. "Man I got myself into some sticky shit this time Rich. I need some advice about how I should handle this one." I said. "Talk to me." Rich responded. "I ain't shit Rich. I've been living a lie for way too long. Ever since I said "I do" to my wife, I've been "doing" everything and everybody. I know better than anybody out here that Sole` is beautiful and special, so I don't need to hear that shit again." I said to let Rich know I didn't want to hear the obvious. I then continued.

"I truly do love my wife but remaining faithful has always been a problem for me. No matter how hard I try, I always break down and end up in some woman's bed. But Rich this time I did the unimaginable. I have now bit that forbidden fruit. Now someone is using what we did to get what I have.

"My marriage, reputation, and finances are all on the line. I've been thinking about telling Sole` but I'm afraid she'll leave me this time. Rich I've really fucked up." I said as a tear rolled down my face. "I really don't want to judge or preach to you Kil, you know that ain't my MO. Just know you are better than the mistakes you make. Every man lies on one level or another we just reap different consequences for our lies. I know you're real sweet on the ladies. I also know that you really do love Sole`.

"Love ain't your problem my nigga. I think your problem is lust. Once you learn how to love Sole` more than you lust other women your problem will be solved." Rich said in his slick style.

"That shit all sounds good but how do I do that Rich?" I asked as another tear hit my slacks. "It sounds like it's real easy for you to say "I do", but you need to learn how to say "I don't". When your ass said "I do" to Sole` at the alter that was only half the battle. From that moment on you would have to say, "I don't" to every other woman that interest you. We both know that there are always gonna be other women that interest you. Shit, everyday I see at least three women I wouldn't mind tasting, and that's before I get to the office. I've learned many years ago that there are only two decisions a man can make, but there are many consequences he can face." Rich said then got dead quiet.

"Two decisions you say Rich. So what are they?" I said hanging onto the edge of my seat in anticipation. They are "yes" and "no". Once you decide "yes", you'll have to continue to choose "no" to reap the rewards of that "yes". Think about that my nigga.

Talking to Rich is always refreshing because he's honest and full of principle. Rich said that he was moving back to the city because he is starting a men's organization for prisoners. I told him to definitely holla at me when he gets to town, but I'll probably talk to him before then...

CHAPTER 8

<u>YES</u>

I decided that me and Amerie needed a little weekend getaway, so I'm taking her to Cancun for the next four days. Amerie has no idea what I have in store for her while on this trip. These last seven months have taught me that not all women are ho's, paper chasing, sneaky, and all those others qualities I used to see in every woman, regardless if it was true or not.

Amerie has entered into my heart. I want to make it official, showing her that I appreciate what she has brought to my world. The last four months that we've been officially committed, I've somehow managed to be faithful to her, even though we don't sex. I've been shooting chicks down like I'm gay or on some married shit.

It's funny, because it's like I'm already fulfilled and don't need another chick for anything. Amerie just does it for me in every way. Life is crazy, because at the New Years Eve party when Akil gave Sole` that new wedding band, me and Amerie's eyes met. Although I had only known her for twenty minutes at the time, I heard a voice in my head say, "she's the first one."

Now I'm not a religious dude, but if I ever heard from above it was then. I have probably slept with over a thousand women and never once have I ever thought about only sleeping with one. Shit, since I was fourteen, I've always had at least five broads in my stable. Yet with Amerie none of that seems to matter. It feels like our souls were prepared and purposed to meet on December 31, 1999 at approximately 11:40PM. It's like regardless of our motivations going in we were meant to be together in the end.

I'm quite sure Amerie has some dirt underneath her fingernails. She probably wanted from me the same things every other chick I meet in the club wants: Some dick and some money. She probably wanted to turn me out and get in my pockets, thinking she would be the first chick to go shopping with my money. Look at us now. This whole shit is crazy to me whenever I really think about it...

AMERIE

I'm too much in love with Yes to keep hiding important things from him. I've somehow managed to keep Tony a little secret and it's killing me. I know Yes is still out there fucking around especially since I haven't given him any pussy yet. I just hope he's using protection because when we finally do get it on I want to feel him all up in me, naturally.

It's crazy because I always make a nigga strap up and put a condom on. I don't care how horny I'm feeling. I always practice safe sex. But with Yes it's different. I want him to be one of only two men that I let sex me without protection. With Yes I don't want him to only sex me, I want him to make love to me.

Yes has no idea that I've been seeing Tony on the side from time to time. For the two to three grand Tony always leaves with me whenever we do see each other, I usually let him have a taste. Tony loves to eat a pussy so whenever I'm feeling up to it I'll sit on his face and let him feast on my sweet stuff. Tony is one of those short thick dick niggas with no stamina. So whenever I really give him some, it's over for him before I even get started.

Tony always hits me with the,"Damn girl your pussy is so good". The truth is that although my stuff is good, his little dick is so bad.

I hate fucking with little dick niggas. Lucky for Tony he has money. If he didn't have money, his little dick ass would have been dismissed at the door. Since me and Yes have really gotten serious, four months ago, I've only seen Tony twice. Only once have I let him get his freak on.

Lately, Tony has been calling and stressing me out. He's been talking crazy, saying he's in love with me and wants for us to be together. I'm gonna have to tell Yes about Tony. I don't want Tony showing up unexpectedly and causing a scene. I know that Yes has a wild side and I don't know what he would do in a confrontational situation. Tony is only five nine one hundred and sixty pounds soak and wet. Meanwhile, Yes is six two, two hundred and twenty pounds, so it's best that I keep them apart.

Tony is actually the nigga that paid for my duplex loft, so he has the mind set that he can just show up at anytime, unannounced. Lately I've been thinking about moving out. I thought about moving into Yes' townhouse, but who knows. I've also been having a lot of regret about the things I've done in my past.

I've done played more than a few games with men and every time I got what I wanted, a little dick action and a whole lot of money. But somehow I'm now finally starting to think about the consequences of all that. With all that I've done in the past, it has to come back to me sooner or later in one form or another. I just know it will come back around, I can almost feel it. That's why I have been taking my time with Yes because if he hurts me it will probably kill me, I mean it would literally kill me.

I know it may sound crazy but it's true. Yes has finally allowed me to feel again. He has broken my emotional wall down.

So if he takes that away from me I will definitely go crazy. Damn, I hate feeling so exposed and vulnerable like this, especially for a man. It's like I don't have any control over my feelings anymore but I'm not afraid anymore. I just want Yes to know how much he means to me. He's opened me up, and completely changed my whole world around. Damn I love my man...

DENALI

Since I've been going to church with India lately I decided that I would also attend the manhood empowerment network at the church. One of the reasons I decided to attend was because the minister seemed to be so real and down to earth at the church, I figured the men's meetings would be the same.

The fellas meet on Wednesday nights, so I'm gonna slide on through tonight. Once I got to the meeting, I was pleasantly surprised by what I saw. Although it was a Wednesday summer night and ass was on every New York City street corner, there stood about fifteen hundred brothers from all walks of life in the hall unified. There wasn't any bow tie wearing, bean pie selling brothers just regular Joe Blows.

Some dudes were professionally dressed, looking like GQ models. Some were still in their work uniforms from earlier. But the majority of the cats were in jeans, shorts, sweats, and more white tees than boot camp. The meetings were held in the hall of the church, which made it more welcoming and created a more relaxed vibe.

When the minister walked out you could tell that he had the attention, affection, and admiration of every pair of eyes in the hall. Minister Gilmore looked about twenty three but I knew he couldn't be that young doing what he does.

I do know, that the dude can't be over thirty though. Minister Gilmore was casually dressed in a grey and blue rocawear summer sweat suit and had on some white on white Adidas classics.

During the church services, I always bug out by how young dude looks, now he really looks like one of the cats from the block. When he stood up at the podium he began with, "Will every man in the house greet his brother with love". And for the next ten minutes brothers walked around and embraced each other with the same spirit and sincerity that me, Kil, and Yes express towards each other. I was definitely touched because everything and everyone seemed so real in the hall. No ego's, no pretenders, it didn't matter if you had a Buick or a Benz, one dollar in your pocket or millions of dollars in the bank. We were all brothers, well at least for the night. There was a common male camaraderie in the air but this time it wasn't in a strip club, on a court or field, or in a locker room.

"Manhood is spiritual and mental. Although biologically we change and our bodies mature with age, unless there's a maturity and transformation mentally you are still a boy. Society is attacking,

74

contradicting, and confusing the image of manhood in this country. Traditionally the African American man has been destructive to his own. The black man in America has been taught, trained, and tricked into thinking of himself as a slave, menace, boy, Mandingo, and every other negative element of society. We have been taught how to be pimps, playas, entertainers, hustlers, everything they want us to be, except men. I'm here to tell y'all that shit must change." The minister said causing the hall to go crazy.

Oh shit, I know the minister didn't just let one go, like he's gansta? See this is why I like this brother so much he speaks to men like men. *"What God created is positive and good. As men we can not go out into this confused world and expect to find our manhood. Don't y'all know that America's systems want us to be suckers, it wants the black woman to be a slut, and it wants our children to be stupid? Only God can give us what is released from his hands. Therefore as men we must return to God to get our manhood."* Minister said as the brothers started applauding and yelling, like we were at the Knicks game.

Wow, this brother is sharp. He has every type of nigga in here convinced that God is the source and Jesus the answer. I've been to more churches than a successful evangelist. And I always walk into a church full of old washed up slave acting women, who force their husbands to join the church and become deacons or something. That's one of the reasons why I don't go to church. They don't know how to empower people. But what this dude is doing is different. He's touching the Wall Street brother, street corner brother, and blue collar man, all in the name of the Lord. Now this I can get with, it's that other shit that ain't for me…

YES

After we arrived in Cancun, me and Amerie decided to settle into our luxurious hotel suite. We napped for about thirty minutes and showered as we prepared for a romantic evening in the lovely Cancun. The scenery was perfect for what I had planned. It was a warm but comfortable eighty degrees with clear skies. And as the water that surrounded the hotel joined together with the gentle breeze coming into shore, it made the weather feel magical; like paradise.

As Amerie unpacked and headed for the shower, I laid out her attire for the evening on the king size waterbed that sat in our presidential suite. She didn't know but I had bought her that fifteen thousand dollar Chanel dress and the platinum tennis bracelet I saw her admiring on Angela Bassett. The one she was wide eyed over, as we watched some red carpet special a few weeks back. Except for the times when we go out, I haven't really spent any money on Amerie.

What I love the most about Amerie is that she doesn't ask me for a thing. Her hair salon has to be making a killing, because she wants for nothing, and babygirl lives a luxurious lifestyle. Her salon must be bringing in the dough or she must have some sucker ass nigga on the side tricking on her. I know she probably thinks that I don't know what time it is out here, but I have been dealing with women for far too long not to know.

So this is the first time she is actually seeing how long my money really is. I know she's gonna be surprised when she sees how deep my pocket's run. It's funny, because Amerie has been patient with giving up the sex and I have been patient with giving up the money. But here we are anyway in love vacationing in paradise.

I figured I would leave the 7000sqft. Presidential suite that covered the entire thirty second floor and allow Amerie to get ready for the evening alone. I also left her a note, which read. "This is only the beginning. Meet me out front in one hour" I signed it "Your future…

AMERIE

This shower feels so good, I almost wish this warm water could wash away the anxiety I'm feeling. I don't know why, but I have a feeling that something special is going to happen. Yes has been so gentle with me and I've never had a man look at me the way he's been looking into me lately. It looks as if Yes has found something that he's been looking for all his life.

It's hard for me to believe, that this is the same man Porche said was as cold as ice when it came down to expressing his emotions towards women. She said he'll give you some dick and nothing more. She said he was more about getting money and having sex, than settling down and building a family. Yet, now when he looks at me there is purity, a confidence, and a loving affection in his eyes, that is breath taking. I can barely stand to look him in the eyes without tears of joy and happiness overtaking my eyes.

On the airplane ride over here, Yes just held my hand so lovingly the whole time making me feel so secure. I hate flying but somehow I felt safe flying with Yes by my side there holding my hand. He has been kissing me so softly and seductively, that I'm about to die if he doesn't make love to me already.

"Yes…Yes, why don't you come and wash my back baby." I yelled softly from the hot shower as it steamed up the huge bathroom. I was hoping he would join me in the shower and finally make love to me while I was dripping wet in the steamy bathroom. "Yes…Yes are you there honey?" I asked listening for a response from him. Maybe he stepped out to get some ice, I thought. Then I realized this suite already has everything in it with extra service a dial away.

After I exited the shower, I dried my wet body off. I then wrapped a large towel around my body and headed for the bedroom portion of the suite. As I looked to the bed, I was overwhelmed and it started happening again. That feeling of love, joy, and happiness overtook my body and the tears started to fall from my eyes again. I have probably cried more in the last few months since I've been with Yes, than in all of my years combined.

How did he remember I wanted this dress and this bracelet? I thought he was sleep during the award show. Where did he go? What is he up to? Do I actually deserve all of this? All of these questions were running through my mind, as I sat there looking at the bed.

Is this God's way of making amends for my dysfunctional upbringing? This really cannot be happening to me. This is for all of those romantics, not me. Is this really going down like this? I thought as the tears fell onto the bed. At that moment, I was having the years of fear, the pain, and the hate I had towards my father, the men who raped me, and all men in general, leave my body with each tear drop from my eye.

As I stood there crying, suddenly a warm feeling of trust and security settled in. I started to feel like everything was gonna be alright, that it was okay to let go and allow myself to feel everything that was happening. I started to feel like a two hundred pound dead body had just been lifted from off of my back. Maybe that was the dead weight of bitterness, manipulation, and rage I was holding against men for all of these years? It could be all of the dead weight of those deadly relationships I was apart of in my past. For the first time, I finally felt free, like there wasn't anything holding me back. Is this what love feels like...

CHAPTER 9

SOLE`

I have made it official, today is the last day I will be running the business from the office. I went over the game plan with my staff, so everyone knows what I expect and what to do while I'm gone. Today they actually threw me a surprise baby shower in the office. What should I have expected from an office of six females and two homosexuals?

My staff is great. I really appreciate all that they do for me. I hope I'll be able to stay away from the office peacefully. Being that I'm such a perfectionist and driven about my business, this new mommy role is a major step for me.

Just as I was preparing to leave the office, I noticed the day's mail and this huge "something important" envelope underneath some junk mail. When I picked up the envelope I looked at the name Tracy Williams. Immediately I got excited because I thought it was my sorority sister Tre` from Maryland. I haven't heard from Tre' since she got married to some cop named Bobby that was also in Law school. I then noticed that the envelope had a New York City address. Has Tre` moved to New York? I thought as I opened the package.

[Dear Mrs. Butler I know that all of this may come as a surprise to you but I think this is something you need to know. I hope that you'll understand, this was not sent to intentionally hurt you. I actually want to help. I am sending this in love because love never lies. I'm sorry that someone who says that they "love you" has been living a lie.]

What in the hell is going on? I thought to myself. As I opened the second envelope my world as I knew it came to a sudden end. I can not believe what my eyes are telling my heart.

This can't be the husband I've been faithful to for all these year? This is not the man who's baby I'm about to bring into this world? Is this the same man who I have forgiven countless times? The man that always said he has changed? This is not Akil in these pictures receiving oral sex from another man, who's dressed like a woman? Oh Lord, this is not the same man who makes love to me? This is not the same dick that I suck practically every night.

How could he do this to me, to us, to our soon to be family? After all that I've done for this man: This is the fruit of it? The financial support I gave him when times weren't so prosperous with his career. All of the crazy things I do sexually for this man. I cook, clean, and serve him like a fucking king and this is what I get back in return? My mind was working over drive as I sat there asking myself thousands of questions. But then I noticed what appeared to be blood staining the crotch area of my maternity dress.

Oh shit, I'm bleeding down there I hope my baby is alright. Oh my God my stomach, the pain is excruciating. I think my baby is coming. "Hello Pam, can you come in here? I think I'm going into labor." I said to Pam my assistant and friend, as I did my best to do what I've learned in Lamaze class.

As Pamela entered my office, I noticed she was in a panic. Her eyes did happen to gaze upon the photos that sat next to me on the floor. I dropped them as I sat in my lazy boy office chair in shock and in pain. Pam did her best to ignore what her eyes saw in those pictures. But I saw the shock all in her eyes. "It's gonna be alright Sole`. Just breathe and relax. I'll get you to the hospital safely. Don't worry about a thing. It's all gonna be alright girlfriend, just relax…

AKIL

"Jim I need to take my ass on home to the wife." I said to Jim the bartender, as I swallowed down another shot of Brandi. "Let me call you a cab because you're in no shape to drive home. Damn son, are you trying to drink your problems away? I hope you realize that when you sober up they will still be there waiting for you to handle them." Jim said as he cleaned off the bar top with his left hand.

"Nah Jim, just every now and then a man needs a drink. If we didn't, you would be out of business, right Jim Brownski?" I said as I was feeling the earth rotate around her axis. "I hear that. But you've been here since twelve o' clock drinking everything in stock. I hope your ass don't get sick because of this." Jim said with a fatherly concern on his face. "My truck is in the parking lot so it will be okay. Just make sure I get home in one piece Jim," I said.

"Don't worry, I got you youngblood." Jim responded. Jim is a real cool middle aged white dude. My father put me on to Jim's bar years ago. My pops and Jim go way back. I'm quite sure Jim is a former hippie or something. He's one of those white people that you forget they're white when you're around them.

Jim has to be the greatest listener in the world. He always has an available ear for a running mouth, and today it was my mouth that was running. As Jim was walking me to catch a cab, I noticed that I forgot to turn my cell phone back on. When I finally turned it back on I realized I had nine voice messages awaiting me. I'm way too fucked up and tired for conversation. I just want to get my black ass home to Sole` and get some sleep. Tomorrow is another day and I'll return calls then. But right now, I have an important appointment with my Stearns and Foster mattress.

After the cab dropped me off, I stumbled into our penthouse door and noticed that Sole` wasn't home. From what I could remember there were no signs of her being in since this morning. I looked at the clock and it was only eight thirty six. So I figured Sole` was still at her office or out with her booshi ass AKA sisters. They get on my damn nerve with all of that sorority chirping and stepping bullshit.

As I'm lying on the floor in our oversized bedroom, I hear the telephone start ringing. Damn I forgot to turn the muthafuckin` ringer off. Damn, who the fuck could this be?

"Hello." I answered half aggravated and half dead. "Akil this is Pamela." The soft voice on the other end responded. "Hey Pam, Sole` ain't here right now." I said ready to bang the phone down on her ass. I was also trying to fight off the Congo band that was setting up shop in my head. "I know she's not there. I've been calling you all evening. Sole` is in labor and she is having major complications. We are at St. Vincent, why don't you head on over here, she really needs your support right now." Pam said in a concerned tone. "Yea okay, I'm on my way now. Thanks Pam, I appreciate what you've done." I said before hanging up the phone.

Right after I hung up the phone it hit me like a stray bullet. I'm as drunk as a skunk. I'm in no shape to do anything. I can't even get up off the damn floor, let alone drive or hail down a cab. So I just sat there throwing up with my head kicking my ass. My wife was in a complicated labor procedure. And I was there paralyzed, sitting in my own vomit, with my thumb in my ass. At the most crucial time, my wife couldn't count on me.

There I was stuck, while Sole` was fighting for the survival of our family. Women have died during complicated labor procedures, I just hoped that my wife and baby would be alright.

How did my day turn out like this? I went from just going to get a drink to ease my mind before I confessed and came clean with Sole`, to this. Before I knew what had hit me, I was in la, la, land, sleeping like a baby. Maybe this whole Tracey scandal and Sole's complications are one long bad dream…

DENALI

Wednesday nights at the Boom Boom Room, my jazz and R&B spot, is definitely for my professional "just want to get their swerve on" older crowd. The Boom Boom Room has a more intimate and personal vibe than the Kingdome. I usually get a lot of couples who come to have a nice time out on the town in here. After the men's meeting, I figured I would stop by and just check up on some things.

As I was strolling through the club, making sure every one was enjoying themselves, I made serious eye contact with this fine ass female. Since I've been attending the manhood empowerment network and rebuilding my relationship with India, I've been slowing down on my one night "wam bam thank you mams". But whoever this woman is has me drawn.

India has said that she wants to wait before we get intimate and I respect that. I'm quite sure India knows me well enough to understand that I still do what I do. I don't know why it is, but the kitty cat be calling a nigga. I usually don't approach women in my club, mainly because I never have to. They all usually know my status and approach me like groupies. I hate a gold digging bitch or a chick that doesn't have any sense of purpose or direction about herself. So I usually just treat a groupie bitch for what she is, some head or some sex. Nothing more than that.

I definitely don't go out of my way to meet women but babydoll is different. I have to spit at honey. When I stepped to her, I realized she was prettier the closer I got to her. She was tall, with a bodacious one hundred and thirty five pound figure and extremely pretty, like I prefer my women to be. She was light skinned with a very short short haircut and was groomed to perfection.

She had on some booty hugging Earl jeans with a cream top and matching Gucci shoes. Shorty was definitely looking worth my approach, so I had to step to her. When I finally made my way over to her she was trying to play like she didn't see me. It never fails women are always trying to play the "I don't know who you are" game, if I approach them.

"Good evening sweetheart. Are you enjoying yourself?" I asked giving her my bedroom smile.

"Yea I'm having a wonderful time, what about yourself?" She asked, still not making eye contact with me. Honey is definitely playing this game. "I always enjoy myself in here. My name is Denali and yours?" I asked taking her softly by the hand. When I touched her, I saw a burst of excitement hit her eyes but then she went back to the game playing. "So do you always walk around the club like you own it, looking for women to hit on?" She asked blowing her cover.

"So that's how I'm walking around, like I own the club? That is definitely a first for me. Well I do know the owner pretty well. Why don't you join me upstairs? The owner gives me special privileges, I think he'll let me use his special lounge area upstairs." I said as I pointed up to my secluded lounge area in the club. "Okay, just give me a second, I have to tell my girl what's going on. She's in the bathroom right now." Shorty said with a huge smile on her pretty face.

After John, one of my security guards brought her upstairs into my secluded VIP room, the truth started to come out. "This is real nice Denali I'm happy I'm finally up in here." Shorty said realizing she was blowing her own spot up. "Excuse me?" I asked letting honey shoot herself in the ass. "I said this is real nice." She said then got real quiet. By honey's excitement I kind of thought she was young for a hot second.

"So when are you gonna tell me your name?" I asked as the band was playing Melissa Morgan's "Do me baby" instrumental. "My name is Meisha, it's really nice to finally meet you Denali. I can't front, I know who you are. I just wanted to see if what I hear about you was true or not." Meisha said sparking my curiosity. "What is it that you hear?" I asked remaining calm. "I hear that you act as if you can have anything and anyone." She said with a little sass in her demeanor.

Being that shorty knew the order, I had no need to bullshit and act like she didn't know what this was all about. "So Ms. Lady, it's obvious that you know who I am, so let's not play games. What I just did by approaching you, I don't do. I only stepped to you because I'm feeling what you got happening. Do you understand what I'm saying? Do you feel where I'm coming from Ms. Lady?" I whispered in her ear, while my left hand ran along her soft thigh.

"Yea baby I understand and I feel where you're coming from. I just want you to be clear on something. I'm not a ho or some freak chick. So I'm not about to suck or fuck you in some club, just because you own it. That ain't how this is going down. You feel *me*? So if you want me, treat me like you do." Meisha said so confidently that my dick started to get hard.

There is one thing that always impresses me about a female. It's when she carries herself like a lady. "I like your style baby and would have it no other way. Is there anything you would like to drink?" I asked her graciously, respecting how she held herself down. "Yes, I would love a glass of Cristal." She said as she crossed her long and thick legs. Damn shorty is bad, I'm gonna fuck the shit out of her ass tonight and she knows it...

AMERIE
[This is only the beginning meet me out front in one hour]
What is Yes up to, I thought as I put the note down. After I dressed and put on my new platinum and diamond filled bracelet, I looked at myself in the full body length mirror and started to think. I am a beautiful woman. For twenty nine years I've looked at myself as sexy, a diva, in every way possible, but as a beautiful woman. I've never felt beautiful before. I've never felt innocent, precious, and gentle. I now feel soft and like a beautiful woman. I now feel alive, like God does care about me.

As I exit our Presidential suite and take the long elevator ride down the thirty two stories that feeling of excitement and anticipation started to overwhelm me again. When I finally got to the front where Yes said for me to meet him, there stood the longest and slickest limo I had ever seen. There was also a short little chubby Mexican man, with curly hair, dressed in a tuxedo holding a sign that said, "Ms. Amerie Black". My last name is Taylor but Yes' last name is Black.

"Mrs. Black, how are you doing on this picture perfect evening? I am Sal your driver." The chubby driver politely asked me with his Latin accent, as he introduced himself. "I am fine. How are you feeling Sal?" I asked returning his polite greeting. "I'm fine, thanks. Mr. Black has arranged for me to escort you to a secret location where he awaits your arrival." Sal said as he took my hand and gently helped me into the limo, like I was a queen.

When I sat down inside of the limo there were white, pink, and purple roses all over the place. There also sat a pink jewelry box next to a huge box of my favorite chocolates. When I opened the jewelry box, there was a beautiful pink diamond necklace sitting there for me to put on. I couldn't believe what was happening to me. I couldn't believe Yes would spend so much money on a gift for me. Isn't he the same man that was tough on the ladies, never giving up the dollars? Doesn't he know that I was coming after his money, when we first met?

I couldn't help but to start crying as Sade played softly in the limo while we drove up the beautiful majestic coast. After about a twenty minute drive up the coast, the limo stopped and Sal opened up my door. "Mrs. Black this is as far as I can take you. But there's your other ride." Sal said pointing to the private helicopter that stood waiting for me. At that point, my eyes were all puffy and my face was a mess. I had makeup everywhere and could barely see out of my eyes.

How beautiful is this, I thought, as we flew over the crystal clear waters and towering grassy mountains on our way to this secret location. When we finally landed to what appeared to be a private retreat there was a heavenly view of the mountains and waterfalls. I felt like I had just died and went to heaven. Everything was so magical. As I exited the helicopter I realized that it was the only property for as far as my eyes could see. For a moment, I had a feeling of fear shoot through my body, but then I was put at ease as my man came slowly walking out of the house.

Yes came walking towards me looking as handsome as I had ever remembered seeing him. His hair was cut razor sharply and he was wearing a cream linen summer suit with tan sandals. All of which complimented his caramel complexion and masculine features to perfection. There he was, the man that was so tough on the ladies. The man who's pockets I was scheming on. There he was, the man who has changed my world, the man I love. There he was, my man for life...

YES

Wow, look at how beautiful my baby looks. "Wow baby, you are so beautiful." I said to Amerie as we stood face to face in the heavenly scenery. I couldn't have asked for a better setting than this. In all of my years, I never thought I would experience something so wonderful with a woman. Remember, my uncle sugar taught me to never trust or give your all to a bitch. "Thanks honey. You look beautiful too." Amerie said as we stood there looking at each other in awe.

"Let's go inside, I have a surprise for you." I said taking Amerie by the hand as I tried to lead her into the house. She suddenly stopped and started crying, right there on the spot. "What's the matter baby? Is something wrong?" I asked puzzled by her tears. "No honey nothing is wrong. For the very first time in my life everything is right. For the first time everything is perfect and I don't know if I deserve all of this. I have done a lot of things in my past that I'm now ashamed of because of how good you make me feel. I have used men, abused my body, and my intentions were on doing the same to you baby. Now here I stand looking you in the eyes and knowing that you are the only man I want." Amerie said crying as I held her close, wiping her precious tears away.

Amerie was actually becoming more and more beautiful as she cried and came clean with me about the things I already knew anyway. It made me feel so good to know that now there wasn't anything hidden between us. "Baby we both have a past and have done things we would rather forget about. I love you today regardless of your yesterdays. I just hope you will let me love you tomorrow." I said as my eyes started to water, because I was serious with mine. "So let's leave the past in the past. Will you do that for me baby…

DENALI

After I made sure things were running smoothly in the club, I turned everything over to my manager Ted as me and Meisha headed on out. "So would you like for me to drop you off at your place?" I politely asked, as one of my assistants Chris brought my jet black Lamborghini Diablo around the corner. "Is this your car?" Meisha asked as her jaw dropped. She was looking as if her panties were getting wet. "Yea, this is me." I answered as I gave Chris a pound and opened the vertical motioned passenger side door for Meisha to get in.

"So what's up baby? You never answered my question. Do you want me to take you home or what?" I asked as Dave Hollister's "The Program" was playing in the car, as I skirted off. "Nah, I'm cool. I was thinking that we should go back to your place." Meisha said as she rubbed my leg while I drove. I knew once she jumped Into my Diablo, she wouldn't want to leave. "So where do you live baby?" Meisha asked me as she was giving up more and more rhythm by the minute. "I live on 76th and West End Ave." I answered as we waited at the red light.

My condo in the city, is really my "spot". I never ever take women out to my house which is in Jersey. I never let them see my 14000sqft. mansion out in Essex county. I have too much nice and expensive shit in my layout to just bring any and everybody to my home. "So let's go to your place and relax." Meisha said looking at me with those chinky eyes of hers.

In Meisha's eyes, I saw excitement, confidence, and the determination of a prizefighter. It's similar to what I first saw in India. That look of a young woman trying to prove she's older than she really is. Back in the days, I ran through my share of high school tenders, and I have never forgotten that look every young girl has. It doesn't matter how old they pretend to be you can always see what time it really is in their eyes. After I turned twenty five, those young chicks stopped turning me on so much. I got tired of dealing with their inexperience. Besides, I stand to lose too much fucking around with a young mind and body. But even to this day, I still kinda have a thing for them young thangs. But for the last couple of years I haven't slipped up...

CHAPTER 10

AMERIE

As Yes led me into his private retreat, I couldn't help but to think about my favorite scene in the movie Jason's Lyric. The scene when Allan Payne's character Jason, takes Jade Pickett's character Lyric, to this old museum where they have lunch and spend a romantic day together in the beauty of nature. "This house is beautiful honey." I said to Yes as I stood in awe of all the antique furniture and the ancient Indian vibe that was in the house.

"Yea, but I don't come out here much. I bought this house three years ago as a vacation spot. I just haven't found anyone to share it with. That is until you came along. I'm a man with a lot to give and I want to share it all with you Amerie Taylor." Yes said as he kissed me softly on the lips. "I want to give you all of me and share my life with you too honey." I said as I stood in Yes' strong arms feeling adored and precious. "Let's have our dinner." Yes said as we walked out to the patio, which had a perfect view of the rain forrest and giant waterfalls?

As we ate dinner my eyes started to tear again causing me to feel a little embarrassed by my sensitivity. "Why do you keep crying baby? I didn't want you to be sad. I thought this would all make you happy." Yes said misunderstanding the nature of my cries. "I am happy. In fact I've never been happier. This one night has already made up for all of the miserable birthdays I had as a little girl, expecting to hear from my father. This one night, has made up for all of the nights I laid in the bed, with men I cared nothing about who just wanted to have sex with me." I was saying before Yes interrupted me...

YES

Damn, I had no idea of all the shit Amerie has gone through. It just goes to show you never really know what a person has gone through to become the person that they are. I know she didn't grow up with a loving father or father figure, but damn. I now doubt if my baby has every received a man's love before.

"Look baby, I understand that your past was rough. I realize that you may not have had the loving you needed as a young lady growing up, but there is nothing we can do about that now." I said, gently holding her hand across the table. "There is something that I want to do that will insure the past will remain your past and that your future will be one of love and happiness." I said as I stood up and then got down on one knee. "Oh my God, Yes what are you doing baby?" Amerie asked trying not to hyperventilate and pass out by the power of the moment. "I'm doing what my heart has told me to do. Baby, if someone would have told me that there was a woman especially made for me, I wouldn't have believed them. I'm a man that knows when he knows. You are what I've been looking for and were afraid of having. Baby, would you do me the honor of allowing me to be your husband, and you be my wife for the rest of our lives. Amerie will you marry me...

DENALI

"So what, you don't have to punch the clock tomorrow?" I asked Meisha as we drove up Broadway on our way to my spot. "No I don't have to work tomorrow, I'm doing the school thing right now." She said as we felt the power and finesse of my Lamborghini while we maneuvered on the city street. "Oh yea, what school do you go to and what are you studying?" I asked. "I go to John Jay and I'm a criminal justice major. I want to be a civil attorney." Meisha answered as she looked out of the window.

After we talked a bit, I realized that Meisha was a lot younger than I usually order, but she still had a lot of class, maturity, and direction about herself. "So how old are you baby?" I asked needing to know for legal purposes. "I'm twenty." She said as we were ten

90

minutes away from my condo. "Twenty?" I asked in shock. "I know...I know, I wasn't supposed to be in the club. But whenever there is some thirsty ass bouncer at the door, all I have to do is flirt a little and they always let me in. Men, no offense to you baby, tend to get stupid and weak when they see a pretty face and big ass." Meisha said as my twelve disc CD changer automatically jumped to my Donell Jones CD.

I'm sure my bouncer Ray let her in the club because he saw the same things I saw in Meisha. Meisha has a presence and aura that not every chick possesses. "You definitely are a mature twenty." I said as we were three blocks away from my house. "Yea, I hear that a lot. So what's up Denali, you want to get up like adults or small talk like kids?" She said as she started to unbuckle the belt on my slacks. "What do you think?" I said as Meisha went reaching for my long dog. Meisha's straightforwardness and aggression had my dick harder than Chinese Algebra.

Once she managed to pull all of my stuff from out of my slacks, she bent down and started to slowly lick and suck me off, like I tasted like a pint of chocolate fudge Haagen-Dazs. "Damn boo, you really know how to do that shit." I said looking down and messaging Meisha's head, as she went down deep on me.

After getting head in the whip, we arrived to my spot. Once we got to my apartment, Meisha asked me for the bathroom, a washcloth, and a towel. I was impressed because most chicks I bring back to the spot just want to fuck, with their pussy smelling like a little bit of everything. But just like I thought honey had class.

After I gave her a wash clothe and towel, Meisha slowly undressed right in front of me, like it wasn't shit. She was definitely letting a nigga see a sample of her goods. She then turned and walked to the bathroom, butt naked, making sure I saw all of the ass she was working with.

While Meisha showered up, I lit some candles and popped open a bottle of Moet that I had in my champagne collection. Whenever I'm in the city, I always bring women here. I learned years ago, that I have to be smart with what I show a broad. I think I showed

Veronica way too much, too soon, and that's why she saw so much opportunity with me. "Denali can you do me a favor?" Meisha called out from the shower. "What's up shorty?" I answered, halfway cracking the bathroom door. "Can you wash my back for me baby?" Meisha asked.

Honey has more game than Kobe Bryant, because once I completely opened the bathroom door she had lit the candles I forgot I had in the bathroom. Meisha even turned the CD player on. When I stepped into that bathroom, I walked right into Meisha's seduction. "Take them clothes off and get in here." Meisha commanded me. Once in the shower, we washed each other down while the hot shower water steamed up the entire bathroom. The steam from the water was fogging up every one of the ten mirrors I have covering the bathroom.

"Damn, you look so good baby." I said to Meisha as I stepped back to look at her perfectly shaped body. "Come here!" I said pulling Meisha's soaking wet body into mine, so that we were both underneath the showerhead. As the water came down, we kissed forcefully like we have wanted each other for years. I started kissing her neck, naval, and continued to work my way down into Meisha's loving.

"Oh baby…eat my pussy daddy." Meisha moaned as she clutched and caressed my baldhead, trying to keep herself from fainting. I must have eaten Meisha's pussy for a steamy fifteen minutes before she just collapsed.

"What are you doing to me?" Meisha asked gasping for breath as she looked me in the eye. She then started to kiss and suck my bottom lip. Meisha made sure she also had a taste of her juices.

"Let me have some more of that big dick." Meisha said as I laid down with the shower water pouring down on me. She then started sucking my tender dick, like I was Prince Charles. I then stood up and watched Meisha enjoy my flavor like she was my sex slave. Meisha had skills with hers almost like she sucked dick for a living.

As all of this was going on it dawned on me, that we were licking and sucking while butt naked in the shower with no protection. Now I'm one who always practices safe sex. I've never been a dirty dick nigga. But as Meisha was on her knees and the warm shower water was beating down on the back of my neck, Meisha stood up, looked me square in the eyes, and commanded me to, "Fuck her warm pussy." I couldn't believe that this young twenty year old tender had me mesmerized.

As we started to kiss, I then picked Meisha up and gently placed her on top of me for the long dick ride. "Oh my God daddy, it's so big. It feels so strong." Meisha cried out as she rode me up and down around and around. No condom barely knowing Meisha I was nine inches deep inside of her. The candle light, warm shower water romancing our stimulated bodies, and the R-Kelly "Honey Love" playing in the background, had me more focused on the pleasure of her juicy walls, than the pain of a STD, unwanted pregnancy, or HIV…

AMERIE

"Yes, I will marry you baby." I said as the tears rolled down my cheeks. Yes then placed a heart shaped five carat pink colored diamond engagement ring on my finger, and gave me a kiss I felt in my soul…

YES

"I love you so much baby. Thank you for saying yes. I now feel complete, like I now have that piece of me that was missing. I know I can do anything with you by my side Amerie, you're my missing link booboo." I said as I held Americ and let a tear go myself, under the full moons crystal clear sky. "Will you make love to me honey?" Amerie whispered in my ear as she started to unbutton my shirt, like she couldn't take it anymore.

"That's all I want to do baby." I said as I picked Amerie up and carried her into the bedroom, and softly laid her down on the bed full of rose peddles. I then opened the wall size windows and moved the linen curtains to the side, allowing the moon light and fresh scent of the rain forrest to romance the room. Before I laid a finger on Amerie, I lit the candles that were surrounding the bed and pressed play, so that Luther Vandross could serenade us as we made love.

I then started to kiss Amerie and slowly undress her as she cried. "Take your time with me baby. Will you please do it to me slow?" Amerie asked, like it was gonna be her first time. "Yes baby I'll be gentle... I'll take my time." I said as we started to explore each others bodies and make love to each other. Never before has so much of my being been involved during sex. I actually felt Amerie's heart beat, while I penetrated her deeply. Wow I never thought I would ever feel all of this with a woman. "I love you baby. Amerie, I love you so much...

DENALI

After three hours of unprotected, spine tingling "wanting to call my mother and high five my father" sex, Meisha turned and said to me as we laid hugged up in the bed. "Denali you are a wonderful lover. You made me feel like a woman all over but there is something I have to tell you." "What is it?" I asked as I tried to stay awake. "Although I gave you the pleasure and fulfillment that every man craves from a woman, I have to confess to you, I'm not twenty years old." She said looking more and more innocent as she spoke.

"What the fuck you mean you are not twenty? Yo, how old are you nineteen, eighteen?" I asked, like she had just poured a bucket of ice cold water on my butt naked body. "No Denali, I'm afraid to tell you that I'm not a junior at John Jay College, but a junior at Manhattan Center High school. In fact, I know my mother is gonna trip when I get home. Hopefully she'll be all wrapped up in her boyfriend when I get there. I'm sorry for lying to you but I had to have you tonight. Ever since I was fourteen, I've wanted you all up inside of my young sugarwalls. Tonight, my wet dream for the last two years became a reality." She said looking like she had played the dirtiest trick on me.

Now I've always been good with math, especially arithmetic. But my mind was too distracted by the fact that I was a thirty one year old man who had just slept with a possible minor. All I was thinking about was that long handcuffed bus trip Upstate. "So how old are you shorty?" I asked holding my breath. "I'm sixteen." She said.

"What the fuck you mean you're **SIXTEEN**?" I answered. Oh shit, this bitch set me up. Oh shit, this little young bitch set me up...

CHAPTER 11

AKIL

It's been four long months since the day Sole` left me and took little Akil with her. That happened to have been the best and worst day of my life. After Sole's c-section, while she was recovering from the procedure, I then showed up to hospital. I was hung over from the day before, busted, disgusted, and all out of character. When I finally made it to the hospital, there were many of our family and friends there. Yes couldn't make it because he was out of town. Denali, somehow managed to show up before me, despite his hectic schedule.

When I walked into her room, it was full of balloons and love, but I knew I had fucked up. Sole` remained civil towards me because so many people were there in high spirits. Besides, it's not her style to wild out in public, but I knew that something was wrong. As I went to kiss her she said, "Don't you dare put your dirty fuckin` lips on me!" I thought her anger was the result of me missing the delivery, but boy was I wrong. After everyone left the room and left me and Sole` to ourselves, the truth came out.

"What's your problem honey? I told you I had one too many drinks yesterday and I couldn't hold my liquor?" I said as I sat next to her bed, while she just stared up at the ceiling. But regardless of what I said or how I said it, Sole` just sat there motionless. She didn't say a word, didn't even look at me. For a second, I didn't even know if she was breathing. But then she finally moved, went into her red coach bag, and threw some pictures at me. Oh shit, that bitch Tracey set me up. I was caught out there with my dick in the wrong place at the wrong time.

There it was right in front of me. There wasn't anything I could say. There wasn't anything I could do, because I was stuck.

I was caught out there with my dick in my hand and Sole` was finished with me. Sole` then turned to me, giving me a Mafia stare that pierced my soul to the core. I then knew that it was over. I knew that I had lost my wife. I knew that I had finally lost my family, because of my bullshit.

I then just stayed in the hospital's nursery and hugged and kissed my newborn son, like it would be for the last time. I had no idea what was in store for me and Sole`. When Sole` finally came home from the hospital, three days later with little Kil, she told me to leave and that she wanted a divorce immediately. She didn't want to talk about it. She didn't even let me hold my son. She just told me to get the fuck out of her house.

Just when I was ready to confess and come clean. Just when I had chosen to correct my wrong, I got caught and lost my chance. I guess Rich was right after all, the truth will be told whether we face it or not, whether we tell it or not.

I've now been staying out in Brooklyn since the separation. I'm renting out this three bedrooms, two baths loft in Clinton Hills. Since me and Sole's separation, I've been doing a lot of reflecting and praying. I still can't get over the fact that I fucked up. My wife and family are gone because of some shit that I did...

DENALI

"Every man is entitled to make his life mistakes. In fact every man is guaranteed to miss his mark from time to time. No matter how good you may be no man is perfect. Even Michael Jordan misses shots and Barry Bonds strikes out from time to time. The key to effectiveness is being responsible for your own actions and to always learn from your mistakes.

"When you miss a shot or strike out in life, don't blame the person who passed you the ball, the defender, or the pitcher. When you fail in life as a man, as a husband, and as a father, don't blame your parents, wife, children, or the white man. When you make a

mistake, forgive yourself and then ask for forgiveness. Learn from your inexperience, ignorance, and strengthen your weaknesses. Learn from your mistakes and turn them into mastery. Become a master man, a master husband, and a master father. Master whatever it is that you do." Minister Gilmore said to a hall of about two thousand men.

"Yo thanks Lee for inviting me. I really needed to hear this but I have to go. I'll get up with you later." Akil said to me as he started making his way out of the hall, like his pants were on fire. Maybe what the minister said shook him at his core, especially with all that he is going through. "Okay Kil. You stay up now it will all get better." I said trying to affirm him. I decided to invite Akil to a men's meeting because Minister Gilmore has a preaching and teaching style that is so practical and full of principle. I knew that Akil would benefit from it.

Since that night with Meisha's little young ass, I haven't heard anything else from her. I've been to the doctor's office twice and each time there were no positive signs of anything negative. It's too much shit out here killing niggas today. I had to make sure Meisha didn't give me anything extra to keep. Lately, all I've been able to do is think about Meisha. That was the best head action and piece of ass that I have had in a long while, but shorty is only sixteen.

Me and India have been moving closer and closer to a committed relationship. We go out on a romantic date at least once a week. We even study the Proverbs together. I have been there by India's side in the studio as she records her first Gospel CD. It's funny, because whenever I'm in the studio with India and she starts singing, the woman sends chills all through my body. A few of the songs that she sings, make me feel like God is speaking directly to me, through her.

Of all the things we have done these last four months none have been better than when we spend time together with our daughter, as a family and end the day listening to some jazz, while we talk and cuddle by the fireplace. India has really got me on some cool, calm, and relaxed romantic tip. But it's all good with me.

YES

Being engaged has been nothing but a good thing for me. Had I known that love was gonna feel this good, I would have stopped my Robocop ways with women years ago. All that tough man shit I was on with women was all for nothing. Amerie is so beautiful and supportive. I feel like I'm sitting on top of the world because of her. We plan on buying a house some time next month. We still haven't decided on if we want to remain New York residents or move to New Jersey, with Denali.

I think Jersey is a better fit. I know we can get more land and square footage for the two million dollar home we are looking to purchase, than if we remain in New York. I don't know why we settled on two million dollars but that is the most we are looking to invest into our home.

For the meantime, we go back and forth, staying in my townhouse and her loft. I like the current arrangement because it's preparing us for what living together will be like. Once we find a house, I know living with Amerie's ass, we are gonna need multiple bathrooms and a lot of closet space.

Between my clothes and collection of over one thousand shoes, coupled with Amerie's gear and shoes, we might have to convert two rooms in our home into closet space. One room for her and one room for me...

AMERIE

"Hello." I said as I ran and picked up the phone. "I thought you couldn't turn a ho into a housewife." The deep baritone said on the other end. "Excuse me?" I asked trying to keep my cool. "You heard me bitch. So what you're playing house now?" The mystery person added. "Who is this?" I asked doing my best to recognize the voice. "What, you've done sucked so many dicks you don't remember me?" The voice said starting to sound like my ex-boyfriend Troy from Virginia.

Troy was a hustler, but also thought he was a pimp on the side. "If you don't let me know who it is that I am talking to I will slam this phone down on your fuckin` ass." I calmly spoke into the phone. "Fuck you bitch!" Then the other end hung up. Who could that be, I started to think? With a past like mine that could be one out of the hundreds and hundreds of men I've met and got to know.

Now this is more of what I'm used to, the bullshit and the drama. After all, that is all my life has been about: The bullshit and the drama…

SOLE`

I will never understand in a million years how Akil could do this to me after all that I have given him. Why would a man cheat on a woman that has been so good to him? I guess only God knows that answer. My mother really wants to spend some time with little Akil and agrees with Michelle and Dana in that I should get out of the house and have some fun.

So tonight will be the first time in a very long time that I will be out hanging with my girls.

"Where are we going tonight Michelle? I'm already missing my baby?" I said to Michelle as she put on more lipstick, while we drove. "We're going to Tony's this nice jazz spot out in Brooklyn. The place is always packed with professional, good looking, got it going on brothers." Michelle said as she tripled checked her face in my car's mirror. "That sounds good for you and Dana but I'm not interested in a man right now. Remember, I'm still married." I said looking back at Dana through my rear view, as she sat sitting pretty in the back seat.

"Married, whatever Sole`. A friend of mine at work told me that her sister Mercedes was seeing some fine brother named Akil. After I investigated a bit, come to find out that that fine brother Akil, is your "husband" Akil. So stop with the bullshit already, you are single like the rest of us." Dana said sounding like she had a bone to pick.

Michelle and Dana are my girls, my highest and lowest self. Michelle is a dermatologist, who's been seeing the same man Lance for the last three years. Michelle is the ultimate optimist and a huge wave of positive energy. She always sees the glass as half full, so her advice is always refreshing. Michelle is beautiful, a young Lena Horne, but she is so spiritual that her physical attributes are the last thing on her mind. It's strange, being that Michelle is a successful dermatologist.

Dana on the other hand, is the polar opposite of Michelle. Dana is a realist. Dana is in advertising and definitely has a way with words. Dana tells you how it is, unlike Michelle who focuses on what can be. Dana is always in and out of a relationships. And maybe it's because of her slick mouth.

Even I know that no real man wants a verbally abusive or vulgar woman. I guess the experience Jason, her son's father put her through has caused her to be so fearful, impatient, and unrealistic, in my opinion, when it comes to men and relationships. Dana and Jason had a child at seventeen, so they were both young and dumb, but she fails to see it that way.

I think Dana has let her mother convince her that all males, regardless of age, should be responsible, mature, and stable. I tell her all of the time that life doesn't work like that. I tell Dana that men grow and mature at different rates but she doesn't listen to me. She believes even a twenty year boy is suppose to be a thirty five year old man.

"Well Dana, I hope Akil is happy with Ms. Mercedes because as you can see I'm the one pushing his Mercedes and living large." I said to burst Dana's bubble, but I'm no fool. I would rather have a good relationship with my husband over any car or amount of money, any day. That's how we got to this point to begin with, we worked together. "Whatever bitch." Dana said then cracked a friendly smile, I saw through my rear view. "But you're right about that girl, this car is lovely." Dana added.

"Look at the line ladies. I told y'all that it would be full of

Michael Jordan, Morris Chestnut, type of brothers." Michelle said as her eyes lit up. "Well I hope they have Michael Jordan and Morris Chestnut type of money. Shit, I don't have the time for a broke ass man." Dana sarcastically said. "Girl you are crazy." I said laughing at Dana's comment. "I might be, but I'm also real." Dana added.

As we pulled up in the brand new silver colored S600 Mercedes Benz, Akil left me, heads were spinning as usual. Everyone was looking to see who was inside of the expensive ass car, with the rims that wouldn't stop spinning. Everyone was looking to spot a celebrity.

As I was surveying who was who on the line, I noticed him looking as good as a man can possibly look. He had his waves spinning so much so that I was getting seasick. His goatee was nicely trimmed and he looked like he added an extra ten pounds of muscle to that tall and athletic frame.

How could a man look so damn good? I was surprised but happy to see him, because for some strange reason he's been on my mind since the last time I saw him. It was "what's his name", that I met in Jamaica. For a minute, I thought maybe Stella doesn't have to travel to Jamaica in order to get her groove back...

DENALI

"It's sad what happened to Akil and Sole's marriage. But when I really think about it for what it is, Akil did it to himself. I love Kil but he did wrong." I said to Yes as we waited in the Galla for Kil to join us. "I told that nigga not to get married until his heart, mind, pockets, and dick was ready. But Kil has always had a hard head. That's his problem now, no pun intended." Yes said as he sipped his beer then continued. "Here comes Hugh Hefner now...

AKIL

"What's good Mr. 2LiveCrew? How are the video ho's treating you pimp?" Denali said as I joined him and Yes at our favorite table. "Ask your mother nigga, she'll tell you all about it." I said as I sat down beside Yes. "Look at him Lee, the nigga is losing weight and everything. Didn't I tell you, for every two nuts you bust you're suppose to drink one and two teaspoons of a Nutriment." Yes said as he burst out laughing, causing Denali to cough up his Heineken.

"Are you trying it Christopher Williams? Didn't I tell you that light skinned niggas went out in the 80's? And why is your man laughing so hard, looking like a fake ass Lou Gosset Jr." I said throwing back at the assault. "Fuck you dawg." Yes said chuckling. I then ordered some barbeque chicken and a Corona.

"We were just talking about your situation with Sole` before you walked in." Denali said as his cell phone started to ring, as usual. The man's phone is always ringing. If it ain't business he has to handle, then it's some female stalking him. "I know you're tired of talking about it, but what about little Kil? I know you are missing your little man." Yes said as Denali started yelling at someone on his cell phone. "Damn dawg let a nigga sip his beer before you start will all the Wendy Williams questions. Be easy…

YES

Akil had no idea how important his marriage was until it was gone. I don't ever want to feel the regret and emptiness he must be feeling in his gut right now. Dudes are always getting caught out there chasing ass. Akil had everything men search for: A beautiful loyal woman, a son, enough money to live by choice, recognition for what he does. He had it all. Not to mention he's tall and good looking. Now that Sole` and his son are gone he wants to humble himself and be thankful. It's just like a nigga.

"Yo, I'm sorry to be jumping all on you Kil. You know, it's all love. I can just look at you and see your heart aches. The shit is bothering me. Damn, why do we fuck up so much? I said loudly out of frustration. "I don't know Yes. That is something that I don't know partner…

103

DENALI

We were having our usual good time in the hall, when all of a sudden Akil started talking recklessly. "Lee, I'll put it to you like this, if you can't keep your dick at home then the pussy of the house will walk right out of the door." Akil said with a slurred speech. "Preach on Kil, preach on." I encouraged him, like he was preaching from the pulpit. "I mean, I've done crushed many a honey but it never caught up to me. At least not until I slipped up and slept with another nigga." Akil said sounding like a wino.

"This alcohol has got this fool trippin`. Let me call him a cab and get his drunk ass home and in the bed, before he says some more stupid shit out of his mouth." I said looking at Yes like Akil was really really drunk. As I went to grab Akil's arm to escort him to his taxi, he shrugged me away and started crying...

AKIL

"I'm drunk, but not that drunk. Y'all heard me correctly, I meant exactly what I said. Remember that bitch Tracy, that I told y'all about?" I asked Lee and Yes as they looked at me like I was crazy. "Yea of course we remember. The Tracy who mailed those pictures to Sole` and blew your spot up." Yes confirmed. "Of course we remember that bitch." Lee added. "Well, y'all know how we met, right? This whole situation is complicated and long. So to make a long story short that bitch tricked me into thinking everything was sweet. The Tracy that I stepped to was really a T.R.A.C.E.Y. That bitch turned out to be a nigga...

YES

I couldn't believe what my ears were hearing. My best friend, the dude I have seen grow from a boy into a man. The man, who growing up I would let sleep in the same bed as me. The man, who I'll give my life for, didn't just tell me what I think my ears heard. Did Akil just ruin his marriage to a beautiful and faithful woman? A woman who loved his dirty ass through thick and thin.

I know I'm far from being perfect but I couldn't take it any longer. Before I had the chance to restrain myself and think my actions through I turned and punch Akil right in the pit of his stomach...

DENALI

"What the fuck is your problem Yes? What, you can't hold your liquor either nigga?" I said trying to make sense out of what was jumping off. "Fuck that Lee, this nigga needs his ass kicked and I got what he needs." Yes said angrily as he side stepped my attempt at stopping him and started kicking Akil's drunk ass.

Now on a sober day, this would have been another Ali vs. Frazier classic but Kil had been drinking Coronas and Heinekens like a camel, so the nigga didn't have his balance. So homeboy didn't stand a chance. "Yo Yes, chill the fuck out, you made your point." I said then realized myself that Kil needed his ass kicked in. So I let Yes give it to him. Sometimes a man needs to feel it...

YES

After Akil threw up after my first blow, I sent another three piece combination to his body. I then gave the nigga a right hook to his chin. And my right hook is text book, so it sent Akil down to the canvass immediately. Akil was crying, throwing up, I think he was so drunk and out of it that he pissed on himself.

After Kil recovered a bit from the hook, he stood up on his feet and threw his hands up ready to fight back. But at that point he was too drunk for what I had in store for him. "Oh so you want some for real nigga. Huh you faggot?" I said, as I was doing my Sugar Ray Leonard shuffle on his ass.

If Denali and Ray didn't intervene, I would probably still be kicking Akil's ass right now. I was that mad. "How the fuck could you do something like that? So what you're a fucking faggot now? You nasty muthafucka. I could kill your ass in here Kil!" I yelled as Ray pushed me violently out of the Galla's doors...

105

DENALI

I had no idea that Yes was so homophobic. Maybe it was due to the fact that his biological father walked out on his moms for another man? Maybe it was because of that gay priest that came onto him in elementary school? Whatever did it, really did it. If me and Ray had not stopped him, Yes would have tried to put Akil out of business for good. Yes just snapped and beat Akil's ass like Kil tried to come onto him or something...

"When I get my shit together I am gonna kick Yes' ass. He got this one tonight but it's far from over, bet that shit. Yo, call me a cab and get me home safely Lee. I'm all messed up right now man." Akil murmured as he held the tissue up against his busted lip. "I said I got you. Just shut the hell up because I'm a few seconds off your ass myself." I said to Kil taking a deep breath before I ended up getting in his ass.

"Y'all niggas are suckers anyway. Why do y'all want to beat my ass when I'm drunk? Let Yes try that same shit when I got my legs. I'll kick his and your ass." Kil said as he stumbled to keep his balance.

"I made a mistake. I slept with a nigga that I thought was a bitch, just like you slept with a little girl that you thought was a woman. So if I deserve to get my ass beat so do you and that nigga Yes. Shit, all of the married women he's done slept with. See that's the problem, we are so disillusioned that we can't distinguish what's right from what's wrong anymore." Akil said as he moved his mouth in a circular motion making sure that his jaw was still in place.

"How can you even fix your mouth to say, you're a few seconds off my ass. You want to know how I could slip up and sleep with a dude? It was with the same mentality you had when you slept with that little hot ass Meisha. So you and your man Yes can get the hell on with y'all self righteous bullshit. Lust is lust, wrong is wrong. So fuck you too..."

106

CHAPTER 12

<u>SOLE`</u>

Tony's is definitely everything Michelle advertised. Besides the India Irie and Angie Stone looking sisters in here, the vibe is wonderful. This is a let your hair down, relaxation, everything is gonna be alright type of vibe. This is exactly what I need right now, I thought as we entered the place.

Once we sat down and ordered our drinks, I had a long island ice tea, the band Nuvu took the stage. And there he stood, all six foot four inches of him making sweet love to that bass. By the way he so masterfully and passionately played, I just knew he was one of those take time to make love to your whole body type of brothers. Not having a man in my life and in my bed at night, probably had me more curious and intrigued than normal.

"Ain't that Todd from Jamaica?" Dana said excitedly, getting wet in her pants "I think so Dana but I'm not sure." I said trying to down play the situation. "Maybe if he takes that shirt off and let's us see that perfectly sculpted body, you'll recognize him then." Michelle said then started laughing. "Shut up Michelle. I think that is him. He did say he was a jazz musician, I do remember that much." I said doing my best to play cool. But I recognized oh boy from the door. That smooth "I'm in control" presence that he has, how could I forget, especially since it reminded me of Akil so much.

As we were watching the band play some attractive brother wearing a dashiki approached us at our table. "Good evening ladies, my name is Muluba. How are you all doing?" He said politely as he introduced himself to us. "We are fine Muluba. My name is Michelle, that's Dana, and this is Sole`." Michelle said in her usual friendly demeanor. Michelle has to be the warmest person in the world. She would sit and talk to anybody at anytime. Dana tells her to stop doing that. Dana says men think courtesy means "she wants me". But Michelle can not stop being who she is, regardless of what Dana says.

"I was watching you all from the other side of the room. And I had to come over here and introduce myself. You ladies are all so beautiful and full of energy. You all are lighting up the room." Muluba said as he was staring at me. "Thank you sweety." Michelle said, as Dana gave me a "what does he really want" type of look.

"So what's really going on? I know you didn't walk all the way over here to small talk. So which one of us do you want?" Dana said abruptly. "What makes you think I have a hidden agenda?" Muluba asked, surprised by Dana's straightforwardness. "Because we are three pretty ladies sitting over here alone. I saw you outside, drooling all over yourself while you were looking at our asses." Dana said with her all in your face mannerism.

That must have scared Muluba off because he then stood up and said. "Damn babygirl, you need to ease up a little bit. You will catch more bees with honey than with that shit. Y'all have a nice evening." He said as he walked away, giving Dana a disgusted look. "Why do you always do that?" Michelle asked Dana in astonishment. "Because men are out of control. If you don't check them they will try to run all over you." Dana answered.

As Dana and Michelle were talking back and forth about men and how you have to treat them, me and Todd made serious eye contact. He then gave me a wink as his band was playing. "Well damn Sole`, what is all that about? I told you about smiling at niggas with your pussy, bitch" Dana said noticing our connection.

"I don't know girl, but if he doesn't stop looking over here like that I'm gonna have to take him home and give him some tonight." I said then started to laugh as I realized what I was saying. After their set was over, I saw Todd heading our way. Before he made it to our table, he shook hands and took what appeared to be phone numbers from the many female admirers who filled up the front portion of the club.

It seemed like every single lady in the club had come to see Todd. Females were all dressed in short skirts and tight shirts seated in front of the club, like groupies.

"Hello ladies. It's good to see you are all still looking good." Todd said while looking down straight at me. "Thank you honey, I really enjoyed the set." Dana said as she grabbed his hand.

Dana is funny like that because just a few minutes ago she was talking all of that smack about men. Now she's all up in Todd's face, smiling at him with *her* pussy. When Dana sees a fine man, she always feels that she has to beat the next woman to the punch. She thinks her fat ass and hips are her wild card. I have to admit it, my girl plays her hand to perfection.

"So how have you been Sole`?" Todd said staring at me while Dana was still holding his hand. *Damn he remembered my name.* "I'm managing to live through it all." I said as I marveled at how fine he still was. "Why don't we let you two talk? Come on Dana, let's go to the little girls room." Michelle said pulling Dana away from the table. Michelle is always so smooth and on point with hers. She always knows what to do and how to do it.

"Well, I see you're not wearing your marriage symbol anymore. Is everything stable back at the ranch?" Todd asked as his admirers stared at our table while we talked. I almost forgot that I had taken off my wedding and engagement rings. I threw them at Akil, as he walked out of the door. "I'm going through a situation right now, but it's nothing that I won't handle." I managed to say confidently. *Damn how could he be finer now than he was in Jamaica where he was damn near naked,* I thought?

"As long as you're "going" through, it won't last forever. It will all work out for you beautiful." Todd said with his smooth and melodic voice. "Thanks sweety." I responded taking another sip of my second ice tea. "Look after this next set, I'm free for the night. How about we get to know each other under a different setting? I have the perfect place in mind. After my sets, it always gets crazy in here for me. And I really want for you to have my undivided attention." Todd said.

I know he ain't trying to get at my booty, or is he, I thought? "That sounds great sweety, just let me inform my girls." I said giving him my own sexy smile, to match his. "Perfect." He responded, then gently kissed my hand, stood up tall, and headed back for the stage. When Dana and Michelle returned to our table they were all excited, like school girls all over again. I then told them what was up with me and Todd, and they immediately started giving advice.

"You better get that man or someone else will." Dana said with lust all in her eyes as she watched Todd and his band set up for the next set. Knowing Dana, I knew exactly what she meant. "I think he already has a woman. A man that fine is never single, even if he says he is." I said trying to maintain.

After their set finished, Todd shook more hands and came back over to the table, and politely greeting the ladies again. He then excused us for the evening. "It was nice seeing you two again. Y'all ladies have a lovely night. Thanks for stopping by the club. Make sure I see y'all again." Todd said as he took me by the hand and led the way through the crowd of horny ladies and fanatic men that wanted to talk and touch him. *There is nothing more attractive than a gentleman,* I thought to myself.

By the time Todd's set was over, I had already checked up on little Kil three times. My mother said that she was enjoying him and for me to pick Kil up in the morning. I gave my car keys to Michelle and told them I'll see them in the morning. I had no idea what had gotten into me, but if Mr. Jamaica doesn't say or do anything stupid, he can definitely have some of me tonight. My body is yearning for some loving, and right now Todd will more than do…

AMERIE

"Troy, don't call me out of my name again. If you're gonna be in my house, you will respect me or you will have to leave." I said as me and my ex- boyfriend Troy stood arguing in my entertainment room. It was Troy who called in that disrespectful manner the other day.

"Respect you, pll..ease. You don't even respect yourself. So why do I need to respect you? I don't know who you think you're talking to with this new and improved shit you're on." Troy said as he walked around my house looking for something.

Troy was the last person that I expected to show up in my new world. Troy was the man on the streets of Virginia before he got knocked on a federal charge. I just knew he would die behind bars like many from his clique did. Troy was a cold blooded hustler, who would do anything to get what he wanted.

I only gave Troy the time of day because he was the first dude out in VA pushing Bentleys, Big boy trucks, and Aston Martins, like it wasn't a thing.

Rumor had it, that Troy was worth close to eighty million dollars before he got knocked. But he never let me see just how much money he had. I hooked up with Troy during an All Star weekend trip me and a few of my girls took to DC. I put my nasty on Troy so bad, that he fell in love, which was the best and the worst thing that could have happened for me. It was the best thing because Troy showered me with the best money could buy. It was the worst thing because Troy was the most possessive and controlling man in the world.

Troy would have a personal driver escort me around whenever I left the house. He always wanted to know where I was, who I was with, and what I was doing, whenever I wasn't underneath him. At first it was kinda cute to have a man cater to me and be so protective of me, like a father. But then it went too far when Troy started to isolate me from my friends and my own little personal world.

I guess the fact that every man who was anybody in the

111

Virginia and DC area wanting me by their side, drove Troy crazy. Before I left VA, I was the bitch all other bitches wanted to be like, but hated because they couldn't be me. Two years before I moved to New York, Troy was shot in a drug bust and got knocked by the feds on some heavy charges. I should have known that he would be back in the world sooner than later. Troy's money is longer than Virginia's entire economy. But I never thought he would be home so soon though.

"Troy, why did you come to New York to harass me?" I asked trying to have a conversation rather than argue with him.

"I have some business to handle out here before I move out of the country. So while I'm here, I figured that I'll pick up all that is mine and take it with me." Troy said as he headed for the kitchen. *Does he still think we are together? It has been a little over three years now and I'm engaged to my new man.*

"What are you talking about?" I asked following Troy into the kitchen, making sure my eyes were on his crazy ass at all times. "I know you ain't trippin` Meme. I heard you're supposed to be engaged to some square ass, suit and tie nigga. Congratulations on that. That sure is a nice ring he bought you. I bet his broke ass spent all that he had on that ring. But we both know that the nigga can't afford to fuck with you anyway, right booboo?" Troy said as he started laughing, holding the belly he developed while in jail. "I figured you thought I wasn't coming home so I understand that you had to move on. But daddydick is back in the building. Daddydick is now home baby. I couldn't wait to taste some of my pussy again." Troy said, moving up close on me. "Troy it's not like that. I'm really in love with my man. I have never been happier." I said courageously, knowing Troy's temper.

In the past it wasn't unusual for Troy to get physical when his emotions got too hot for him. "What do you mean you are serious? You really want to be with that tight ass nigga, after all I've done for your ass. Fuck that you are my woman." Troy yelled, as he started to rip my clothes off of me. Immediately I had flashes of my childhood and the many times I was raped and violated by the anger and perversion of those men. I always remembered the evil look in the eyes of the perpetrators as they violently took my sexuality and innocence.

So what, you're gonna rape me now because I'm in love with another man? Are you gonna rape me Troy because I don't want to be with you?" I said looking Troy eye to eye, heart to heart. I was almost daring him to say "yes"...

CHAPTER 13

SOLE`

    "So Todd where are you taking me?" I asked as he opened the door to his Range Rover. "It's a surprise. What are you afraid or something? I'm not a Jeffery Dama or killer type, you'll be alright babygirl." Todd said then closed my door. "No, I just want to know where in the hell are we going." I responded as we started to pull off.

    "I'm taking you to the property my grandparents left to me. It's real cozy and comfortable, I think you will really like it." Todd said as we pulled off onto Brooklyn's bumpy streets. I was a little thrown off by how casual and coy he was. Did he expect to sleep with me? I mean, I barely know the brother. He is fine and sharper than a razor, but I ain't no ho, I'm still a married woman. We did have a nice conversation out in Jamaica, but I don't get down like that.

    It has been a while since I've felt the presence of a man within me, but that man has always been Akil. Damn I miss my husband, I thought privately as Todd drove. As we drove, Todd kept looking over at me with those bedroom eyes, while he sung the lyrics to the Carl Thomas CD that was bumping in his truck.

    Why am I riding in the car with a man I barely know, going to an unknown destination? I must really be vulnerable and in need of some TLC. Once we settled in, I had to admit Todd was right. He had a cozy lodge out in Tarrytown, NY. It looked like one of those weekend getaway spots in the Pocono's. It was decorated with fine hand made African artwork and had Persian wall to wall carpeting all throughout the place.

There was also a huge fireplace that could be viewed from the living room as well as the master bedroom. Todd gave me a quick tour of the place and said for me to get comfortable because he was going to take a shower.

As I heard the shower water running, I made it my business to have a second look around the place and get a better feel for my surroundings. There was cultural artwork and pictures of jazz greats like Miles Davis and of great men like Malcolm X and Gandhi, everywhere.

I also noticed the pictures of who appeared to be Todd's grandmother and parents. I could see where he got his good looks from because the pictures displayed at least three generations of fine men in the family. "Sole' would you like a glass of wine or something?" Todd politely asked me as he returned from the shower. "Yes please." I answered nervously, giving Todd a smile.

Todd had changed into some soft cotton ENYCE sweat pants and into a clear white t-shirt, that made him look comfortable, but five years younger. "So what do you think of the place?" Todd asked as he returned from the kitchen and handed me my glass of wine. He then sat next to me on the sofa. "I think you were right, it's cozy, intimate, and romantic here." I responded. "Good because you are the first person I've ever invited up here. This place has a lot of my family history in it." Todd said.

"Wow, you sure do know how to make someone feel real special. Why me and why so soon?" I asked trying to feel him out "Sole' I have to be real with you. Do you remember how I looked at you when we first met?" He asked. "Of course I do. You looked like you wanted to eat me up." I answered and started laughing. "I knew that you were the one for me the very first time I laid eyes on you. When I saw you and your girlfriends there sunbathing in that Jamaican sun, I knew that I had laid eyes on something special.

"That's why, when I stepped to you I was heart broken when I found out that you were married. But after talking to you and looking into your eyes, I knew you were settling with your marriage.

"I knew you were in a situation that wasn't giving you all that you deserve. You are beautiful, intelligent, independent, all of the things that I want in a woman. I wanted you then and I want you even more now." Todd said while holding my hand, putting the pressure on me.

"But… but like I was telling you in the car on the way over here, my situation is still foggy and I don't want to walk you into uncertain grounds." I said feeling my heart rate going up. "I respect your situation and wishes but I have to level with you. Your husband didn't deserve a woman as precious as you. That's why he lost you. I'm not gonna force anything on you, but I have to let you know where I stand." Todd said looking at me with this passionate look in his eyes. His eyes told me that he was certain about what he wanted...and it was definitely me.

"Look Sole`, I'm a patient man. I've learned how to wait for my blessings. I don't want to force you into anything but I'm done looking. I don't want to date another woman or even look at another woman for that matter. I just hope that one day you'll be all mine." Todd said, then moved in and gave me a nonsexual kiss. That meant a lot to me because it showed me that although he could've had my body right then and there, he wanted more than just my physical. Todd wanted all of me.

With all that I've been through with Akil, a big part of me was willing to give myself to Todd. But I knew the timing wasn't right. If I were to get with Todd now, all I would be giving him is my body…

YES

My feelings are hurt. All of this time my man has been a fag. I know that the whole gay and bisexual thing is suppose to be cool and PC. But I'm from the old school, where men are men and women are women.

God made Adam and Eve not Adam and Steve. There is

nothing natural about two grown muthafuckas making love to one another. There isn't anything a person could say for me to think otherwise. I could've killed Akil's ass in there if it wasn't for Denali.

I really need to go see my baby and calm myself down. I know she'll make me feel a whole lot better about this situation, I thought as I headed for Amerie's house. When I got to Amerie's block there where cop cars and an ambulance parked right in front of her loft. Seeing all of that, sent a chill up my body. But I calmed myself down as I tried to find a parking spot.

It is always bumper to bumper on Amerie's block. Now that the cops and EMS workers were there, taking up half of the block, I had to drive four blocks down before I found a spot. As I started walking towards Amerie's building, that chilling "something ain't right" feeling returned. I became so uncomfortable that I started to jog back to the building. Mrs. Miller, Amerie's nosy ass neighbor and building gazette, stopped me before I could make it to the building. She started to tell me that she heard arguing and what appeared to be fighting going on in Amerie's loft, so she decided to call the cops.

She said, as she was dialing 911 she heard gun shots go off from within the apartment. She was talking so fast and was so emotionally distraught that I couldn't grasp all of what she was saying. The cops had the building sealed off, making it evident that it was a crime scene on sight. People were watching from their windows, the side walk, and gathering on the sides of Amerie's building waiting to see who would be lying dead on the gurney. I couldn't help but to run right through the police tape and up the stairs to Amerie's floor. I needed to know what in the world was going on with my baby. Before the cops could apprehend me, I saw my future wife, the love of my life being carried out on the gurney as a death statistic.

What the fuck happened? Did someone come to rob the apartment then shot her dead? Did she commit suicide? I know my baby was overcoming some emotional scars from the past, but she wasn't suicidal. All types of questions were running through my head as I tried to make sense out of what I saw. Just then my answers were kinda answered. I saw the EMT's carrying out another body on the gurney, taking the body count to two.

I know this is all a bad dream. I must be asleep. Akil couldn't have slept with another man and Amerie is still alive. Amerie is still alive, we are still getting married. My baby isn't dead on a stretcher, not when our love is just getting started. I know life wouldn't do me like this, I thought before I passed out...

DENALI

The nerve of that nigga Akil, there is no way me sleeping with Meisha is anything close to him sleeping with some transsexual. That nigga is on some gay shit. I just got caught up with a young bitch.

When I finally got home at around two in the morning, I was still full of energy, so I decided to do some pushups and sit-ups. I usually do around five hundred pushups and sit-ups a day, but today I ended up doing around a thousand. Akil had me so amped I had plenty of energy to burn.

I usually always stick by my brothers Akil and Yes, but right now Kil needs to be confronted and corrected. He gets no support from me on this one. Damn, I should've kicked his ass too! Akil fucked up real bad and he deserves to live with it.

Just as I was about to get into the shower, my cell phone started ringing. When I looked at the number, I didn't recognize those digits, so I wasn't gonna answer the phone. But I followed my gut and picked it up anyway. Maybe it was Yes or Akil?

"Hello." I answered as I took the phone and walked out onto my deck. "What's up daddy, this is Meisha?" The voice on the other end said. I knew it was only a matter of time before I would hear from Meisha's little young ass again. "What do you want shorty? Don't you have school in the morning or something?" I said as if I didn't want to be bothered.

"Don't try to play me now, because it wasn't like that when

118

you were all up in me." She responded. "Whatever shorty. I was about to get in the shower. So what do you want?" I asked impatiently. "Ooh, can I join you? You know how I feel about you and showers baby." She said trying to seduce me. "Yo, shorty I made a mistake by sleeping with you. And the games you're playing, I'm too grown to be playing. So why don't you slow your little young ass down. You are a beautiful girl Meisha for real. Why don't you focus on your education or something important towards your future? Don't you have your SAT's or Act's to take?" I said on some serious shit.

"I told you, I was sorry about how I tricked you. How many times do I have to say it? I was wrong, I admit that. But by the way you looked at me it didn't seem like my age would matter." Meisha said ever so sweetly. "Look Meisha, I'm a grown ass man who could spend a lot of time behind bars protecting my manhood because I fucked around with you. So why don't you do me a favor and be easy. Stop chasing men and playing a grown woman's game. By the time you're twenty five, you'll be all washed up with two or three kids by four or five different niggas. I'm telling you shorty, I've seen it happen to many females, so be easy. I'm not gonna front, you got it going all the way on, but that can be here today and gone tomorrow, so don't rush to get old shorty. What's the deal, are you looking for a daddy or father figure sweetheart?" I said as I looked at my Olympic size swimming pool, and ninety four foot basketball court from my deck.

"How dare you come at me like I'm some chickenhead who doesn't know what time it is out here? I've been dealing with older niggas ever since I was thirteen. So I know all too well what a man wants. Like I said to you before, men get stupid around a pretty face and fat ass. I've been turning niggas out since I was fourteen. Y'all nigga's get so stupid that age, health status, personality, you know all of those things that matter, go right out of the window when y'all are dealing with a chick. All y'all want is some ass. So I give to get what I want. And for your information

I'm not looking for a daddy. But you better get ready to be one." She said trying to put me in my place.

"Yo shorty, didn't you hear me? I don't have time for the bullshit, so stop being young and acting silly." I said very sternly. "I'm not playing with you Denali. I'm pregnant with your baby. I told you not to cum inside of me, but you didn't listen. So now listen to this... I'm expecting a baby…

CHAPTER 14

AKIL

After hearing about what happened to Amerie, I knew that Yes was going through it. Denali and India tried to convince me that I should go see him, or at least call, but I just couldn't do it. I figured I was the last person Yes would want to see. So I just did nothing about the situation. Well I did send him some flowers with a card, but that ain't shit. I really need someone to talk to, let me give Rich a call.

"Rich, it's me Kil again. What's going on playa?" I said as I spoke into the phone. "Damn Akil, you think I'm your therapist or something nigga?" He responded. "Nah, it's nothing like that. I just feel like you are the only person that I can talk to, who won't play God with me." I said. "I hear you homey but what's crackin`? I'm on my way to pick up the wife and little princess." Rich said.

"Yo, you were right about a lot of things, especially about our lies and fears being the greatest evils we face. Rich, I really want to do something to make things right between me and my wife. I want to do something to make things peace again between me and my friends. I have no idea what I should do. I know that there is a step I can take. I just don't know in what direction I should go." I said sounding like a man lost.

"I would never tell another man what he "should" do concerning his own affairs. I do however have some suggestions. The first is that you be completely honest with yourself. Kil you do what you do because you choose to do it. Your infidelities to Sole` are no accident. You are an intelligent brother but you make stupid decisions when it comes down to the ladies. Maybe its best that you remain separated from Sole` until you are ready to truly be united.

"I mean until you are ready to be faithful let her be alone. It's funny to me because when you were with Sole` you wanted to be with other women. Now that you can be with as many women as you want to be with, you now only want to be with Sole`.

"I know right now you feel real guilty and regret all that has happened. But if your guilt and regret is because you got caught and not because of what you did, you'll do the same things again. I don't believe Sole`, Denali, Yes, me, or any other person can change you. I know first hand that you are out of control, especially for a married man. Why don't you focus on you right now and the decisions you make. You are your problem, you are your own worst enemy. Once you get right, things will fall back into place for you dawg." Rich said then said he had to go.

After talking to Rich, I walked over to the mirror and just looked at myself for about two hours. I stood there crying, laughing, dancing, and doing whatever came to mind. There is something very therapeutic about facing oneself in the mirror. Afterwards, I started to smile and feel good again. I just knew from that moment on that everything had started to turn around for me. From that moment on, I knew things were getting better in my world...

YES

It has been a couple of months since Amerie was murdered but to me it still feels like it all happened yesterday. The newspapers ran the story like it was some love triangle gone bad. The truth is, Amerie was murdered by her ex-boyfriend after he viciously raped her. The autopsy report stated that he was HIV positive. So I guess the fact that he had probably given her the virus and had escaped from prison drove dude over the deep end.

After viciously raping Amerie, the nigga then turned the gun on himself, shooting himself dead with a bullet through his mouth and out of the back of his head.

I'll never forget the crime scene in her apartment. The blood and guts that were splattered all over the pictures we took while in Cancun. I feel like someone has ripped my heart right out of my chest. How could someone be here one minute and gone the next? Life is really a fragile and precious opportunity we receive from the Maker. My baby is dead. Damn, it hurts so much to even think about it.

Denali, Sole`, along with every and anyone who cares about me showed their respects and expressed nothing but love; everyone except Kil. I figured he was too ashamed or afraid to show up, but I've already forgiven him. It wasn't me that he married or slept with. Besides, I realize that every man does wrong. I now realize that life is too short to allow a mistake or difference of opinion to ruin a friendship. Kil is already dealing with the consequences of his actions anyhow. I'm Akil's friend not his God. I know in my heart that Kil will get things together and do right. He is too much of a man not to. I just hope he forgives me…

SOLE`

I have been missing Akil like crazy; his smile, his laugh, his touch, his playful demeanor...everything. Dana makes it her business to let me know what he's doing and who he's doing it with. It's almost as if she gets some satisfaction out of seeing my marriage like this and knowing how badly it hurts me. I know that Dana is my girl, but her issues with men have never been my issues. Well at least not until now and I think she feels it brings us closer together. Maybe it does but I would rather we become closer on some more positive terms.

Women can be very spiteful, especially when hurt. I just overlook Dana's bullshit and pray that she will grow out of it, because she can get on some little girl shit when she wants to. My son brings me so much joy, but everyday he is looking more and more like his father. He has Akil's thin nose, peanut head, and bushy eyebrows.

I know in my heart that it's wrong for me to keep little Kil from his father. But like I said, women can be spiteful. Akil hurt me and this is my way of hurting him. Some nights I think that I'm hurting everybody because I'm not feeling any better, and I want my son to know his father.

My mother always said a family is a team, and a team is only as strong as its weakest player. I'm not sure how that philosophy may apply to my situation, but I do think there is some correlation. I have been dealing with Todd lately and he has been great. He really makes it hard for me to hate all men because he is such a good man. He takes me out, has stimulating conversation, and treats me like a lady. He doesn't seem to have any hidden motives and is patiently getting to know me. I still haven't introduced him to my little Kil.

I think the only men little Akil should know are those in his family. Denali and Yes come by often and check up on me. I think Denali shows up as often as he does because he's making sure that no one is sleeping in Akil's bed. Denali comes over, makes sure that all of the toilet seats are down, and then leaves. Denali thinks he's slick, but I've known him for too long not to know how protective he is of me.

Todd and I have been on several dates and we do a lot of talking on the phone, but right now I'm not ready for another relationship. Todd is so understanding and considerate towards my feelings that it's making me want him all the more. Every time we go out in public, women are always staring at him and whispering. I even saw one dude pimp slap his woman for looking at Todd so hard. The man is just that fine.

My body is aching for some loving. I guess I'm still going through sexual withdrawal. Akil and I used to have sex, if not everyday, then every other day. It was like Akil couldn't keep his hands off of me. I definitely need some sex and TLC. Whenever Todd wears some sweat pants, my eyes can't seem to stay away from the bulge that is always calling my name.

I know the brother is packing and very soon I'm gonna

have me some of that sweet dick. Tonight Dana and Michelle were supposed to come over for dinner and to watch some movies. Michelle just called and said she couldn't make it. She said Lance isn't feeling well, so she's staying in tonight playing nurse. Michelle is too good to Lance. She'll do anything for that damn man.

So I guess me and Dana are gonna have to kick it alone. I hope she doesn't bring her male bashing ass over here with the bullshit. Right now I'm really not in the mood to debate.

When Dana got to the house I was just finished putting little Kil to sleep. "What's up girl?" I said as I gave Dana a hug and kiss. "I like those shoes and your hair looks fierce" I added, complimenting Dana on how good she looked. One thing I have to say about Dana is that she's probably the most stylish woman I know. "Damn it sure does smell good up in here. What did you cook?" Dana asked as she took off here brand new Ralph Lauren shoes that matched her Marc Jacobs bag. "There's some baked chicken, steamed vegetables and salad in the kitchen. Go and help yourself girl. I'm about to jump in the shower." I said as I walked off.

While I was in the shower, I couldn't help but to start fantasizing about Todd and what it would feel like having him make love to me. The more I thought about having Todd's long and toned arms holding me tight as I rode his pony, the hornier I became. So I did what any real bitch in my position would do. I masturbated until I exploded. Shh..it, there's no reason to suffer just because there isn't a dick around. Ahh, …ahh… ahh… I now feel ten pounds lighter.

After I got out of the shower, Dana made an unusual suggestion to me and it threw me way off. "Sole` do you want me to give you a massage?" Dana asked. "What?" I said like she had just bumped her head. "I said do you want a massage. I know your muscles are tense. You've been doing a lot lately, so I know it will make you feel better." Dana said making perfect sense to me. "Yea, maybe you're right girl. Between my son and running my business from home, I've been neglecting my own well being. I don't remember when was the last time I went to the gym. And my ass and hips are spreading like biscuits girl." I said.

"It looks good on you. You know niggas can't get enough of a big ass." Dana replied as she slapped me firmly on the ass. She slapped it hard enough that it caused my booty to clap. "Stop Dee, that shit turns me on." I said jokingly then continued. "So give me my massage already, bitch." I demanded. "Okay I have some massage oils in my bag." Dana said. "Ill, in your bag? What kind of freak are you bitch. I bet you have a home pregnancy test and a pap smear in there too." I said as I laid down on my chest, trying to relax.

"You never know when you're gonna need some extras. I'm always prepared girl. Let's do it like they do it at the parlor." Dana said. For some strange reason, Dana started massaging the lower portion of my back first, touching very close to my ass. For a second I was about to trip, but it actually felt good to have my lower back massaged. She then traveled up my back and as she did, I really started to relax all the more.

I then started imaging that it was Akil's hands caressing my back, shoulders, and legs. The more Dana massaged, the more, relaxed I became. I then started to zone out to the thousands of times Akil and I made love. The strength he possessed as he maneuvered me so easily during sex. Most of all, I envisioned how good it made me feel as a woman to have my man make love to me.

Dana then turned me over and very sensually started massaging my legs, which sent me into a trance or deep meditation. My meditation was very strong. I actually started to feel the moisture of Akil's presence as he caressed my clitoris with his long tongue.

"Damn baby that feels good. I've missed you so much. Do that thing baby." I moaned zoned out in my erotic meditation as Akil ate my pussy. Just then it started to feel too good. So good, that I decided to open my eyes. I wanted to see Akil's face buried in my pussy as I came all over his chin. But when I opened my eyes, I didn't see Akil's dreads. I saw Dana's blond braids and head stuck in between my legs, eating my pussy like she loved it.

"Bitch are you muthafuckin crazy? Did you just lose your fuckin` mind?" I screamed at the top of my lungs, but then I realized my son was asleep down the hall. "Sole` I'm so sorry. I don't know what came over me." Dana said in a state of shock. As I was reaching for my panties, Dana ran out of the house faster than Flo Jo. Just as I was about to beat her ass she took off running. Is that bitch crazy? Doesn't she know I'm strictly dickly? I don't care how much shit I go through with a nigga, I'll never turn to a bitch. Ain't shit a woman can do for me sexually, or romantically. She knows I don't get down like that.

Damn, I wish she hadn't ran out of here so fast. I would have beat the freak out of Dana's nasty ass. Maybe that's why she's always bashing men. Her gay ass wants to be one. Damn, I feel so violated. Dana better pray I don't ever see her again, because I owe her an ass whupping on site...

CHAPTER 15

DENALI

I'm sure glad that I have more than enough money to get what I want. It's true that money talks and bullshit walks. Whenever the deck is stacked against you, buy the house if you can afford it. I offered Meisha ten grand to have an abortion and she went right along with it.

It's true, everybody has a price. I'm happy that Meisha's price was so low compared to what she could have gotten from me, if her game was half as tight as she thought it was. Meisha is young just like I thought. So when I offered her more money than she had ever seen in her young life, she bit. I learned many years ago that once you buy someone, you can control them.

Early on in my business career, I would sell myself short and give up my control to some more experienced business person. Now I know better than to sell myself to anyone, for any price. With Meisha she didn't know any better, so for ten grand she went to the clinic to lay on that table. Her young ass probably went shopping to heal right after. I know the Meisha type very well, that looking for money any way they can get it type. That's why I played her game and beat her at it. I do feel bad about what I did, but there was no way she was having that baby. I don't care what y'all think.

I've finally convinced Yes to come with me to a manhood meeting tonight. I'm sure it will lift his spirits. "Lee this better be worth it, I could have stayed my ass at home and figured my own shit out." Yes said as we drove in my Bentley Azure. "Be easy black man. Trust me, I wouldn't stir you in the wrong direction.

The minister always deals with real life issues in a spiritual way. I think it will help to change your perspective on some things." I said as I parked my car on the city street.

"Nigga are you crazy? You better put this bitch in a garage." Yes said trippin` at how I could just park such an expensive car on the street, so carefree. "Calm down young fella I have insurance. Besides, what's the worst that can happen?" I said as we walked towards the hall. "What's the worst that can happen? You better stop bullshittin` with yourself." Yes said as we continued to walk. When we walked into the hall, I could tell Yes was feeling the same thing that I felt when I first walked in the hall. There is a presence in this place that grabs you immediately.

"Are you all right dawg?" I asked Yes. "Yea I'm cool dawg. I just didn't expect to see so many black men together like this. It looks like a million man rally up in here." Yes said as the minister took the stage.

"Tonight we will discuss the treatment of our women as men. Soldiers you must come to understand that God made the woman to help man fulfill God's purpose in the earth. Women make men stronger and enhance our capacity to live, once we connect with them on the right levels. Until you treat the women in your life right, a lot of things will continue to go wrong for you as a man. I understand that some of you may be sitting there thinking that not every woman is deserving of your respect. The truth is, even the stripper girl and the prostitute is to be respected. As men we are the first principle, therefore we set the stage for what's to follow. Women are the last principle and they manage and multiply that which we give them. So as men, it's our responsibility and duty to treat our women right first, if we want our lives, households, and community to be blessed. Give our women the best and they'll multiply it into greatness. If you want to become a great man, give your woman your best and watch what she gives back to you. Keep in mind, that she is gonna put a woman's touch on your life. So let that woman, do her womanly thing." Minister Gilmore preached.

129

After his sermon the minister led us into prayer. He always stresses that a praying man is a prosperous and powerful man...

YES

I'm so glad I decided to come out tonight with Denali. He was right, the minister is good and seems like a regular dude. "How often do they meet?" I asked Denali. "Every Wednesday." He responded. I don't know why it took Denali so long to put me on. I could have used this years ago.

After prayer, I turned around and was surprised to see Akil sitting in the back row of the hall, like a lost soul. God sure does answer prayer...

AKIL

As I'm walking into the hall, this strong and hot presence came over me. It was so strong that it forced me to collapse and drop to my knees. I then sat in the back of the hall, praying to God for forgiveness and the chance to correct my wrongs. I have finally reached my point of no return. Here I am face to face with God, dealing with the sins I've committed as a man and husband.

As the minister talked about the treatment of our women, I sat there getting warmer and warmer. I will make things right: Now being the husband, the father, the friend, the man God created me to be. Thank you Jesus, I cried out to the Lord. After the meeting, I sat there praying and noticed Denali and Yes walking towards me. This is a sure sign that things are getting better...

SOLE`

Dana and I haven't spoken to each other for several weeks now. I guess she knows she was dead wrong for what she did. I told Michelle and she said I should've kicked Dana's ass. I told her that before I had a chance the bitch was out the front door. Dana must really feel bad for what she did, Michelle hasn't even heard from her.

Tonight is Todd's 28th birthday and I've decided to take him out to dinner and then out dancing. Maybe tonight I'll give him some. The man has been so thoughtful and patient with me, he deserves some of this loving. After dinner, as me and Todd were pulling out of the parking lot, I noticed Denali's Bentley parking down the block. As Todd's truck moved closer, I saw Akil, Denali, and Yes, all get out of the car and walk towards the restaurant.

When I saw Akil my stomach jumped with excitement. It had been months since I saw my baby. He had on a gray velour Sean Jean sweat suit and was looking real good. He also let his beard fill out more, just how I like it. He was definitely looking sexier. I could spot Akil out of a crowd any day by that slow and confident walk he has.

A big part of me wanted Todd to stop his truck so that I could get out and run into the arms of my husband. But if Akil, Denali, and Yes were to see me jumping out of another man's truck, they would probably beat Todd's ass with his own hands.

As Todd made a left turn my view of Akil vanished. I then just sat there motionless while Todd continued to drive. "Are you alright baby?" Todd asked as he put his right hand on my left shoulder and massaged it a little. "Yea I'm fine. I just had a crazy thought." I said trying to recover from my shock with a smile.

Thank God Akil didn't see me. I wonder what would have happened if he did. I'm quite sure it would have been problems, especially for Todd. "Sole' I want to thank you for the dinner and for making this such a wonderful day for me. The watch is beautiful. I know it cost a grip." Todd said. *I wonder if Akil is still sexing Tracey?* "Don't worry about price when something comes from the heart." I responded doing my best to stay focused on what Todd was saying.

"I'm just saying, no woman has ever given me such an expensive gift. It's not everyday that a man receives a 24 carat diamond filled Rolex, from a "friend", Todd said. *I wonder if Akil is living with someone.* "Todd these last five months you've listen to my cries, made me laugh, and lifted my spirits. It's because of you that I didn't lose it. You know how much it hurts me to be separated from the only man that I've loved." I said looking over at Todd, now holding his hand as we drove out to Tarrytown.

Once we got to Todd's place, we sat out back on his porch.

"Sole` I must admit it, I am in love with you and want nothing more than for you to be mine. I do know what time it is and realize that you still are in love with your husband. I recently met your husband, Akil. He goes to the same men's organization as me. I realize that he is a good man who made some bad decisions.

"As a man of God, I have to honor what belongs to another man and he clearly has your heart. Tonight I had my heart set on making love to you, but that's impossible to do if your heart isn't with me. I strongly believe in the beauty of marriage and I refuse to disrupt you and your husband's possibility at reconciliation. I saw your eyes when you recognized him at the restaurant. So I will fall back and let you do the right thing." Todd said very gently.

"So what are you saying Todd?" I asked as Todd wiped away the tears from my eyes. "I'm saying that I love you Sole`. I would love to have you as my woman but not nearly as much as Akil does.

"Maybe you can find it in your heart to forgive Akil and close that chapter in y'all marriage." Todd said as he held me close. We then just sat on Todd's porch looking out at the trees and river. After two hours of conversation, I fell asleep in Todd's warm, strong, and securing arms…

DENALI

"It's good to have our family back together. We've been through too much shit for us to allow anything to separate us." I said, being the one to set the tone. "Akil, I'm sorry man. I just snapped and before I had a chance to consider what I was doing, it was too late." Yes said looking right at Akil. "Look, there is no need to apologize for doing what needed to be done. I was wrong and I had it coming. I only wish someone would have beat my ass the first time I dipped out on Sole`." Akil said looking deep in thought…

YES

"I hear you Kil. Think about how much different our lives would be if every time we did something wrong, we got our ass kicked?" I said smiling at the thought of it. "Shit, don't wish that on me. My dick is always getting me into trouble. I ain't trying to walk around fucked up like Rodney King, my nigga." Denali said crackin' up. Having Akil and Lee around me again made me really feel good. "Y'all know I love y'all niggas right?" I said doing my best not to get sentimental on them.

"I love y'all too. Dawgs, I'm so sorry for not coming through for you when Amerie died. I was all fucked up and didn't know what angle to take. If I could do it all over I would've at least called. I just want you to know that I was with you in spirit." Akil said to me very sincerely.

"There's no need to dwell on our pains and mistakes of the past. I know you better than to think that you were ever against me. We are brothers. I want us to vow to be better men and friends to one another. No more allowing one of us to knowingly do wrong. Let's stop supporting each others destruction. If we see one of us walking off a cliff, don't push him over, but stop him. As friends we need to bring the best out of each other and put this little boy shit behind us...

AKIL

"I'm feeling that. No more bullshit from this moment on. Damn, it took us twenty five years of friendship before we decided to be more than just homeys, but men. That's what's up. Here's to being men." I said as we toasted to our new level of commitment. "But one more thing. Never forget that no man is perfect. No matter how well intentioned he may be, no man is perfect in what he does. May God bless us...

CHAPTER 16

DENALI

Why every time I take two steps forward there's something that tries to pull me one step back. Veronica has somehow decided that the $5K I send her on a monthly basis, which is for Donte`, isn't enough any more to cover her expenses. She must really think I'm Booboo the Fool, if she thinks I'm gonna dig any deeper for her money hungry ass.

I told Veronica that I ain't going for the bullshit any more. I told her that if she wants more money to take me to court. She knows that if we go to court, she'll end up getting a whole lot less than the $5K I give her now. So whenever I play that "let's go see the judge" card, Veronica somehow manages to get by with the money I'm giving her now. Besides, the money I send her now is basically for her pocket. I pay her mortgage and buy my son whatever he needs, so Veronica should know better than that.

I did find out that Veronica's new man has a serious gambling problem and is on the run ducking bullets. I heard dude owes everybody and there mother some money. If she's using my money to cover that niggas debt, she can forget about getting another dime from me. I'll have legal custody of Donte` and have her sending me money monthly.

India has really been on my ass about where we stand. India has made it clear to me that if I want back into her life, I have to get my shit together. No more questionable phone calls. No more "she's just a friend from the club", or any of the stunts I used to pull when we were together. I know that at the end of the day India is who I want to be with. I know I have to step up to the plate sooner or later. But when I step up I want to hit a game winning home run…

INDIA

Denali must think he can just string me along like some puppet. I know better than to force a man into a commitment. I know it must be something that he chooses. I am getting a little aggravated with how convenient I'm making it for him. He comes over unannounced, eats, showers, plays with Imani, and leaves. I know Denali is still out there dealing with every big booty in a skirt, but ain't no woman like the one I am. I'm too confident in mine to be jealous or threatened by another woman.

Denali better decide what it is he really wants, because I want and will have more with or without him. I PROMISE…

AKIL

I've been on my knees more than a hooker on a good night praying to God for another chance with Sole`. I've been sporadically seeing this chick Mercedes for the last few months, just to get by. But she's now catching feelings, talking about she's in love with me. Why is it that whenever I dick a chick down and spend a few dollars on them, they start talking that love shit? How can I love another woman when I'm in love with my wife?

I'm gonna have to kick Mercedes pretty ass to the curb, before she starts getting all possessive on a nigga. I'm really working on cleaning my act up. But like with anything I have to crawl before I walk. I can't help the fact that I love to make love. For now, Mercedes has been able to keep up.

Lately, I've been a regular at the network. I have met some real cool brothers over there. I met this one dude named Todd and the brother seemed unusually curious about my personal life. I've been so nervous lately that at first I thought word had gotten out about me and Tracey. Initially, I thought son had a gay angle. So I was quick to establish that it wasn't that type of party.

Once I made it clear that I didn't have any sugar in my

135

tank, Todd made it clear to me that he wasn't on that gay shit either. That relieved me because you never know nowadays. It's like being gay is fashionable. After that whole Tracey experience, I know just how nasty that gay shit is. Two niggas are a nasty ass sight.

Todd told me that he was having women problems, so we sat to rap a taste. "Man I'm dealing with this bad bitch right now. But the bitch is still all wrapped up in her lame ass husband." Todd said very colorfully. I was a little taken a back at how easily he could be so disrespectful towards women, especially since we just left a prayer meeting.

"Oh yea, it seems like that women problems disease is going around right now." I said still measuring the dude out. "I put it to you like this playa, I'm a pimp. I got bitches paying my bills, buying me clothes. Do you see that brand new Range Rover I'm pushing? One of my white broads bought that for me. You see this Rolex I'm rocking?" He said as he stuck his left arm out so that I could see his bling bling. "My baddest bitch bought this for me. I haven't even laid the smack down on her ass yet and she already made a visit to see Jacob the jeweler for a nigga." He said trying to give me a pound.

Damn, this is one dirty muthafucka I thought. I bet he has women clawing and praising his dirty ass. On the surface the brother is sharp. He has everything going on physically that women have wet dreams over. He's tall, dark, clean cut, and strikingly handsome. Dude has the model look happening to perfection. So it's easy to perceive him as a "good man". Especially since women think that a good looking man equates into a good one.

I know a snake when I see one. I don't trust this nigga as far as I can throw him. Whenever a man takes pride in dominating and manipulating women, he is weak and lacks good judgment. And I keep getting a funny vibe from this dude. It's like my spirit man is trying to tell me something about him.

He has that "I'm hiding something" look in his eyes. The

same look I had on my face when I was hiding my skeletons from my wife and friends. I just know that his dirty ass is up to something and until I find out what it is I'll play the "buddy, buddy, friend, friend" game, just to keep this nigga close...

SOLE`

Akil has been calling the house and left several messages about how sorry he is and that he understands how I feel. I have really considered forgiving Akil so that we can be a family again. The dozen white roses he sends to the house everyday, helps me to want to move forward.

My mother said that I made an "until death due us part" commitment to Akil so I should always be willing to fight for what's mine. My mother still has those, "always stick by your man no matter what" values. That old school let a man run all over you bullshit I refuse to accept. If a man can't be a man, he isn't fit to be with a good woman. Akil jeopardized my health, broke the purity of our union, and destroyed my trust in him. It's gonna take an act of God for me to forgive Akil for what he did...

DENALI

Every month I have a business meeting with my financial advisors, accountants, and business managers to discuss the overall status of my finances and business affairs.

I make sure that I surround myself with good people from the hood. Everyone from my lawyers to my business managers are African American men and women from the block. I think it's important that we make each other and our own community rich. That's why I hire the best black people for the job and pay the best money for their services.

"So Mr. Shaw, according to our calculations your net worth is now thirty seven million dollars. The real estate, print shops, laundry mats, and car dealerships are all performing better than projected. If all remains steady you should net another five million dollars of income this year." Raymond Wise, my accountant for the last six years said to me, as we all sat in the conference room of my corporate office.

It always makes me laugh whenever I hear how much I'm worth or how much money I make. I laugh because I think about where I came from and think about the fact that I don't rap, dance, act and I've never sold a drug or anything illegal in my life. I haven't played ball seriously in years, yet I'm a thirty two year old brother still getting that NBA money. I'm living proof that a young black man can succeed in business. That's why I stay in the hood, showing the youngings how to really get it in America. I show them how to really "keep it real".

After my business meeting with my money team, I decided to go to the gym to get my work out on. Lately I've been boxing and I love the work out. On my way to the gym, I accidentally bumped into Meisha's young ass.

"Hey daddy, you still looking good." Meisha said as she opened her arms for me to hug her. "What's up shorty?" I said, noticing that Meisha had put on some weight, but was still looking great.

"Have you changed your cell phone number? "I've been trying to get in touch with you for the last few weeks. You haven't been at the clubs, what's going on?" Meisha asked as we stood talking three blocks away from the gym. "I change my cell number every six months or so whenever it starts to get too hectic for me." I said still noticing she looked more beautiful than usual. "Did you just get off the train? I know you don't ride the train, Mr. Lamborghini?" Meisha asked still small talking.

"Yea, I just got off of the train. Come on now you know how I do, no Hollywood with me. I take the train whenever I don't feel like driving in this hectic ass city." I answered. "I'm surprised you don't have a personal driver or something, Mr. nightclub owner." Meisha said still trying to bust my balls. "Shorty my name is Denali, not Puffy. I don't need all that extra shit, I'm not a rap star." I said looking at all the people as they walked by.

"Damn shorty you look like you're putting on some

138

weight, but you look good though." I said gazing at Meisha's ass, that looked to be filling out even more. Then I thought to myself, I need to be easy because shorty is still a minor, but damn. "Of course I'm putting on weight, I'm pregnant silly." Meisha said as she playfully slapped me on the chest. "Congratulations. How far along are you?" I asked expressing genuine concern. "I'm four months pregnant by this dude named Doug from uptown. That's why I've been trying to call you. You were right about me needing to slow down, because I was on the wrong track in the fast lane.

"Doug just got knocked and is facing a seven to ten year bid. I don't know what to do right now. It's too late for me to have an abortion. And I don't want to give my baby up for adoption. My moms moved to Chicago with some young nigga a couple of weeks ago.

"Right now I don't have anything or anyone." Meisha said with tears in her eyes. This is the shit that pisses me off. Women always want to play the victim when they reap the situations and circumstances from their bad choices. I'm usually numb to the cries of a woman in this situation, but Meisha is not a woman. Meisha is a misguided little girl.

"So where are you staying at now?" I asked with a big brother's concern. "I'm staying with my cousin in the Polo Grounds. But it's too many heads in that household." She answered, looking so innocent.

"Look you don't have to explain everything to me. Here is my new number. Give me a call tomorrow morning. I'm gonna make it right for you and that baby, okay." I said giving Meisha a big warm hug and smile.

This is probably the best part of being rich. I can help people get on their feet and find their way. I'm gonna help Meisha get her life in order. It's the least I can do after all the bullshit and drama I've brought to the lives of women…

YES

I remember thinking I wouldn't be able to handle the loss

of a loved one. Especially the lost of Amerie, who had become my world. It's amazing that I'm still standing and living life. After her death I took a lot of time to think and learn about myself. I think not dating and having sex for a few months has probably been one of the best things that has ever happened to me. Lately I'm getting that sexual itch again. I'm starting to want some ass again.

I pray that God blesses me with a woman worthy of becoming my wife, like he did with Amerie. I finally understand the difference between sex and love. I know the difference between having a girlfriend and wanting a wife. After my relationship with Amerie, I've been touched by the beauty of love from a woman, and that I still crave…

SOLE`

After Todd suggested that I forgive and forget in order to restore my marriage, he hasn't been coming around as often as he use to. He now just calls to check up on me, and I'm missing him.

Tonight I've invited him over for dinner. I'm preparing some baked ziti, garlic bread, salad and his favorite strawberry cheesecake for desert. Well, I actually bought the cheesecake, but who cares. Not having Todd around has made me want him even more. There have been many nights when I was a second away from calling him over at one 'o clock in the morning so he could come and rock my world. But somehow I never made the call.

When Todd arrived at my door he was looking so suave and debonair. He had on all black, which made his six foot four athletic frame look even sleeker. One of the things that drive me crazy, is a tall and slender man, with good posture and a confident walk. Todd exemplifies what I like in a man physically.

"Hi baby, I've missed you." Todd said as he greeted me with a bear hug and sensual tongue kiss at the door. "I've missed you too." I responded still blushing from the energy of his presence and the kiss he just laid on me. Todd has never kissed me in such a way before. I know he hasn't because I'm starting to get wet in my thong. Damn, who knows where this is leading…

TODD

I'm done playing games with Sole's fine ass, I want some of that pussy. I got her just where I want her. She trusts me, cares for me, wants me, and I'm quite sure she can not resist the heat I'm about to put on her ass. I don't know what has happened, but being away from her has shown me that I really do care for her, and want Sole` as my woman.

I can care less about that nigga Akil. Son lost his spot. He struck out and now I'm up to bat. I want what I want, no if ands or buts about it. Sole` is bad and that stupid ass nigga couldn't do right. So its Akil's lost and not mine. Besides, what's gonna stop me from getting off…

CHAPTER 17

INDIA

"Lord, I've been steadfast and obedient to your Word. I'm in love with a man who is still battling with the strongholds of an illusionary world. Your Word says that you are love, so I know my love for Denali is a godly thing. Lord, grant me the patience to stay out of your way and the wisdom to know how. I believe that all you have for me is good and perfect. I know that my connection with this man is Divine and for your purpose. May your perfect Will govern our lives and affairs." Amen...

DENALI

I have never been big on prayer but since I've been attending those meetings at the network and been talking with India, I now find myself praying more often. Since I've been praying regularly, I notice that I'm doing things I would have never done before. I'm also not doing some of the things I used to. I cut out smoking trees all together and I don't know how that happened. I just don't crave many things anymore.

The situation with Meisha is a perfect example of my change. I ended up letting Meisha stay rent free in one of the brownstones I own in Harlem. I even gave Meisha some money to furnish the place. I also connected her with a business associate that was looking for a receptionist to help run his modeling agency. I think that will inspire Meisha to channel her good looks and charismatic ways into a more positive outlet.

Last night at the Kingdome I ran into Pumpkin this chick from Brooklyn. Pumpkin said she's been wanting to suck my dick

142

for years, but said she has always been in a relationship. She went on to tell me that she's single now, then went into explicit detail about how she can swallow a nut and take it up the butt.

On any other day, I would have taken Pumpkin to my private room in the club and let her walk her talk. But things are different now. I don't know why but I do know I'm thinking and feeling different as a man...

SOLE`

"So how's the business? Are you still working from home?" Todd asked as we had a candlelight dinner. "Business is great. I'm lucky that I have good people working for me. They are doing such a good job that I'm considering starting another business. I've always wanted to run a day care center and maybe that will be my next move." I said as I took a sip of the Don Pier ion that we were drinking. "Speaking of which, where is the little one?" Todd asked as he wiped the tomato sauce off of his mouth.

"He's with his grandmother." I responded. "So we're here alone?" Todd so smoothly asked, as he stood up from the table and started walking towards me. "Yes baby, we are here all alone." I said looking up into his bedroom stare. "Great, lets go into the living room and get a little bit more comfortable." Todd said taken my hand and leading me into the living room. I am always taking a back by Todd's mannerisms. He is a perfect gentlemen, he even leads us in prayer before a meal. I always feel respected and like a lady whenever I am with Todd.

After dinner, as we sat listening to some Anita Baker, Todd started his confession. "Sole` you have been nothing but a good thing to me and I thank God everyday for putting you in my path. Lately, I've been making an effort to create some space between us in order to protect my feelings. But what I feel for you I can no longer control. I've been fantasizing about what it would be like if I could make love to you." Todd said as he stroked my long hair.

I wasn't surprised by what Todd was saying. I was more

143

relieved than anything. Finally he was coming at me in a sexual way. "Well, I like having you around and close to me. My husband was the first and only man I have ever been with. Until you came along, I thought he would be the last. But I've been sexually attracted to you Todd since you introduced yourself to me in..." Before I could finish my nervous thoughts, Todd gently caressed the sides of my face with his big hands and hypnotically kissed me with those full soft lips.

As he kissed me, a burst of electric energy shot through my body and I welcomed his moist tongue into my mouth. As we kissed, Todd firmly but gently placed me on top of him. Todd then placed his strong masculine hands on my shoulders, while he gave me a sensual rub down. Todd then proceeded to kiss and suck my neck, while he slowly unbuttoned my blouse. "Can I make love to you, Sole'?" Todd whispered in my ear, as he unfastened the hooks on my bra with his teeth. With my girl Anita blowing in the background, and me sitting straddled on top of Todd, my mind and body was on fire with passion for this man.

"Can I make love to you baby?" Todd whispered again, as he licked in a circular motion around my nipples. "Yes you can make love to me." I moaned. By then Todd had my shirt and bra off. So I proceeded to undress him. Todd has the most muscular and ripped body. He looked so good with his washboard stomach and chiseled physique that I had to have some of him. Todd gently laid me down on my mink carpet and then disappered as he went into the kitchen. He then brought back some strawberries, whip cream, and the bottle of champagne we were drinking.

As I laid there in anticipation, Todd removed my stretch pants and slowly stripped me down to my thong. He then just sat there for a moment, admiring my body. Since having my son, my ass has gotten juicer and I'm more curvaceous now than I have ever been.

"You are so beautiful. Wow baby, you are so beautiful." Todd kept saying while shaking his head in disbelief. He then poured champagne and whip cream all over my breast, stomach, and on the front of my thong. Todd started to masterfully licked and suck the whip cream off of me, slowly. He was being so patient and erotic with his love making that it's almost as if he did it for a living...

AKIL

Tonight, I'm gonna make it special. I know Sole` will be surprised to see me. I can't wait to see my beautiful wife and kiss my son again...

TODD

Sole` is so beautiful. She has the perfect figure eight body. Her skin is so soft and flawless. That honey brown complexion, just makes me want to lick her up and down, never stopping. As I'm licking the whip cream off of the front of Sole's thong, I noticed that she has the juiciest pussy I have ever seen. "Damn baby, I want to eat you up." I said to Sole` still in awe of how sexy she was. "You can have as much as you want, it's all yours tonight." Sole` moaned, looking down at me with a sexy look.

Sole's sexy encouragement was so inspirational, I had to bury my face into her wet pussy...

SOLE`

"Oh my God Todd." I moaned. "Is it good to you baby?" Todd asked as he glanced up at me with my womanly juices all over his mouth.

"Yes baby it's good...don't you think about stopping." I sighed as Todd's tongue action was sending me to ecstasy.

As my temperature kept rising, I noticed that Todd had taken all of his clothes off and was hung like a horse. "You want some of this?" Todd teased me as he stroked my wet spot with his long thick black dick. "Don't tease me, please me daddy." I said as I put the condom on him and then slid all of that dick, gently inside of me. As he entered my body, I couldn't help but to shout. "Ahh baby that dick feels so good."

As Todd rhythmically penetrated me satisfying every ounce of me, my body began to peak.

As I started to count down to explosion 10, 9, 8… I noticed a figure of what appeared to be Akil, slowly walking towards us. "Ah… I'm cumming baby" I moaned 7, 6, 5… Damn this dick has really got me trippin' because I clearly see Akil getting closer, looking as if he just saw a ghost. "Ah… ah… ah baby, I'm cumming." I continued to moan, feeling my body getting ready to erupt. But for every second 4, 3… that I got closer to climaxing, the figure got closer. "Yes baby, here I go, here I cum" 2, 1… oh shit, *AKIL*…

AKIL

After I cracked Todd over the head with the champagne bottle, which broke into little pieces once it hit him, I stomped him unconscious with my size thirteen gators. How dare this nigga look me in the eyes and then turn around and fuck my wife…in my house? "So this is what your dirty ass has been up too. Huh, you bitch ass nigga. This is the bad ass married bitch you were talking about…my wife you dirty muthafucka?" I yelled as I tried to kick his nuts through his brain.

As I was working on putting that nigga Todd out of commission for good, Sole` sat there screaming. The whole time I was stomping a mud hole into Todd's ass, Sole` sat there butt naked, screaming at the top of her lungs for me to stop before I killed him.

After about her tenth desperate cry, I stopped. Although I had every intention on killing that bitch ass nigga Todd right then and there. I just didn't want to spend the rest of my life behind bars, because I let my emotions get the best of me for a moment. "So he's the reason why you won't return any of my calls, bitch?" I yelled at Sole` as I ran after her before she made it to the bathroom. She then locked the door behind herself to escape my fury.

"Honey, it's not what you think. I can explain everything

later. But you'll have to calm down Akil." Sole` said. "It's not what I think! So you're telling me I didn't just see you fuckin` that nigga? You're telling me that muthafucka wasn't in my pussy?" I roared causing the whole house to shake, as I tried to kick the bathroom door down.

"Akil please leave. Please leave honey. I'm sure one of the neighbors has called the cops by now. If you're still here when they show up it will get even uglier." Sole` pleaded with me, crying from inside of the bathroom door.

If I would've had a gun when I walked in here, I also would have had two dead bodies on my hands. The rage I was feeling was demonic.

"I could kill you and that nigga right now. You're lucky this door is keeping me from you. But you really fucked up Sole`. How could you fuck some nigga you don't even know? You better believe I'll be back and I want my son, bitch." I said as I kicked the bathroom door one last time. My kick caused the huge wedding picture of me and Sole` that was in the hallway to come crashing down.

As I was walking outside of the apartment, I saw Mrs. Pearlstein, with her nosy ass, sniffing for some drama. "Is everything alright Mr. Butler? I heard some yelling and screaming coming from your apartment?" She asked with her cat woman glasses hanging off the bottom of her nose. "That's what it sounds like when people are fighting. Now mind your business, old lady. Just take your ass back in the house." I answered as I walked right past her still enraged by what I just saw.

As I was walking to my car in the pouring rain, I noticed that my entire body was shaking uncontrollably and my mind was racing. Once I finally sat down behind the wheel, I almost decided on going back upstairs with the Louisville slugger I had in my trunk, and getting my Sammy Sosa on Todd's wavy carnium. Just then, I saw those lights and heard the sirens of the pigs in blue, coming to save the day. So using my better judgment, I sped off into the city's traffic.

As I'm driving, all I could think about was Todd's back and Sole's face as he was fuckin' my wife. How could she look so turned on by another man? The more I thought about it, the faster I drove. As I'm driving the rage I was feeling had me blinded to the hazardous road conditions I was speeding in. While I'm dipping and diving through traffic, I started picking up more and more speed in my Excursion truck.

All of a sudden, I started hydroplaning along the slick road and lost complete control over my truck. As I'm clocking speeds over one hundred miles per hour and hydroplaning on the FDR, I noticed a thick piece of metal in the road. I did my best to gain control of my truck and avoid running over the metal object. But all it did was cause more problems for me and I collided with an Acura that was also speeding in the rain. All I then heard was a loud screech, a scream, and then the lights went out on me…BEEEEEEEEEEEEEEEEEEEEEP

CHAPTER 18

<u>YES</u>

Peace I leave with you; my peace I give you. I do not give to you as the world gives. Do not let your hearts be troubled and do not be afraid."(John 14:27)

Since I've been going to the meetings, I've also been reading the Bible again. I forgot just how inspirational and therapeutic it is.

As I was laying on my California size bed, looking up at the mirror that rested on my ceiling, the phone started ringing. "Hello." I answered. "Yes, what's going on?" "What's good Lee, is everything cool?" I asked immediately recognizing his voice, but also hearing concern in it. "No it's not. Akil has just been in a serious car accident. They said he's in critical condition." Denali nervously responded. "What?" I asked. "He's at NYU hospital. Meet me over there." Denali said sounding like he was about to cry. "I'm on my way now." I responded as I hurried out of my door.

As I got into my truck and was headed for the hospital, I said a short prayer.

"Lord you have authority over all things. You know the hearts of men and have the wisdom to understand every action. I know that you are a just and perfect God. Lord please allow Akil to remain in good health and give him the strength to get through this." May God's Will be done...

DENALI

When India and I arrived at the hospital, I suddenly remembered why I despise hospitals so much. The smell and all the signs of sickness, injury, and disease are enough to make anybody sick. When we finally located Akil the nurse told us he was rushed to the ER. She said a team of specialist were working overtime to stabilize him.

The nurse said that he had suffered major injuries to his head, spinal cord, and broke several bones. I asked if there was a chance that he may be paralyzed. And the nurse said that it is common in this type of case.

"Don't worry for one second baby. Akil will be fine." India said as she hugged me. As me and India were sitting in the waiting room holding hands, Yes arrived and was just as heartbroken as I was, when I heard the news. "So do they think he'll make it?" Yes asked nervously.

"The nurse said the doctors are working hard." India said in a comforting tone, to ease Yes' nerves. Just then I thought I should call Sole` and let her know what was going on with her husband. I know that regardless of what they were going through, she still loves that man. I know Sole` would be concerned about her son's father. It was almost as if my thoughts were in the air because India picked right up on it. She asked for Sole's number so she could give her a call...

INDIA

"Hello Sole`, this is India, Denali's girl. How are you doing sweety?" I asked after Sole` picked up the phone on the fourth ring. "Not so good, I'm going through something right now." Sole` said sounding like she just lost her dog. "Well I really don't like being the bearer of more bad news but there is something that you need to know. Akil has just been in a near fatal car accident on the FDR." I said "He's WHAT?" Sole` asked in a panic. "He's here at NYU hospital in surgery. I just wanted to let you know what is going on." I said softly. "Thanks India, I really appreciate the call girl...

SOLE`

It hasn't been an hour since the EMT's and cops left my apartment questioning me about what happened to Todd. After I gave them some bogus story about an old boyfriend coming over and beating him up, they took some notes down and left the apartment. One night and all of this.

They just rolled Todd out of here to St. Mary's and now Akil is in NYU hospital. Two men, right now both laying in a hospital bed needing me by their sides. One man that represents my past and all that I've grown comfortable with over the last ten years. The other representing possibility and what my life can become. One man, my husband, the other a special friend. One man, the father of my son, the other a good brother.

Despite all that Akil and I are going through, I didn't have to think twice about what to do. Before I realized what I was doing, I was in a sweat suit and baseball cap hailing down a cab on my way to NYU hospital. There is no way I was gonna leave my husband and the father of our son in a hospital room alone, fighting for his life. Regardless of what we've been through, I still love my husband. I still love Akil with all my heart.

I was too rattled to drive myself, so I took a cab. While in the cab, I didn't know what to think or what to expect. I decided to do the only thing a person should do in this predicament. I started praying.

"Lord please be merciful towards my call and forgive me of my confused and fearful ways. My husband, the man I vowed to love for better or for worst is fighting for his life on a hospital bed. Right now we are in the worst of times. We need your strength and love to get us through this together and to restore our good times. Lord give us the wisdom and grace to rebuild our marriage and raise our son. In Jesus name Amen...

YES

Why do bad things happen to good people? The serial killers, murderers, and rapists never get shot by stray bullets or end

151

up in serious car accidents. It's the hard working, decent, tax paying people that shit like this happens to." I said to Denali and India as we sat waiting to hear something new from the doctors.

"What did Sole` say India? Is she on her way or not?" I asked India, as she rubbed Denali's back, while he sat bent over with his head in his hands. "She didn't say what she was gonna do. She didn't sound too good though." India said as she started to rub Denali's baldhead. Knowing the type of woman Sole` is, I knew she would show.

When I stepped into the hallway, on my way to the bathroom, there she was talking with the doctors looking so worried and concerned about her husband. "Sole` it will be alright. Lord knows he will be alright. Akil is in God's perfect hands. Lets stay positive and strong. Let God use the doctors to make Akil strong again." I said holding Sole` firmly, consoling my sister. "I just want to see him Yes, I really just want to see him." She said as her tears hit my sweater...

DENALI

It's sure good to see Sole` here at the hospital pulling for Akil, right along side his parents, who took a flight up from Maryland. Akil has been in surgery for the last five hours but the doctors said he'll pull through. Looking at Akil's parents with their thirty plus years of marriage and love that radiates for one another, made me think. What do they know and what are they doing to make their marriage and lives work so well?

"Mr. B, can I talk to you for a second?" I asked as we took a walk outside to smoke a square. "Sure son, what's on your mind?" He responded as he passed me a Newport, looking just like Akil from the side. "I know this might not seem like the appropriate time to ask but sitting here watching you and Mrs. Butler is amazing.

"After all those years together, y'all still so lovingly interact with one another, looking like kids in love. Tell me what is the formula? How do you still do it?" I asked shaking my head in amazement, as I took another long drag on my cigarette. I really need to give these damn cigarettes up.

"Growing up, I was raised to be a different type of man than what we raise today. I was raised to honor my word and to keep my commitments, regardless of temporary setbacks or discomfort.

"In my day, marriage was perceived as a lifetime commitment and partnership. As men and women we understood commitment a little differently than you all do today. We approached marriage with a different attitude. Back then black people didn't have so much materially, so we valued people and our relationships more than silver and gold. To us, family and friends were symbols of wealth and success. Today it's titles, cars, homes and all that other shit, so relationships aren't as important.

"Back then we were hardworking, committed to the end, do whatever it takes, type of people. Today young people want everything by yesterday. You all think that commitment means, I'll do this for as long as I'm comfortable and not challenged. A real commitment makes things solid, stable, and strong, which is needed in those tough times.

"With Gloria and I, there is no such thing as how we "still" do what we do. We never had the mentality of not doing it. When I asked that woman to marry me, it was because it was something that I wanted for the rest of my life. Marriage was something that I chose to have. I thought marrying Gloria would make me a better man, and guess what... I was right.

"Everything I am, everything I do, everything I have, is fifty percent because of that woman. So my question to you is, how could I not "still", as you put it, love someone that makes me rich, successful, and prosperous?" Mr. Butler said as he put his hand on my shoulder.

"I see how you're looking at that young lady India in there. She is a good woman, I can see it all in her eyes. The way she looks at you and caresses you, shows me that she supports you Denali. In your eyes I see two things son. I see love and I see fear.

153

You are in love with that woman but you are afraid of the responsibilities of commitment. But I'll tell you the same thing I tell Akil. The rewards of commitment far out weigh the responsibilities.

"You are not as successful as you are in business without commitment. Right now you are committed to making your business prosperous right?" He asked. "Of course I am." I answered. "It's the same thing with loving a woman son.

"You're a smart man, I have always known that. Every since you were a kid, you have always been three steps ahead of the bunch. So I'll put it to you like this. If you give a hundred percent of yourself to one thing or to one person, you are guaranteed to succeed, for there won't be anything to confuse you or dilute your effectiveness." Mr. Butler said giving me that huge white smile of his.

"I do love India, but there are so many other women out here. I'm still a young man Mr. B." I said sounding like I was fifteen all over again. "See that's the greatest lie the devil ever told a single man. You think that it's hard and a sacrifice to be with only one woman. The truth is, it's harder for a man to be with more than one. It's also far more of a sacrifice to your health and well being.

"When God made Adam, his perfect match was Eve, not Eve, Shelia, Tanya, and Carmen. A real man only needs one woman, a boy needs many." Mr. Butler said, dropping that old school wisdom on me.

Damn, with all of this wisdom at home, I never understood why Akil made so many foolish decisions. "Damn Mr. B, it's always good to talk to you." I said as we started walking back into the hospital. "Oh yea, so why don't you call or visit nigga?" Mr. Butler said as he threw some playful punches my way.

"I don't know, maybe for the same reasons Akil don't listen." I said blocking his blows. "Akil is a very stubborn and independent thinker, so until he learns these truths and principles for himself, it's all just jargon to him." Mr. Butler said as we walked back into the waiting room.

Mr. Butler is an old-G, one of those men that all men respect and admire. He has seen it all and has lived to talk about it. Mr. Butler walks his talk, he is a man of integrity, so I always hang onto every word that comes out of his experienced mouth...

DOCTOR

Good morning, I'm Doctor Williams the head surgeon on the team. Mr. Butler is now out of surgery and is in good shape. He is a very strong willed man and he'll be just fine. He will be able to see guest shortly. I have let him know that his family and friends are here, which brought a huge smile to his face.

Mr. Butler is pleased to know that you have all shown up, but he has asked to see Mrs. Butler, his wife, first. Just be warned, that we had to stabilize his spine and he's still in a lot of pain, so don't excite him. Remember, he can hear and comprehend fully, but his words may be limited. Mrs. Butler, nurse Brown will escort you in shortly. You all have a lovely and blessed day. Mr. Butler will be alright ...

SOLE`

Akil's parents have been nothing but supportive of me and our marriage since we've married. Here at the hospital they have been angels. I'm surprised that even though Akil's parents and best friends are here it's me that he wants to see first. After all that we are dealing with, he wants the first familiar voice he hears and face he sees to be mine. Especially with all that we just experienced, with the Todd situation and all.

As nurse Brown, this short older woman, gave me the okay to enter the room, I became terrified. What would he look like? What would I say to him? Just twelve hours ago he was on his way back home to make things right and walked in on another man screwing his wife. I know that I've witnessed his infidelity by photo but he witnessed mine in the flesh. A big part of me feels

155

like this is all my fault. I don't know how to face him. Lord guide me...

AKIL

Am I dead? Where in the hell am I, I thought as I walked down this long bright path. As I get to the end of the walkway this huge door opened up. As I enter, I see these huge three dimensional giant size mirrors, lined up perfectly. There was a mirror resting on each step of this stairway that went up as far as I could see. Is this the stairway to heaven? Damn, I must be dead.

As I took my first step up the stairway, I saw an image of my mother and father walking together holding hands. They appeared to be thirty years younger. As I took the second step I saw images of a baby that appeared to be me being born. As I took the third step I saw my first day of school and images of that stage in my life.

For every step I took up the stairway, I saw different stages of my life. I saw when I turned thirteen and lost my virginity. I saw when I decided to follow my heart's desire to become a writer. I even saw the day I meet Sole` at Madison Square Garden. She was looking so cute, dressed in pink. I saw our wedding day and the many, many beautiful times we had together. I almost forgot all of the good times Sole` and I shared.

After about the seventh step I took, I saw the image of a terrible car accident. I then heard a loud but extremely gentle and comforting voice speak to me. *"I am not finished with you. These remaining steps you are not to see in here but to live out there. I have given you another chance for I am not finished with you my son. I will greatly increase you if you will follow me. Come follow me Son. I am the Truth, Love, and Life you have been seeking your whole life. Come follow me...*

SOLE`

As I'm slowly and gingerly walking into Akil's room, I was surprised by what I saw. Even though Akil was connected to every machine and tube in the hospital, he looked at peace. Not that peace of a dead body in a casket, but the peace of a man that was in paradise. "Hey baby." I said as I stood over Akil's bed and kissed his forehead. Once I kissed Akil his eyes opened up.

"Hey booboo." He mumbled as he tried to crack a smile. I then just held his hand as we looked at each other. We just stood there, looking at one another for the next ten minutes, asking for each other's forgiveness, without saying a word. As I looked into my husband's eyes, I didn't see the man I was used to seeing. In his eyes I saw a change, I saw a different man within Akil's body. Although he was lying in a hospital bed he looked strong and assured.

As he sat there looking into me, I couldn't take it any longer. "Oh baby, I am so sorry for all of the harm I have caused." I said as my eyes started to water. "I never set out to hurt you, all I ever wanted to do was love you daddy. I made a big mistake and I'm truly sorry for the whole thing. Will you forgive me Akil?" I asked as I clinched his hand tightly.

"Baby there is no need for you to apologize for what has happened. You didn't do anything to me that I haven't done to myself. What I saw at the house was largely because I gave up my right to be there. I messed up first honey, and I'm truly sorry for everything. Will you forgive me Sole`?" He asked of me with this new look in his eyes.

"Yes Akil, I forgive you baby. I have missed you so much. It felt like I couldn't breathe without you. Being apart this long has taught me a lot, and there is one thing I know for sure Akil. I know that I don't ever want to live my life without you again…

AKIL

My wife is so beautiful and special to me. Why did I ever jeopardize our marriage? Seeing Sole's pretty eyes and dimpled smile again brought the ultimate joy to my spirit. I realize now that as a man I need to serve the Lord, as a husband and father, I need to serve my family.

"Baby I haven't been living life without you. I felt like half of my body was gone or something. I missed your smile, lying next to you at nights, hearing your squeaky voice in the morning. I missed you so much Sole`. I want you now like never before booboo." I said as the tears were rolling down the sides of my face. "We have a lot of talking to do and so much we need to re-establish. We have so much to discuss. There is so much that I have to say to you.

"There is so much that I need for you to know, but none more important than I am still in love with you baby. Sole` I love you so much baby, more than life itself boo. I hope that you believe me when I say that you're one of the main reasons why I'm still alive. You inspire me to live baby." I said crying and holding her hand as tightly as I could muster. For the next twenty minutes we just sat there holding hands looking into each other's teary eyes communicating with our souls. We just sat there in that hospital room making love to one another...

CHAPTER 19

DENALI

Since Akil's car accident, and finding out about all that he and Sole` have gone through, my appreciation and respect for love has grown. The conversation I had with Mr. Butler at the hospital has stuck to my conscience like a moth to a flame. He really challenged me with some of the things he said, especially about a real man only needed one woman, but a boy needing many.

I've decided to take my kids and India to Disneyworld. I have now been spending more quality time with my love ones, and that begins with my son and daughter. After seeing my man Kil lay halfway dead on a hospital bed, shit really fell into perspective for me. So my kids are top priority and Disneyworld is the next move.

Veronica's simple ass wanted to be difficult but after I threw a grand her way for some shoes, she miraculously became supportive of our trip.

"As long as nothing happens to my baby, he can go with you." Veronica said as we stood in her kitchen talking. "First of all, he's my baby too Veronica. As his father, I would never allow anything to happen to my little man." I replied frustrated by the nature of the whole conversation. The worst decision I ever made was not pulling out of Veronica. I love my son more than life itself but this bitch knows how to keep a nigga away.

If the courts would somehow allow it, I would love to have full custody of Donte`. I do know that when he gets a little older, he will be coming to live with me. I think young boys need to see how a man lives on a day to day basis. And that's exactly what my son will have.

159

"We'll be back in two weeks. Enjoy yourself and don't party too hard." I said. "You wild bitch." I mumbled to myself.

Me and Donte` then walked outside and hopped into my tricked out Yukon Denali truck.

"How's my little man doing?" I asked Donte` as I strapped on his seat belt. "I'm fine daddy. We going to see Mickey Mouse?" He asked with those innocent eyes of his. "Yes little man, daddy is taking you and your sister to Disney World. We're gonna get on a plane and have fun. Do you like the sound of that?" I asked Donte` as I put on his Spiderman DVD, so he could watch it as we drove. "My sister is going with us? I miss my little sister daddy. Can we go get her now, uh daddy?" Donte` asked as he watched his DVD that played in the headrest.

"Yes little man, we are going to pick up Imani but after we spend some time together and do the things men do. You do want to spend some time alone with daddy, right?" I asked Donte` as I looked over at my little face. "Yea daddy, let's go get on your boat…

<u>YES</u>

I frequently do lunch at this spot called Vasco's, right off of Wall Street. They are the best and least expensive Italian restaurant, in the business, as far I'm concern. I'm quite sure that over the years I have spent tens of thousands of dollars in there ever since I became a Wall Street man.

As I walked into Vasco's with Jeff, a fellow broker from the firm, I had no idea what I was about to get into. Minister Gilmore once said, "A man attracts his compliment, that woman who completes who he is and what he expects." I have changed and matured a lot over these last three to four years. That must be the reason why I was able to recognize it when I saw it; although I didn't expect it to happen right here and right now.

As we were walking to sit at our favorite lunch table, I accidentally bumped into her. She was five five with a butter pecan colored complexion and was wearing a navy blue Donna Karan power suit.

"Excuse me Ms. Lady. I'm sorry, I didn't mean it." I politely said looking down to meet her eyes. When our eyes met every nerve in my stomach jumped. "Maybe I wanted that to happen." She girlishly responded, as she licked her glossy lips.

"Oh really?" I added. "Maybe just maybe." She responded. "So are you leaving? I know you're not gonna hit and run like that. My name is Yes Black." I said extending my hand for her to shake, not wanting this conversation to end. "Unfortunately, I have to get back to the office. I'm Adrienne Waters, it's a pleasure to meet you Mr. Yes Black." She said.

"Well I don't want to hold you up but I also don't want you to go. Well not until I know, when I will be able to see you again." I said as we stood face to face and body to body. "My thoughts exactly. Here take my business card but use it for pleasure." Adrienne said as she gave me a smile that looked like she had never missed a dentist appointment in her life. After we exchanged business cards with the excitement of junior high school kids, I watched Adrienne walk out of Vasco's into the rainy hustle and bustle of downtown's financial district at midday.

Sitting there eating my lasagna with Jeff, I couldn't help but to recognize the butterflies that were in my stomach. The same butterflies I felt when I first saw Amerie. "Damn Yes you in love already. I know you're not one of those "love at first sight" suckers." Jeff said as he laughed with his goofy cornball laugh. "Come on Jeff, you've known me ever since we were interns. You've seen some of the women I have knocked down. But honey is special Jeff, I just know it. What, you didn't see it in those pretty light brown eyes?" I asked.

"Did I see it in those pretty light brown eyes? Are you kidding me? How could I with you all in baby's face like that?" Jeff said as he drank his Sprite. "You're a funny guy Jeff. All I know is that Adrienne has got it. Remember I have dealt with plenty of women and only two have ever moved me. One I asked to marry me but she was murdered, the other one I just met, so who knows…

AKIL

They kept me in the hospital for only three days. It was a miracle, considering they said it would take at least two weeks before I could be released. Little did the doctors know, I was in God's perfect hands.

Since I have been home again, me and Sole` have spent the entire time "talking talking, and listening, listening". We've been forgiving, correcting, and planning our new life together. We are doing all the things to make our relationship and marriage strong again. I've learned more about Sole` in the three weeks that I've been back home, than in the ten plus years I've previously known her.

Something powerful happens between a man and a woman when they communicate openly, respecting the other's point of view, in a nonjudgmental way. I don't know why we've never talked like this before. I guess all that we've been through has really changed us as individuals. Therefore, our relationship has to feel the effects of that. Little Kil has been in Maryland with my parents the last two weeks. My parents suggested that me and Sole` spend some quality time alone. So we decided to stay at our little vacation home, up in Bear Mountains, NY.

I'm still recovering from my injuries but at an incredible pace. The vision that I had in the hospital is holding true. My bones are healing faster than we thought possible.

My marriage and relationship with Sole` is also unlike before. It's like we have this newfound desire to please and love one another. Our relationship is growing faster than our son, and we smile and laugh so much now, that I've been busting stomach muscles.

Me and Sole` have been chilling; watching movies, playing cards, listening to music, just really having a good time doing the simple things again. While out here, I've been thinking a lot about starting the magazine I dreamed about as a kid. Funny thing is, Sole` must feel it as well. She has said the same thing I've been hearing in my head, word for word. "Now is the time for you to go

162

to the next level and start that magazine…

SOLE`
Prayer sure does work. My mother didn't raise us up in the church, but the spiritual foundation she instilled is really starting to pay off. With all that has happened, only God could turn such a chaotic and destructive situation into order and construction. Akil and I have talked about everything, from our fears, dreams, marriage, to our fantasies. It feels like we just met yesterday.

"I think young girls are having sex way too early and too often." I said as me and Akil were having a deep conversation. "They are only doing what they see and hear their older sisters, aunts, and girlfriends doing." Akil said as we sat out back just shooting the breeze. "I hope our son doesn't grow up, looking to hump every girl with a butt." I said, a little concerned about the idea. "Nah not our little man. Kil is gonna know how to treat a lady and respect his relationship. I know if there is one thing I will teach him before I leave this earth; that is how to be a man." Akil said as he sipped his lemonade while we talked. "My son will not have to make the same mistakes I made." Akil added.

I almost forgot just how brilliant and intelligent of a man my husband is. Akil is a wonderful man with a lot to offer. Being that he is still experiencing some pain, we haven't gotten physical as of yet, but the pressure is brewing. I do know that as soon as he is able I'm gonna give Akil what he's been missing. He has to have some of his pussy again

"We really need to stop talking so much about sex, especially since I don't have my swagger back yet. Please believe Ms. Lady, that I have something special lined up for your ass once I get my spine back." Akil said talking smack in his usual style. It is sure good to have my man back in the house…

INDIA
"I would love to take a trip to Disneyworld with the kids baby. God knows I need a vacation." I happily said to Denali.

163

Surprisingly Denali isn't the traveling type, unless it's by car or train. Amazingly, someone who conducts so much business is so opposed to travel. So when he decided on flying us out to Florida on a private jet, I was delighted.

Working on this CD has been an arduous process, so I'm looking forward to a break in the routine. "How long will we be staying honey?" I asked Denali. "Seven days and six night's baby." Denali responded as I followed him into the master bedroom. Denali's home and property is wonderful, it's almost like a resort. I really enjoy being over here in this gated community, where all of the celebrities and entertainers live.

On Denali's property he has two pools, a man made pond, a basketball and tennis court. There are enough bedrooms to house a housing project. Plus there is plenty of open space, which creates a serene atmosphere. Whenever I spend the nights over here, I always wake up early in the morning and come outside to talk with God.

"Baby you know you mean the world to me? You do know that, right?" Denali said as he brought his towering body close to mine. "Yes baby, I know that." I affirmed as we stood in the center of his huge bedroom holding each other. The passionate look in Denali's eyes and the emotion I heard in his voice, revealed that he was being sensitive. "I'm feeling different baby. A lot of things I was afraid and confused about, are becoming clear to me. All that I want in life is for my businesses to continue to prosper. I want to raise my kids to become responsible and good people. But more than ever before, I want you by my side India." Denali said as he pulled me even closer to him and started to kiss my bottom lip.

"So…so… so what do you mean by your side?" I stuttered trying to slow my sexual intensity down. As much as I want Denali, I'm saved now. So we have to wait. "I mean I want us to be together forever. Just me and you against the world baby." Denali responded as he dropped down to his knees.

For a second, I thought the moment I had been praying for had arrived. But then I felt Denali's strong hands and long fingers, caressing my curves and thighs, as he lowered my Diesel jeans. "Denali don't take me there baby. You know I want us to wait before we do this...don't take me there please baby." I passionately pleaded with Denali. I was struggling between being firm in what I said with my mouth and submitting to what my soul and body wanted. But Denali's mind was already made up. And nothing can stop a determined man.

Besides, my body was already in complete agreement with the lure of Denali's sexual rapture...

DENALI

I've been understanding and respectful of India's new beliefs about sex before marriage, for as long as I could be. I've patiently took her desires into consideration but I can no longer take this shit. I know that she wants some of this loving. I can barely hold her close without her kitty purring.

After sucking the cinnamon off of India's tongue, I could almost taste the naturalness of her pussy. So it was only right that I satisfied my desert thirst with her life saving juices. As I was on my knees, eating right through India's secret, I thought about one day proposing and putting that rock on her finger. But this time it was all about pleasing India's body.

As I was caressing India's clit with a tornado's fury, she stumbled to the wall, grabbing my baldhead, and started moaning. "Why are you doing this to me baby?" She asked looking as if she couldn't take it. "So do you want me to stop?" I asked teasing her clit with my tongue. "No baby, don't stop. I've missed this so much. Taste all of it." India moaned as she started to grind up and down on the wall, while my face was deep in it.

Like I said before India can dance her ass off. The more she moved, the more the sexual fire increased. "Is this my pussy baby?" I asked. But India's moans told the story. "I'm cumming baby, I...I...ahhh...ahhh...I'm cumming Denali...I'm cumming right now." She cried out growing louder and louder. As India's body was convulsing, I sucked her wet pussy in a circular motion while she cried out like a howling dog.

I then stood up and looked India in her moist eyes and said, "I'm in love with you India so much that it hurts me all over baby." And that must have been what she needed to hear. Because India then pushed me down onto the bed and sucked me off, like she *loved me*.

India then slobbered all over my dick and balls, while moaning the whole time. And right before I exploded, India took the the tip of my dickhead, sucking all of my life juices into her mouth, and down her throat. "Da…da…damn baby." I said after my vision returned.

"I just wanted you to know that I love you too baby." India said then got up and walked off to the bathroom. I just sat there and watched in amazement at how good India's feminine curves looked as her butt jiggled while she walked away. Damn India's has got that good shit, I thought as I continued to lay there. I then heard India turn on the shower. So I decided to join her and proceeded to finish what we started.

We made love in the bathroom, on the kitchen counter, in the pool outside, on the basketball court's bleachers. We made love all over the damn house as the kids slept all through the night. I've been known to get my "freak" on, but me and India made passionate love to one another. "I love you India." I said as we laid out, butt naked on my bed. "I love you too baby." India responded as we laid there thirty pounds lighter.

YES

"Good evening, can I speak with Adrienne?" I asked the sultry voice that picked up the phone. "This is she." The sultry voice responded. "Hello Ms. Lady, this is Yes from earlier today at Vasco's. How are you doing this evening?" I asked. "I'm fine Mr. Sexy. I'm just getting in from work and yourself?" She responded.

I then looked over at my clock and the time read 9:47PM.

"I'm here just relaxing myself. I noticed that your card said attorney at law. What type of law do you practice?" I asked breaking the first conversation's ice. "I'm a corporate lawyer honey. Look sweety, I just walked in the door. I live on 84th and Park Ave. Why don't you come over and see me, we can talk in person." She said rather seductively. "I would love to. In fact, I'm twenty minutes away, so give me an hour. I look forward to seeing you." I said before hanging up the phone with a smile on my face.

After I showered up, making sure I did a thorough cleansing of my body and balls, I got dressed. I put on some of my tailor made black slacks, threw on some black Hugo Boss shoes and a matching black cashmere turtleneck. Oh and I can't forget, I had to throw on some smell goods. Before I walked out of the door, I threw on my black fall leather. I can't front, I was looking like a beige Shaft as I dashed out of the door on my way over to Adrienne's place.

Once I made it over to Adrienne's apartment, I was nervously excited. "You look amazing." Adrienne said as she opened the door, wearing a black cat suit. She had on one of those numbers with the fishnet holes running down her voluptuous left side. The one like the strippers wear. Oh shit, baby is trying to kill a nigga in here, I thought. "Wow." Was all I could utter as I stood there in disbelief.

This cannot be the same woman I met earlier, looking like Hilary Clinton, now looking like Diamond from the Playas Club. "Are you surprised honey? I bet you didn't expect that I would be working with all of this body." Adrienne said as she twirled around, displaying her coke bottle 36-26-42 frame. "Wow." I repeated, as I marveled at how soft her ass cheeks were looking. "Well, let's not stand here in my doorway, come let me show you around." Adrienne said as she took me by the hand.

As Adrienne gave me a quick tour of her lavish apartment, I decided to get a conversation going. I had to because my dick was harder than three construction hard hats. "Your place is lovely.

167

How long have you been living here?" I asked as we admired her expensive collection of European artwork. "I've been living here for the last ten years. The last two I have been here alone." She answered while leading me into her entertainment room, which was decked out in all white. She also had a matching snow white Baby Grand piano resting in the center of the spacious room.

"Do you play?" I asked pointing over to the piano. "Yes I do a little something, something. Would you like to hear something?" Adrienne asked as she sashayed across the room, carefully enhancing my sexual interest with each step. Damn, baby was killing a nigga for real. She had her juicy ass coming all out of her cat suit. She definitely had that sex goddess thing happening and I was drawn. Adrienne then played the piano and sung me a sexy song. Now at that point my dick was so hard my muthafuckin` balls were starting to turn blue on me. As Adrienne sung Patti Labelle's "If only you knew", the emotional and sexual intensity increased and was becoming extreme.

"Oh look honey, it's a full moon out tonight." Adrienne said as she cat walked from the piano out onto her deck. She then signaled with her hand for me to follow her out onto the deck. And like a puppy dog, I obliged.

"Do you want me honey?" Adrienne asked me as she back pedaled to the edge of her deck. "Yes I want you baby." I responded, pushing all two hundred and twenty pounds of myself up against her, while we stood face to face. "Well show me how much you want me. Before I commit to a man he must be able to capture and tame me." Adrienne said slowly rubbing my dick through my slacks.

Oh shit, honey has me feeling like a virgin again and I am… and I am speechless. I just stood there frozen, looking stupid in the face. I'm saying, how many times does it go down like this? I mean, I barely know baby. From what I saw earlier, I would have never thought it would be about this, and so soon.

"See you don't really want me." Adrienne said with a disappointed look on her face. She then tried to side step herself away from me. "Yes I do want you. So don't run now." I said pulling her body into mine. I then threw my tongue down her mouth.

As we were kissing and undressing one another, it started to rain down hard on our naked bodies. While nature's rainy waters were soaking us, I lifted Adrienne up onto the deck's ledge. I made sure that Adrienne's fat pussy was ready for the pleasing. Then with one swift motion, I put the condom on with my left hand, while I held Adrienne's back with my right. "Give me that big monster baby." Adrienne said giving me a freaky look.

With Adrienne's blessing, I then proceeded to see just how much dick I could get inside of her. I then stroked Adrienne down, from thirty two stories up into the New York City skyline. "Yes baby, show me how much you want me." Adrienne yelled loud enough for everyone in the city to hear. "Is that enough for you baby? Can you handle all of me?" I asked as I felt the tip of my dick reaching the back of Adrienne's sexual walls. "I didn't hear you." I said as I pumped Adrienne violently, while she scratched and clawed my back, tearing my skin with her nails.

"Yes daddy… that's more than enough dick…that's more than enough dick. Fuck me hard with that big ass monster dick." Adrienne yelled as the raindrops fell off of her nose and chocolate covered nipples, while she rode me vertically. As me and Adrienne stood out there on that deck, fucking like wild bandits, it would only take fifteen passionate minutes before our bodies erupted, And let me be the first to tell it: I bust the nut of two lifetimes

CHAPTER 20

AKIL

"So Rich, what do you think? Are you in or not?" I asked Rich concerning my business proposal. "Starting your own magazine cost big bucks Akil. That shit can run close to a million dollars if you really want to compete. How will you raise the capital?" Rich asked not realizing that raising the capital would be the easiest part for me. With two best friends worth millions, money is never an issue. Besides, me and Sole` ain't cutting coupons either.

"That won't be a problem. I have some angle investors and plan on landing some quality advertising accounts. My major objective is that I want to formulate a team that will help to make this dream a reality. I have wanted to do this for the last ten years Rich, and now is the moment. All I need to know my brother is if you'll come along for this ride?" I asked Rich as he looked around Justin's restaurant, considering his options.

"God sure does work above our planning. I moved back to the NY, set on starting a prison ministry for men and now this." Rich said as he continued to look around the restaurant. He then continued. "I would love to come along. In fact, I have fifty grand towards the start up, if you need it. When you get all of the details ironed out just let me know where I fit in. I'm there all of the way." Rich added as he shook my hand to seal his commitment.

I have always admired Rich as a man and friend, when we used to work together. Not to mention, the brother is the most insightful and talented writer I know. So having an anchor like Rich provides much stability to the team. It's a great start for me. I know that building a first class organization, I'm gonna need people that possess three winning qualities: Character, talent, and ambition. I want my magazine to be the hottest and realist shit on the stands. So I need the best to produce the best...

DENALI

What a wonderful and much needed family vacation that was for all of us. Me, India, and the kids had the best time of our lives out there in Florida. The whole Walt Disney World experience was real cool and unexpected. We took pictures with Mickey, Minnie, and all of those other characters kids love. Me and India took the kids to damn near every show and rode every ride we could, having a great time all seven days we were there.

One of the things I love so much about India is that she's always willing to have a good time, regardless of how tight her hair is done up at the time. At nights, when the kids were sound asleep, me and India would make love for the history books. Shit, my balls have never felt better and happier. India has been giving me all of the woman that I need and I'm cool with that. But being back in the city is what a nigga also needs right now.

While on vacation I realized that what I've really been craving is more meaning and intimacy in my life. Being with India and my kids brings that to my life. One thing is for sure, I still enjoy the nightlife and it's excitement. I guess I can still party and love my woman and family at the same time.

Tonight, the fellas are supposed to meet me at the club. It is gonna be a good night tonight. Akil hasn't been out partying since his accident and I know my man wants to boggie a bit. I can respect that Akil is on something different now but that nigga wants to party. I can hear it in his voice and see it all in his eyes. That nigga wants to get his two step on...

YES

"So what's up with your new Lady friend? What's baby's name again? Akil asked as we drove in his S600 to the Kingdome.

171

"Man things couldn't be better Kil. Her name is Adrienne. She's a mature and sophisticated woman. I think she might be the one dawg." I said sounding like Adrienne has my nose wide open.

"The one, damn dawg, you need to stop bullshitting like that. What's going on, are you feeling vulnerable my nigga?" Kil said and started laughing. "Baby must have put it on that ass. What she sucked your toes and licked your asshole or something?" Akil said laughing some more taking my confession lightly.

"Kil look at me. Do I look like I'm bullshitting? Baby is all of that. She's sexy as hell, funny, she has her own money, and all she wants is me. Oh, and did I mention that she's forty five." I added looking over at Kil while he drove.

"Damn playboy you went and found some of that Eartha Kit pussy, I see. That's why you're sprung that pussy has got some season on it." Akil responded still laughing from what he had said before. "So how long has it been good to you?" Kil asked trying to be serious. "We have been kicking it hard for the last two weeks, and everyday it's getting better." I said sounding immature with excitement.

"Two weeks…two weeks… I would sure hope that everyday was getting better. Shit I would hate to think things were going downhill after only two muthafuckin` weeks." Kil said laughing real hard this time, but making a valid point in the process.

It's true, I have only known Adrienne for two weeks. But damn it sure does feel like I have known her for a lifetime…

INDIA

Denali has said that he wants to take our relationship to another level. But he has yet to clarify what that means. I hope he doesn't want us to shack up and live together without an official commitment towards our future. I don't care how much I'm in love with him or how much I want our family living in the same household. Denali has to step to the plate and handle his business as a thirty two year old man. I'm talking engagement or marriage if we are to live together. I know ain't no man gonna rush to buy the milk if he can have the cow for free.

I love Denali, but I know that all of his bad habits: The women... the women... and the women, haven't been purged out of his system as of yet. So I'll let God be God and fulfill his Will in his life. As for me, I need to exercise a little bit more control around Denali. At the rate we are going, I'll be pregnant and barefoot in the kitchen by this time next year. Besides, making love to a man without a commitment is like living in Florida without an umbrella. You know that despite how sunny and hot the days may get, the rainstorms will come crashing down on your parade. And not having a protective covering will not only ruin your parade but your hair as well...

AKIL

Damn there is ass everywhere in the Kingdome tonight, I thought as we rolled up on the set, in my brand new S600 Benz, with my Sprewell's spinning non stop. "It looks like some Luke Peep show shit up in here." I said shaking my head like I was seeing ass for the very first time. "Well damn dawg, I don't want to slip on your tongue." Yes said still trying to recover from me cracking on him in the car. " Yea, yea, whatever nigga. But do you see all of the ass in here tonight?" I responded sounding like I just got home from doing a thirty year bid.

"Hell yea nigga I can see all of this ass. I'm not blind. But look who's coming your way. Don't forget that Sole` and little Kil are home waiting on you playboy." Yes said to me before sliding off onto the dance floor's action.

"Ooh, look who is up in the club looking good enough to sex tonight." Shawna, one of my former freaks from Harlem said as she pushed up on me. "Hey Shawna, what's going on?" I said trying my best not to look at her titties as they stood out to shake my hand.

"I can't complain. Ooh, that's my song. Come and dance with me baby." Shawna said trying to pull my hand and lead me to

173

the dance floor. "Oh not to this song baby, I just walked in. Let me get something to drink first." I said trying to avoid the pressure. "Okay go and get a drink, I'll be back for you in a few." Shawna said as she went on the dance floor and started dancing with some young looking dude.

As I watched Shawna dance my mind started working its sexual magic. I then started thinking about those sexual episodes we used to swing. Shawna used to swallow a nut like it was mineral water. And baby can ride a dick like a champion bull rider.

After the DJ changed the song, I saw Shawna motion with her hands that she'd be right back. I waited patiently for Shawna, drinking my mixed drink. When she came back, the DJ started playing that old school R&B, so I had to get my boogie on, doing my infamous two step. As Guy's "Yearning for your love" was bumping, Shawna immediately turned around and started grinding all over me. Damn, her ass feels so good I thought, as my dick started to take notice of what was going on.

"Ooh, don't start something you can't finish." Shawna said, giving me a dick check. She then turned to face me, placing my hands all over her thick booty. "Can you feel all of that? You know I went and took my panties off in the bathroom, just for you right? Remember how we used to do." Shawna said really putting the pressure on. As I'm there reluctantly grinding with Shawna's fat ass on the dance floor, I couldn't believe who I saw at the bar, all loved up in some dudes face. It was Tracey with his bitch ass. I should go push his shit back right now. But that will cause a scene and Denali doesn't need any problems up in here. But damn, I need to do something, especially after what that nigga did to me...

DENALI

It never fails, every night in my clubs there are a gang of women trying to become Mrs. Denali Shaw. Since word got out that I actually owned the clubs and wasn't just some promoter renting out space, my pussy stock increased one thousand fold. After awhile a man gets tired of the "groupies" with their tight jeans, weaves, pretty faces, and phony smiles. But shit, I ain't that man as of yet, I still love the "game".

I ran into Joanna this freak from New Jersey. Joanna definitely has that crack underneath her skirt but baby once asked me to piss on her and that did it for me. So after I pissed on the bitch, I cut her freaky ass off. Joanna's nasty ass had to go. So I've been shutting her down since that night. I do kinda miss how Joanna used to hook me up with her freaky girlfriends and we would bang them out together.

Now that I think about it, of all the times I twisted Joanna out, only twice was it soley about me and her. I've probably ran through her whole crew. I even ran through her twin sister Asia. In fact, a few nights I would hit the both of them off as they freaked off with each other, on some incest shit.

"What's up Kil? You're looking strong again playboy. I'm surprised Sole` let you out. You know she has you on house arrest." I said as I gave Kil a pound and a hug. "Yea, yea, right, right." Akil responded sounding and looking like something was wrong. "You iight?" I asked. "No not even a little bit. I just saw Tracey's tricky ass down stairs, and I'm doing everything in my power not to go to lunch on this nigga up in your club. But I promised myself the next time I saw him he was gonna get it." Akil responded looking dead serious.

"Damn son, I hear what you're saying. So what do you want to do? You know I can make it happen quietly. Shit, no one has to know or find that nigga?" I said thinking of some torture tactics we could use on Tracey. "Yo, let's bring it to this ho ass nigga." Akil shouted like a commanding general. "That's all I needed to hear…

SOLE`

"Yea girl we have been working hard on repairing our marriage and making things right." I said to Michelle as we talked on the phone. "My mother's advice was right, a man and a woman working together, as one, can accomplish the impossible." I added. "That's for sure. I'm so happy that you're happy Sole'. I know how much you love that man. I knew that for all that you were saying with your mouth your heart and soul still yearned for Akil. Everything is gonna work out for y'all. If you two can stick together through what has just happened, y'all can make it through anything." Michelle responded in her usual positive and encouraging spirit.

"Hold on Michelle, I have another call." I said as I clicked over to the other line. "What's up baby? Just calling to say that I'm in love with you and that I'll be home around three. Is my little king asleep?" Akil asked sounding like a loving husband and father. "Ahh, how sweet daddy and yes he's asleep baby. I'm in love with you too Akil Butler." I said to Akil before I clicked back over to finish talking with Michelle.

"Who was that, Dana?" Michelle asked with a smile I could hear over the phone. "No that was Akil just checking in. You know that bitch knows better than to dial my digits. Damn that's my other line again. Can you hold on one more second Michelle?" I said then clicked over.

But this time when I clicked over there was no answer. For the last three days I've been getting prank calls. Maybe something is wrong with the phone line. That storm the other day did cause problems with the phone lines. "What, you have a party line or something girl?" Michelle asked. "I don't know what's going on. Someone's dumb ass keep calling, but ain't saying anything." I answered. "It's probably Dana?" Michelle said sparking a thought I hadn't considered. "It was probably her ass. I should give her a call because I'm past all of that now…

YES

"Yo what's good?" I asked Denali and Akil as they were huddled up looking like they were plotting something serious. "That bitch ass Tracey is about to get what's coming to him." Akil responded looking like he was about to fight for the title. "Oh hell yea let's torture that nigga." I said joining in on the plan.

176

What people don't know about me, Denali, and Akil, is just how gutter we can get when the lights go out. Although we are professional, educated, and wealthy brothers, we still know how to take it to the streets. Young niggas always believe that you have to be a drug pusher, thug, or gangster in order to get dirty. But a real man knows how and when to roll his sleeves up and put his hoody on. "Kil, I'll have Jason go pick Tracey up." Denali said looking like his adrenaline was rising. After Jason brought Tracey downstairs we went to work...

AKIL
"So you thought it was all good bitch? Thought you wouldn't see me again, right? Thought you could ruin my life and never have to look me in the eyes again muthafucka?" I hollered at Tracey in the basement of the club, as I blooded him up, rearranging all of the furniture in his mouth.

Yes and Denali's crazy asses then stripped Tracey butt naked, taking off the wig, padded bra, and all that other shit he had on trying to look like a woman. They even tied him up and pissed all over him. "Should I light this nigga up?" I asked Yes and Denali, as I pointed Denali's 45 to Tracey's head. "Nah don't body him Kil, just keep kicking his ass." Yes said as he slapped Tracey causing him to scream out loud like a bitch.

As we were breaking Tracey down, I decided that I had enough. I'm done with that phase in my life. For every time I hit Tracey, the pain and confusion of my past returned. After about an hour and a half of torturing and beating on Tracey, I decided to leave the club early. I needed to head on home to my wife and son...

SOLE`
"I'm thinking about selling the business and staying home to build my family, like my mother did for us. Maybe I'll even help Akil out with the administrative side of his business." I said to Michelle who I had been on the phone with for hours. "Are you

177

sure that's what you want to do? Staying home is a giant leap from running your own successful business." Michelle asked objectively.

"I'm still thinking about it. I can easily sell the travel agency for two or three million dollars. I have enough money saved and income from our investments coming in that I don't have to work another day. I only work now because it's something that I enjoy doing. But I love my son and husband. And I enjoy being a mother and wife more than anything." I said sounding like my mother. "So what does Akil think about it? He's probably in love with the idea of having his woman at home in the kitchen making biscuits and managing the household." Michelle said, sounding like the typical career woman. "Akil is supportive of whatever I seriously consider. Hold on Michelle, I think that's Akil on the other line." I said to my good friend.

When I clicked over this time, I heard someone breathing into the receiver and then a hang up. Then my doorbell sounded. "I think Akil lost his keys." I said to Michelle as I went to answer the door. But when I got to the door, I couldn't believe who it was standing there…

YES

After Akil broke out, looking like he was battling some mental demons, me and Lee, dumped Tracey's bitch ass out into the alley, butt naked, with the rest of the trash. "Lee, I'm gonna blow it and get some sleep." I said to Denali as he wiped his hands off. "I hear you, things got crazy tonight. I'll holla at you tomorrow then playboy. Stay up, no more trouble tonight." Denali responded, as he walked into the back door of the club.

While I was walking to catch a cab back to my house, I ran into my former girlfriend Venus. Now me and Venus were actually getting serious before I meet Amerie. Once Amerie stepped into my world, that night in the club, Venus fell by the wayside. Maybe me and Venus would be about it today, if Amerie hadn't rock my world.

"Hey stranger, I thought you fell off of the planet or something. I heard you went and got married on me. Is that true?" Venus asked with those radiant eyes she has. "No I didn't quite get married. I was about to... but that's a long story. What about yourself? What have you been up to? You're looking good." I said to Venus as we looked each other over. "I went and had a baby. I have a little girl named Malaysia. She is a beautiful baby." Venus said.

Immediately my stomach jumped. I remembered running through Venus several times unprotected. And I'm quite sure I put some of that sauce in her. Venus had that always oven warm and tight pussy. It always felt like my dick was melting whenever I was inside of her. As a result, I hardly ever put a condom on like I should have.

"Congratulations on the baby. How old is she?" I suspiciously asked. "Thanks, she'll be fourteen months tomorrow." Venus responded like a proud first time mother. "So...so how are things between you and your daughter's father?" I asked still investigating the situation. "Her father has never seen her. In fact, he doesn't even know that she exists." Venus said as she looked down at the floor.

"Damn, I'm sorry to hear that Venus. You know how brothers can be sometimes. Hopefully one day he'll come around and do the right thing." I said doing my best Maury Povich impersonation, trying to lift her spirits. "Well maybe you should talk to him and let him know that there's a beautiful little angel in the world that looks just like him." Venus said looking across the street as more and more people were leaving the Kingdome.

"What...what do you mean I should talk to him? Do I know the brother or something?" I asked still puzzled by what she said. "Yea you definitely know him because my daughter's father is you. Yes, you're my baby's daddy...

SOLE`

"Are you crazy? What are you doing here Todd? My

husband will be home any minute now." I pleaded with Todd from the door. "I just couldn't stay away baby. I have missed you far too much. But more importantly I need to talk to you Sole`." Todd said. "Well that's what telephones are for. Don't you know that me and my husband are back together? Why didn't you just give me a call? You know that's why people have telephones? Did you ever think that my husband could've answered the door?" I asked still in disbelief as to how much nerve Todd had to show up at my door unannounced.

"I know he isn't here, he's at the Kingdome. So can I come in and talk, it's cold out here in this hallway or are you gonna treat me like I ain't worth a quarter?" Todd asked like a lost puppy dog. "You must have fell on your head or must be out of your mind, if you think I'm letting you inside of these doors." I said before I closed the door in his face. I didn't slam the door on him out of disrespect but out of fear.

"What's going on girl, is everything okay? Michelle asked, reminding me that I was still on the phone with her. "Todd is at my door girl looking like an orphan child." I said to Michelle. "What! Is that brother crazy. Didn't Akil try to decapitate his ass? Michelle asked all high pitched. "Hold on girl, this fool is now making a scene in the hallway. I'll call you back Michelle I promise." I said. "Okay girl, I love you." Michelle responded. "I love you too." I said before hanging up.

"Todd if you don't stop banging on the door, I'm gonna call the cops on your ass." I pleaded, realizing that it was a quarter to one in the morning and he would wake the baby and neighbors if he continued. "I just want to talk. I'm not gonna do anything stupid Sole`, you have to trust me. I just want to see you. Don't you miss me?" Todd asked sounding so humble and sincere.

I don't know what came over me or what I was thinking. Maybe it was because Todd is so damn fine? Maybe it was because Todd was so gentle with me, or maybe it was because of the flashback I had of him pleasing me orally? But whatever it was it was enough to persuade me to open up the door and let him in. I guess even women make mistakes too. "You have five minutes Todd what's up?" I demanded as I opened the door and let him in.

"How could you be more beautiful, you look incredible?" Todd said as he admired how my ass filled out the satin night gown I had on, which was to seduce Akil later on. "Let me just cut to the chase. Before I do can I use your bathroom?" Todd asked looking around impatiently. "Todd stop bullshitting! What's going on already?" I said looking back at the door fearing that Akil would walk through those doors and kill us this time. "No seriously I had a six pack of Coronas and they are running through me right now." He responded looking down at me.

By the smell on Todd's breath, I knew he wasn't lying. He had to be drinking Coronas because his breath was hella hot. "Hurry up Todd and I'm not playing." I ordered still looking at the front door, fearing Akil would walk through head hunting this time. While Todd was in the bathroom, I realized just how nervous I was. Then I heard the toilet flush. As Todd came out of the bathroom, I was once again blown away by just how fine he was. "Did you put the toilet seat down?" I asked not wanting Akil coming home tracing his steps. "Yea I dropped the seat." He said as he buckled his leather belt. "So what's up?" I asked Todd.

"Sole` I've been diagnosed with HIV and genital herpes. My whole life is falling apart right now. Sole` I'm not the man I presented myself to be. I'm a liar and manipulator of women. I was someone who played the "role" and the "game". I tried calling you, but I just couldn't tell you something like this over the phone. That's why I'm here. Since we did have a sexual encounter, I thought you should know for you and your family's safety. I'm sorry Sole`. I didn't know and would have never thought something like this would ever happen to me. But this HIV shit isn't a respecter of persons. I found out my status while in the hospital, recovering from the injuries your husband caused me. I'm so sorry I did this to you. Please forgive me." Todd said as he headed for the door.

As Todd walked out of the door, I just stood there frozen in disbelief. Could I be HIV positive...Could I be sick...

YES

"What do you mean I am he?" I asked Venus as seriously as I could. This isn't the first time some woman from my past has resurfaced talking that "baby daddy" shit. "I mean you are the father of my daughter Malaysia. If you don't believe what I'm saying then look at the picture for yourself." Venus said as she went into her Carla Mancini handbag, and passed me a picture of the most beautiful little girl I had ever laid eyes on.

"Wow, she is gorgeous Venus but she can not be my daughter. I don't have any kids." I said still in disbelief. But I couldn't help to notice that the little girl was a splitting image of me as a baby. The little girl looked just like me. "Well look, I'm not about to force you to do anything. I just wanted you to know that there is a beautiful little girl that you helped to bring into this world. A little girl that doesn't know you. I'm doing fine all by myself in raising her but this is bigger than me. I grew up knowing both my mother and father, and that's exactly what I want for our daughter." Venus said sadly.

Listening to Venus talk brought back the memories of my mother raising me and my sisters, alone. There are far too many black children that think their father's name is mommy. Besides, I'm too much of a man to leave my daughter, if she's mine, to fend for her identity in this confused world without a loving father.

"I hear and understand you Venus. If Malaysia is my daughter I have no problems with being a father." I said as I gave Venus a securing embrace. As I held Venus close, she exhaled and started crying. "I didn't want to impose on you but you needed to know Yes. Malaysia is such a wonderful joy and blessing. You just had to know." Venus said as she sobbed on my shoulder.

"Don't worry about it Venus. You don't have to beg or convince me to be a father. I don't have a problem with anything you are telling me. If she is mine, I promise to make things work

182

for everyone. I promise you have my word on that. Don't worry about anything." I said to assure Venus and to ease her worries.

After comforting Venus, we then exchanged numbers, hugged, and I helped her into her Dodge Stratus. "I'll call you tomorrow Venus." I said as she pulled off and drove down the block. If Malaysia is mine and Venus is my baby's mother, the first thing I'm gonna have to do is get Venus into some classier wheels. I can't have my child and baby's mother pushing a Stratus while I'm living large. I'll probably get her a BMW or something....

DENALI

What a crazy ass night, I thought to myself as I jumped into my car. That's why instead of jumping on the Holland Tunnel heading to New Jersey, I jumped on the FDR headed for Mount Vernon. I need to see my daughter and India right now, to calm me down. I know I have a good woman and a good thing going with India. Whenever things get crazy or even when things are really going good, she is the first person I run to.

When I finally got to the house, it was a little after four in the morning. Everything in the neighborhood was asleep, the dogs, the birds, everything. When I opened the door I headed straight for Imani's room to look at my little princess. As Imani slept, I put my hands on her and gently prayed over her, as tears developed in my eyes. Minister Gilmore once said, "That a father's responsibility is more spiritual than physical." He said, "A father is to protect his children from demonic and deceptive forces in this world and to prepare a path of prosperity for them." He added that it all begins with prayer.

It is remarkable that for all the mistakes I've made and for all of the ungodly things I have done to women, God would bless me with a daughter. My daughter is my world and it's truly amazing to watch her grow. Once I walked into the bedroom, India was fast asleep looking so angelic with her Bible by her side. I often just find myself watching India as she sleeps. Watching India sleep makes me think about how precious and special a woman can be to a man, once he acts right and becomes a man…

AKIL

As I got to my door a funny feeling came over me. I didn't know if it was the guilt I felt over beating Tracey's ass or what, but something was up. Surprisingly, the door was opened and Sole' was sitting on the sofa in the family room looking crazy.

"Is everything alright honey?" I asked, cautiously fearing some other shit from my past had resurfaced. But I have told Sole' practically everything. But then again there is so much to tell, I know there are some things I may have left out. "No baby something is wrong and we need to talk." Sole' said with that disturbed look on her face. "**Damn!**" I thought silently.

"Okay baby, just let me jump in the shower. I smell like three butt naked bums." I said trying to get a smile out of her. But Sole' just sat there looking straight through the fireplace, as if she was hypnotized. After my shower, I dried off, threw my Calvin Klein boxer briefs on and headed for the living room for my questioning. But when I got there Sole' was sound asleep like a baby. I then put a blanket on Sole', kissed her soft dimpled cheek, and went off to bed. Whatever it was Sole' had to tell me will have to wait, I thought, as I went into our bedroom and talked to God before I went to sleep…

CHAPTER 21

YES

"Hello can I speak with Adrienne? I asked. "Now you know you really need to cut the act. What's up baby?" Adrienne responded. "I have something on my mind right now baby. I would like to meet you tomorrow for lunch, to discuss what's going on." I said to Adrienne. "That sounds good. What time would you like to meet?" She asked. "How does one thirty at City Crab sound?" I asked confirming a time. "That's fine, I'll see you then honey." Adrienne responded. "Good night baby I'll see you tomorrow." I said as we hung up the phone.

I don't know how I'm gonna break the news to Adrienne that I have a daughter. A daughter I knew nothing about. Especially after Adrienne's ex husband had two kids outside of their marriage. Baby has been through her share of tough times with men and I don't want to add more shit to her experience. I hope she doesn't look at my situation as some more drama and bullshit.

I can't believe it either, but I'm a father. The DNA test made it official. I have a little queen named Malaysia. Denali and Akil are all pumped up and can't wait to meet her. The are happy that I'm now in the "father's club" My mother is so delighted that she's finally a grandmother but I'm still adjusting to the role of father.

Not having my father around, I never thought hindered me. However, right now I would love to have a father figure to model myself behind. Venus is such a terrific woman and great mother, I regret not being there for her and Malaysia from the very beginning. I would have never expected me and Venus to have so much in common. Before I met Amerie, me and Venus were kicking it, but it was mainly a sexual relationship. Now that I'm getting to know more about Venus, I can see why every dude I know has been trying to get with her.

The last three days we have shopped, took pictures, and ate dinner together. We have been doing all of those things that families do. Whenever we're out together we get so much attention. We look like the perfect loving family. Venus is a beautiful African American woman. She stands five feet seven inches tall, has a beautiful bronze complexion with sparkling brown eyes. And like with all of my women Venus has a nice body. But being that her people's are from down south, Venus has more curves than I usually deal with. Venus has one of those showgirls bodies. She has a shape that always has niggas saying, "Daammnn".

Venus is by far the prettiest woman, I have ever dealt with. Like all of my women, Venus is a chocolate lovely. I just can't get enough of those chocolate brownies. Amerie was special but Venus is unbelievable looking. She is also an incredibly intelligent woman, a graduate from Fordham University, like my mother. And she is also very spiritually grounded. I know that my mother is gonna love Venus, I'm glad that she is the mother of my child. She's the type of woman I always wanted for my kids…

SOLE`

My doctor has confirmed the answer to my prayers. I'm HIV negative and free of any STD's. She did find a trace of sickle cell in my blood but that I can manage to live with. Akil has never mentioned the fact that we never had that conversation. I guess he thinks he dodged some bullet from his past. The truth is our marriage was saved once again.

"Hello baby, how was your day?" I asked Akil as he walked in the door giving me a ten second kiss before he headed straight for the bathroom. "My day was hectic as usual. How was your day honey?" He asked while his voice faded out, as he hit the bathroom. Akil has been working like a man on a mission getting his magazine off the ground.

He leaves early in the morning and returns late at night. It's good that he calls me throughout the day telling me that "he's in love with me", because I miss him when he's gone.

After Akil finished taking his shower, he joined me in the kitchen. He was wearing some red cotton FUBU shorts with a wife beater, that showed off his dark muscular arms. "Hey baby, little man is sleep I see." He said as we hugged. "I missed you today. Damn, you smell good as hell." Akil said as he continued to hold me close. Since his accident, Akil has been the most affectionate and loving husband in the world. "Baby did I tell you about your man Yes?" Akil asked jokingly. "Yea you told me that he's somebody's, baby daddy." I answered as we burst out laughing together.

"He said that he was kinda getting serious with homegirl before Amerie came along. So maybe they will be civil for the sake of the baby." Akil said as he sat down to eat the dinner I prepared for him. "Have you seen his daughter? I bet she's adorable." I said as I took a seat at our dinner table next to Akil. "No, I haven't seen her yet. But we are all going to do the "family thing" at the circus next week. Oh, I'm sorry I forgot to ask you baby. That won't be a problem right?" Akil said as he ate his shrimp.

After Akil finished his dinner we went into our bedroom, threw on some Tweet, and snuggled in front of our marble fireplace. "Baby I'm loving you more by the day." Akil softly whispered in my ear. "I feel the same way daddy." I moaned as Akil sent chills up my body, while he kissed the back of my neck, moving down my back and spine. "Damn baby your ass looks tasty." Akil said as he started sucking on my ass cheeks and then slid his tongue into my butt hole. "Ooh…ooh you want it nasty tonight, uh daddy?" I moaned as Akil's face was buried in my phat ass, while I laid on my chest.

"Yea baby… daddy wants to keep it nasty." Akil said as

187

he moved his tongue from my asshole and began to slowly penetrate my wet pussy, with his long and flexible tongue.

"That feels so good." I said as Akil stuck his finger in my ass. While Tweet was telling him to come to her place, Akil was all in mine. As Akil placed all of himself deeply inside of my warm spot, I was feeling like a woman loved.

As a woman there is nothing more intimate and divine than making love to your husband. Being one with the man you vowed to be with before God, in spirit and soul, as he enters your body, is magical. "I love you Sole`." Akil said to me as tears of love fell from his eyes unto my face, while he so rhythmically penetrated the depths of my soul. "I love you Akil." I said, as I thought about all that we had overcome to be back in this position. The tears then rolled down my satisfied face.

As Akil stroked and kissed me so perfectly, with tears streaming down our faces, I had never felt more loved and connected to him in my life. Akil is all the man I want, and all the man I need. I really do love my husband despite all that we had to go through. "Don't ever stop making love to me baby." I said to Akil as he slowed his stroke to a reggae grind. "I won't ever stop making love to you, I won't ever stop...

CHAPTER 22

DENALI

"I got next." I said as I entered the park to get my ball on. Akil and Yes where already doing their Shaq and Kobe impersonation, as their team was on the court getting their ass` cracked. "Looks like these young guns have got y'all on y'all toes." I yelled at Akil, Yes, and our boy Doug, as they did there best to keep up with the nineteen and twenty year old bodies they were running against.

"I'm as tired as a retired Jamaican." Yes said as his man crossed him over and went to the basket and scored with that Allen Iverson precision. "I see my nigga has you on roller blades out there." I said causing the spectators to laugh. As I shot around, waiting for the game to end, I noticed the money green SC400 Lexus pull up bumping that Kelis "I hate you" song. As I looked at the car, I couldn't figure out who it was through the dark tint on the windows. I did recognize that it was at least two females sitting in the car.

"Where are your manners Denali Shaw?" A voice from the passenger side said as the car's horn beeped. "Damn dawg, you still pitching." Doug said as the game stopped because of a foul call. "Not at all playboy. I have a good woman at home. I don't even know who the fuck that is." I said to Doug as I squinted my eyes, trying to get a better look. "Well you need to stop bullshittin` and get on your job before I do playa." One of the young dudes in the park said as he watched the car.

"Yea maybe you're right young fella, maybe you're right." I said making my move towards the car. As I made my way to the

189

car, I realized that every pair of eyes were on me as I did my pimp stroll towards the tricked out money green Lexus.

Once the passenger side window came down, I saw exactly who it was in the car. "Oh shit!" It was Alexus' crazy ass pointing a nine millimeter at me, squaring up to pop my head. Alexus is this white chick, my little snow bunny that I use to dick down. I broke Alexus' heart once I stopped digging her out and that rubbed her the wrong way.

I had told Alexus from jump street that I wasn't interested in getting serious with her, but she thought she could change my mind. She made that mistake most women make when fucking with a playboy. She thought just because I let her play on my team that she could get me to change my game. But that ain't how the game is played.

She left her husband and daughter for a nigga, thinking it was gonna be about me and her. After it dawned on her that I didn't care a rat's ass about her, she went bananas on a nigga. She slashed the tires on my Excursion, broke all the windows on my CL600 Benz, and tried to burn one of my brownstones down. She was caught by one of my tenants Will, who just happened to be a cop. I guess she just got out and still wants to pop my head. Blast... She let off a shot, but it missed me but went straight into someone's Explorer.

"Think you can still use and abuse women. You're not a man, you're a bitch." Blast...Another shot was fired. After the first shot, mayhem broke out in the park. People started running to take cover like a track meet. In the hood, niggas are used to this type of shit. It's like a fire drill or something. "I'm gonna kill your ass." Blast... The third shot was fired, as I hid behind the grey Altima, using it as my fortress. This shit has really hit the fan for a nigga. This bitch is trying to zap my ass.

"You can run but you can't hide muthafucka. And you better believe, you haven't seen or heard the last of me... you *BITCH*." She yelled as the car sped off like a drag race.

Alexus isn't the first woman that has tried to send me for a for a premature dirt nap. But she will definitely be the last. I'm through screwing women over. Especially, since these crazy bitches today ain't playing to lose anymore...

YES

"Damn Lee, honey was trying to decapitate your ass. I told you about trying to be me dawg. That white pussy is deadly. Just ask OJ, my nigga. That was that white broad from Delaware right?" I asked as I tried to calm Denali down. "Yea, that was that crazy bitch." He responded in between deep breaths. "What was that all about Lee?" Akil asked joining us as we sat waiting for our pizza pie to come.

"She left her husband and daughter to be with me and I left her assed out. I told her not to do it. She went straight fatal attraction after she found out that I wasn't bullshitting with not wanting to be with her. She shot Peaches in the ass with a stun gun in the club after she caught us hanging out in my office. She tried to light me up. I had to break her down before having her thrown out and banned from my clubs. Alexus is bugged out. I mean she is really off the hook." Denali told us.

"It's always a woman somewhere losing her damn mind because of what some man had taken her through." I said. "That's some Oprah Winfrey bullshit right there dawg. A man can only do to a woman what she allows to be done. He can only take her where she will follow." Akil responded militantly. "Whatever Kil." I responded, not wanting to get into another debate with him. "Yo, I need to take my ass to the network tonight, y'all with it?" Denali asked. "Of course." Me and Kil responded knowing that we haven't kept up our commitment to the network...

INDIA

With my album almost done and a expected promo tour lined up within the next couple of months, I realize that my life is about to change drastically. Denali still hasn't made any type of symbolic commitment to me and I'm growing impatient. How am I to glorify God and sing Gospel music while I'm fornicating...

YES

"I'm so sorry that I couldn't do lunch with you the other day baby. I got caught up at work. A lot of my clients are losing their shirts in this bear market." I said to Adrienne as we sat in the famous Sammy's seafood restaurant on City Island.

"What's going on baby? Is there another woman or something? You've been acting strange the last few weeks? Adrienne asked as she looked right through me.

"What do you mean?" I asked looking to see just how in tune she was with her woman's intuition. "The first couple of months that we were dating, I could feel that I had your full attention. The amount of time we spent together, the way you would look and listen to me, as well as the energy you would bring as you made love to me, all let me know that I was the one and only. Now there's anxiety in your eyes and you seem distracted. Remember I've been married and divorced twice, so I'm pretty accurate with my assessments of men's behavior.

"I know that a lustful man has a short attention span but I felt a different energy from you when we first met. Now it's like you're hanging on just because you think I'll die or something if you let go. I need you to understand something about me Mr. Black, I am a grown ass woman.

"I know that you are a handsome, successful, and intelligent man that any woman in her right mind would love to be with.

"So anything you have to tell me won't come as a surprise. So just be honest and real with me." Adrienne said as the waiter brought our food to the table.

See this is what separates the women from the girls, the ladies from the rats. Adrienne is strong enough to stand by herself yet so savvy, sexy, and sensitive to a man's needs, that men would kill to be with her. Her level of understanding concerning men's ways is astonishing. Looking into her eyes I could sense her concern and curiosity as to what is going on with me.

"Adrienne, I want you to know that above anything, I want to be with you. I want you in my corner and by my side. I want you to be the woman in my life. But a few weeks back I ran into an old girlfriend of mine. Come to find out, that before we separated, I got her pregnant. I have a little queen named Malaysia. She's fifteen months old and looks just like me. I didn't know how to tell you or approach you with this, without it being devastating to you." I said as I caressed Adrienne's hand.

"Baby that is a wonderful thing. I love kids. I would love to meet your daughter, if her mother doesn't have a problem with it. Speaking of her mother, how are things between you two now that you know y'all are parents?" Adrienne asked calmly. "We…we are getting along well." I answered. "How well?" Adrienne asked raising her neatly trimmed eyebrows. "We have gotten reacquainted and are building a friendship and understanding for the sake of our daughter." I said to Adrienne as we ate our lobster.

"That sounds great. It is exactly what we need more of, partnerships between parents. I do need to know if you two are becoming intimately involved?" Adrienne asked with that sultry voice of hers.

"We have done a lot of talking and stuff, but I haven't slept with her if that's what you're saying." I said trying to avoid Adrienne's eyes. But I can't stop thinking about sleeping with Venus again. "So if that's the case, there isn't anything for you to be ashamed or afraid of. If you have a daughter and a good relationship with your daughter's mother, I have no problems with that. In fact, I respect and can appreciate that. I am way too mature and too much of a woman to be petty. But if you violate what we have going and get involved intimately with another woman, I don't care if she is your daughter's mother, I'll have serious problems with that. I don't do the infidelity thing. I left two husbands that I loved dearly because they lost their focus. So I won't hesitate to leave a boyfriend that I care a whole lot about, if it comes to that. I value myself too much to allow anyone to take my love and faithfulness for granted." Adrienne said as she looked at me sharply.

"I hear you baby and there isn't anything for you to worry about. Like I said, you are who I want to be with and that's that." I said as I leaned over that table and kissed Adrienne's soft lips. "Oh, I don't worry baby. I never worry about what's mine." She added as she bit my bottom lip as we kissed. Damn this is one awesome woman...

CHAPTER 23

AKIL

It's been a minute since I attended a men's meeting at the network. I have kept up with my reading, exercise regimen, and dietary program, even though I haven't been in attendance. Starting this magazine has consumed a lot of my time lately. But I'm happy I made it to the network tonight. As I entered the hall and took my usual seat in the middle rows, I see Denali politicking with Melvin. Melvin is this former hustler who at one time was running all of Jamaica, Queens.

When he was really getting it, Melvin was on some Pablo Escobar shit in the day. He was putting hits out on niggas and was seeing that Scarface money, before anyone in Queens saw a penny.

"What's up Mel, I'm surprised to see you in here." I said as I took a seat next to him and Lee. "So am I, but God has a bigger plan for me." He said as he gave me a pound. "I heard you were doing a lifetime bid up north. I thought they sent you away for good." I said, still amazed that Mel was sitting in the hall looking like this new man.

Mel wasn't wearing any of the platinum and diamond jewelry he was known for rocking. The only piece of jewelry he had on was a gold wedding band, and for Mel that was a miracle. The last time I saw Mel in the world, I didn't know if he was Baby from the Cash Money Millionaires or muthafuckin Mr. T, because the nigga had on so much ice. "So what's going on Mel?" I asked needing answers.

"Man, I was sitting on top of the world when the Lord

195

came knocking on my door. I had a million dollar a week drug business with cops, district attorneys, and judges all on my payroll, when the Lord said, "He had greater things in store for me."

"I battled with that call for like four months before I couldn't take it any longer. It was so crazy because in that four month period of time, three of my key men were murdered, the police raided two of our key spots, and I personally escaped two hits that were out on my life.

"So with all of that going on, I just had to walk away from it all while I could. The entire "world" I left behind. I'm now married to a good spiritual woman. I own some real estate upstate, I have three barbershops in the city, and I'm working as a counselor with the networks prison outreach. Man, when I go out and talk to the brothers on lockdown, they listen to me. When they see how the Lord has changed Mel, they believe in change. I have never felt more powerful than when I can influence the youngsters in a positive way. I mean, the same dudes who I influenced to get money, buy cars, clothes, and jewelry, I am now influencing them to be men, to take care of their families, and to live right." Melvin said looking like the perfect image of peace.

"Wow, that's good to hear Mel." I said all inspired by his transformation myself. "You're still looking good man. How is that beautiful wife of yours? I heard you're a father now, how's the little one?" Mel asked with a warm smile on his chiseled faced. "I'm winning in everyway playa and the wife and little one are my most precious gifts." I responded as we waited for the minister..

As Minister Gilmore greeted the hall, that strong presence overtook the room and he began to speak.

"Tonight we will discuss the power of God's purpose. Many of us make God a man and make men God's. As a result we are in fear of and worshipping men. God the Creator's plan doesn't orginate with man. Therefore no man has the authority to define, control, or limit you in this life.

"Black men and women in this country have created false

196

God's which we've allowed to determine, the who, the what, the why's, and the how's in our lives. The two greatest God's we serve *and worship in this life are: the rich man's lifestyle and the rich man's power."* The minister said causing everyone in the hall to think.

"The Minister was deep tonight." I said to Lee as we walked out of the hall. "I know he is really on that materialistc shit." Denali responded forgetting he just walked out of a church. "What happened to pretty boy? I thought he was meeting us tonight." I said to Denali as we stood outside of the hall just talking.

"I think he got caught up at the office again or he's spending some time with Adrienne." Lee said. "Speaking of which, let me get home to the wife. Tonight we're gonna play scrabble. The loser has to give the winner a full body massage for an hour, and Sole` can definitely rub my bones down." I said smiling at the idea. "Well let me drop you off so that you can hold it down for the homey's...

DENALI

I've been spending a lot of quality time with my kids but Veronica has been trippin' extra hard lately. She is always asking for more and more money, like she has a drug habit or something. I don't know what her deal is, but every time I go to pick up Donte` or drop him off, she's all up in my business trying to dig deeper into my pockets. The other day I found a twenty dollar bill on the coffee table with what appeared to be some cocaine residue left on it. When I brought it to her attention she said that it was Shawna's, her older sister. Now I know how Shawna gets down so I didn't spaz out on her.

I did let Veronica know that if there are people getting high in front of my son, he'll be coming to live with me. I know that Veronica is a weed head, but that cocaine shit I'm not going for, no way, no how. As I was driving out in my Escalade EXT that I dress with twenty four inch heels, my car phone starts to ring.

"Hello." I answered as I spoke into my trucks voice activation phone system.

"Hey Denali, this is Shawna." She said sounding extremely nervous. "What's up girly?" I said turning down my trucks stereo system from the steering wheel. "Lee, the cops just raided the house and took Veronica, Niya, Chris, Ahmed, and confiscated all of the money and drugs that were in the house." Shawna said in a panic.

"What the fuck are you talking about, all of the drugs? Where is my son Shawna? Where the fuck is my son? I roared. "He's here with me at my house." She softly said, sounding intimated by my rage. "Well I'm on my way over there. Tell me everything then." I said really trying to calm down.

After I hung up the phone with Shawna, I floored the accelerator of my truck and flew up I-95 headed north towards Connecticut. When I pulled up to Shawna's townhouse, I was on fire. I couldn't remember when was the last time I was so fired up. After almost knocking Shawna's door down, some chick wearing the tightest pair of jeans I had ever saw opened the door.

"Hello how are you?" Ms. Fatbooty asked me as she greeted me at the door. "I'm fine. Where's Donte` and Shawna at?" I asked looking right past honey. "She's in her bedroom on the phone. Donte` is lying down in the guest room. I'm Success." Babygirl said as she stuck her hand out for me to shake, while she licked her lips and batted her eyes a little bit. "I'm Denali, nice to meet you Success. So you say Donte` is in the bedroom?" I said still ignoring honey's sexual mannerisms.

"Yea he's right down the hall to your left. I think he just went to sleep a few minutes ago. Why don't you let me fix you a drink? Come sit down and relax yourself before you scare someone." Success said softly to me like I was the pimp of the year. "Nah, I need to go check up on my son." I said as my fatherly instincts took over. As I was headed to check on Donte`, I passed by Shawna's room and saw her lying down, whispering sweet nothings on the phone, with her thick ass all in the air.

Shawna was wearing some black stretch pants, which complimented that nice frame of hers to perfection. Once I saw that my little man was secure and fast asleep, I decided on going into the living room to relax, before I did hurt someone.

Besides her little cocaine habit Shawna, is doing good for herself, I thought as I walked through the house. Shawna is a successful entrepreneur, with her own catering business, but by the way she carries herself you would think she was a successful stripper. Shawna is a nice looking woman, but just like her sister Veronica, she is money hungry.

"So what happened?" I asked Success as I took a seat across from her, while she sat on Shawna's suede sofa. "What are you talking about, what happened?" She responded like I rode the Special Ed bus to school as a kid. "What happened over at Veronica's house?" I asked as if she was the retarded one. "I'm not sure. I'll let Shawna tell it, because it's none of my business anyway." Success responded defensively. Is this chick bananas, I thought. She was definitely acting like her shit wasn't together.

As we sat there listening to the radio, drinking some ice cold Pepsi, Mystical's "Shake ya ass" came on and Success got up and started dancing. Damn honey has got it going on just how I like it. But I did notice a wedding ring on her finger.

"So how long have you been married Success?" I asked trying not to look at her juicy ass while she wiggled it. "Too damn long." She said as she grabbed my hand for me to join her. As I reluctantly stood up to dance, Success turned around and put every bit of her forty eight inches of ass, all on the front of my ENYCE sweats.

With all of that big booty action happening on my crotch, it didn't take long before my balls got excited and started dancing along with us. "Oh baby, you must like how I work it." Success said as she bent over and gave me the stripper shake, making her booty clap all over my dick. "Yea that's real nice sweetheart." I whispered to Success, as I held the sides of her hips, making sure she felt just how hard the dick can get.

How the fuck did I end up dancing in the living room with some big butt jump off? I was supposed to be picking up my son, I thought.

"Well I guess the party is over." I said as Mystical went off and Hot97 went to a commercial break. "Come on baby, we are just getting started." Success said as she stuck her tongue in my ear, like we knew each other. Just then, Shawna came out of the bedroom wearing only a pink Polo towel.

"Oh shit, I didn't know you were here Denali. I don't want you looking at all of my loving." Shawna said as her and Success started to laugh. "So what happened to Veronica? How much is the bail set for?" I asked Shawna, as Success sat on my lap and started to slowly grind all over me, like this was how she paid her bills. "I'll tell you after I shower up. Besides, you look preoccupied anyhow." Shawna said as she winked at Success and slowly walked off to the bathroom. What's really going on, I thought to myself? I did know that something sexual was jumping off?

"Damn it's getting hot in here.You don't feel the heat baby?" Success said as she took her shirt off and displayed her size 38D's. At this point it was becoming damn near impossible for me to remain cool. I started to feel like I had walked onto a porno set and I didn't even know that I was the leading man. "I want you to have something as a "nice to get to know you gift." Success said as she stood before me, taking off those skin tight Babyphat jeans.

"Oh, I didn't know that today was my birthday." I said as I licked my lips and massaged my rock hard dick. I watched Success strip down into her Victoria secret seduction. Damn baby has one banging ass body.

"Do you want to taste some of this?" Success said as she climbed up over top of me and placed her love right before my face. "Some of it… act like you know that I want all of it sweetheart." I answered as I stuck my tongue out to have some. "So then have all of that loving baby." Success said as she squatted down and fed me that peach.

200

"Damn boo, it smells and taste so sweet." I said talking dirty right back, as Success bounced on my face. As I sat there face deep in Success' candy, Shawna came out of the bathroom butt naked, still dripping wet from the shower. "Yea I got you now Denali." Shawna said as she pulled my sweats down and started to suck my excited dick. I always knew Shawna was sweet on a nigga, but damn.

"Damn baby, could you be any harder? It feels like I'm sucking on a steel pole, but it taste so good." I heard Shawna say as Success was grinding all over my face, beating the wall, as I was putting it down on her clit.

Life is so funny at times. Just two hours ago I was headed over here madder than a raging bull, now here I am freaking off with my baby's mother sister and her big booty friend; that just happens to be married.

After Success exploded from the tongue action I put on her. I then turned Shawna around and dug her out from the back, while she sucked on Success' fat pussy. As we fucked and sucked, I started to have a nauseating feeling in my stomach. As Success was riding me, I tasted some more of Shawna's bush, which by this time was seasoned with that sex sauce.

What would India say or do if she knew about this? I did promise her that I would be faithful, but this shit "just happened", I thought as I looked at Success. This freaky shit was the last thing on my mind. But what woman would accept that bullshit reasoning? "Damn girl, ride that dick." Shawna cheered as Success was climaxing, while I was long dicking her G-spot.

What about my baby India, I kept thinking? I then started to see images of India's angelic face reading the bible, praying with me, and smiling as I lit up her world. At that point, I couldn't fight the guilt and disgust I was feeling, as Success and Shawna sat on top of me, one on my dick the other on my face, while they kissed each other.

"Damn, I'm so sorry India, but I do love you baby. This means absolutely nothing to me. In fact, I have never felt worst about anything in my life." I said to India, in my head, as I pleaded for her forgiveness. As I was dealing with India mentally, I started to hear her soft voice in my head. "When are you gonna do right by me baby?" was all I heard India saying to me.

The more I saw and heard India, the wilder Success and Shawna became, as we fucked. Just as Success and Shawna were both, crying out in sexual pain, I heard my wake up call sounding. Just as these two freaks were getting off, my sexual high and erotic world came crashing down.

"Daddy... daddy...daddy what are you doing?"... It was Donte`, crying out to me, as he watched me sex his aunt and her friend, with his innocent and precious little eyes. Damn Denali, you have really fucked up now...

YES

My daughter has been the best thing that could have happened to me. Lee and Kil have been spoiling my little princess rotten, doing the "uncle thing" like the big Willy's that they are. Venus is such a wonderful woman and we are getting along a thousand times better than I could have asked for. Between Venus and Adrienne, I have two of the baddest chicks on the streets, in my corner. I have to admit it, I have made a complete one hundred and eighty degree transformation in regards to how I used to think about and treat women.

It took me all of these years to discover that my uncle Sugar was wrong and full of shit. Damn near everything that nigga taught me about women was false. Women are not "dirty bitches that can't be trusted" like he would often put it. But then again in Sugar's world it was true. Sugar was a pimp, and all he ever dealt with were "bitches" and "ho's". Sugar never had the luxury and fortune to ever have experienced the beauty of a woman like I have. The other day I found myself reflecting on all of that bullshit he taught me. I can't believe how much I let Sugar influence me.

I really don't like pointing the finger, but my Uncle Sugar sent me off in the wrong direction. He had my mind all fucked up out here in regards to women.

I now thank God that Amerie, Venus, Sole`, and Adrienne, along with my mother and sisters have been a part of my growth as a man. All of a sudden, I feel guilty and ashamed about my past relationships and experiences with women. I was really on some "stone cold, I don't have a heart" shit. If there were one thing, I would ever tell the next man about the ladies, it would be to never fear feeling or caring for a woman. I have no idea what has gotten into me lately, but I'm on some loverboy romance shit.

Maybe it has been my daughter that changed my world? The innocence and love in Malaysia's eyes make me feel so proud and exposed all at the same time. If a man isn't doing right by his family, it's hard for him to look his children or his women in the eyes. The eyes of children and women will always expose one's manhood. When a nigga ain't right, he ain't trying to intimately connect with his family. That's why I now realize what my pops was feeling when he walked out on us like a sucker; he was living foul.

I do know that when a man is right, his family will be the apple of his eyes. Me and Venus have talked about a lot of things since we officially became a family. Yet with all of our talking we have somehow managed to avoid the topic of me and her. That is until tonight.

"How do you feel about me and you getting back together again? Venus asked as she washed our dinner dishes. "Where did that come from?" I asked trying to sound surprised. "I've been really thinking and struggling with how I feel about you and with what I want from you." Venus said as I got up to help her with the dishes. "So how do you feel and what do you want baby?" I asked as I was magnetically drawn to stand behind Venus, placing my broad chest on her back. I then placed my hands into the soapy water with Venus`, just adding gasoline to the fire.

"I love you Yes. And I want us to be together." Venus said as she turned, looked into me, and kissed me deeply in the mouth. "Ven…Venus you know it's not that simple for me. I'm in a

203

situation right now. I thought you understood that baby." I said thinking about what Adrienne said to me about sleeping with another woman. "I know all about Adrienne. You have made it clear to me how you feel about her. I don't want another woman's man, nor am I trying to take you from her. But your heart feels like it belongs to me.

"Can you honestly tell me that you don't feel something strong between us? The way you are looking at me right now, tells me everything I need to know baby." Venus said all choked up and teary eyed.

"Damn Venus don't do this to me. Don't jam me up like this baby." I said as I was growing weak as she cried. I was never one to be moved or compassionate towards a woman's tears. But ever since Amerie opened my heart up, I can now feel everything. "I really do care about you, and yes, I feel something strong between us. However, I'm in love with another wo..." Before I could finish my sentence, Venus rushed me with passionate kisses, which broke down my wall of resistance. "I want you so bad baby." Venus said as we hugged with our hands full of soapy water. "I want you too Venus." I said finally telling her and myself the truth about what was really going on with me.

"Are you sure you want to do this?" I asked Venus which was my attempt at rethinking the situation. "Yes I'm sure." She answered as we started passionately kissing in the middle of the kitchen. My mind, body, and soul has been wanting Venus again, ever since the first day we spent time together as a family. I guess I couldn't fight the temptation any longer. I then laid Venus down on that dinning room table and made love to her, like I meant every stroke of it. I know... I know what you're probably thinking, so let me say it for you. What the fuck am I gonna do now...

CHAPTER 24

AKIL

    Starting a business is a challenging task. Starting an upscale men's magazine for African American men, is nearly impossible. Finding credible businesses that want to advertise to a primary African American male demographic, isn't easy. The perception is that black men are only interested in sports and scantily dressed women. How did they ever come up with that idea? In addition to all of the negative stereotypes, "they" think that Black men can't or refuse to read anything of substance. My attitude is, fuck "them". I'll prove "them" wrong.

    "I will be investing a hundred grand of my own money into the business. My numbers show that I'll need another four hundred grand, along with some more advertisement accounts in order for us to hit stands correctly." I said to Denali and Yes as we were having a business dinner at the Four Seasons.

    "Your proposal looks good. I would also add another two hundred grand towards your expected start up cost, and expand your marketing campaign to include a discounted subscription rate for thirty six months as well." Denali said adding his business savvy and expertise to my business plan.

    "I agree with Denali. I think that would solidify your plans chances of major success." Yes added as he overlooked the plan himself. "Well great, I'll make the recommended changes. I now need to know just how committed you all are to the project, starting with you Denali." I said, continuing with the closing part of my meeting. "The plan makes good business sense to me. So at the five percent interest in the business you're offering for my initial investment, I accept. I will invest not only the two hundred grand you've asked for, I'll double it to four hundred thousand." Denali responded, giving me his biggest smile as he loosened his silver Van Heusen tie. Which by the way, complimented the black pin stripped custom made suit he was wearing.

Whenever Denall decides to throw a suit and tie on, he really looks like a Michael Jordan body double. "Mr. Black what about you, what is your position?" I asked, remaining professional the whole time. I wasn't gonna take our friendship for granted when asking for this type of financial commitment. Denali and Yes are too intelligent and way too financially sophisticated to invest in a bad deal. I had to come at them correct. Their commitment is also a big sign of confidence for me. If they say it's a go, then it really is a go.

"If my investment of a hundred grand gets me three percent interest in what appears to be a great business enterprise, I'm in. From the looks of things, I believe this magazine is in the best hands possible. So I'm in all of the way." Yes responded as we all started smiling at each other.

Having friends is one of life's greatest gifts. Having rich friends that believe in you, is the greatest. After finishing up our business dinner at the Four Seasons, we all decided to head on home. "So you're going over to India's?" I asked Denali as we walked out of the restaurant, looking like executives. "Nah, I ain't going over there, she's been acting funny lately. I'm going to the spot. I need to just chill out in some intimate quarters tonight." Lee said getting into his Bentley.

"Okay then, y'all ladies stay out of trouble. Kil you make sure you take your bitch ass straight home. I'll get up tomorrow. I'll holla." Denali said as he pulled off, looking worth every million in his accounts...

YES

"Hey baby, I know it's late but can I come over, we need to talk?" I said to Adrienne over the phone, at one thirty in the morning. "Sure honey come on over." Adrienne said, sounding groggy as I woke her up from her beauty sleep. I need to stop bullshitting and come clean with Adrienne about what the deal really is between me and Venus. The last few weeks, I've been seeing and sleeping with the both of them, like it ain't a thing.

I should've never given in and slept with Venus. Now I can't seem to stay out of her. It's like her loving be calling me.

"Hey baby, what's up. I've been missing you?" Adrienne said as she greeted me at the door wearing some sexy lingerie. Damn, how does she manage to always look so good? It's two o' clock in the fuckin' morning?

"Hey babe, I needed to see you tonight." I said as I held Adrienne close. "What did I do to deserve that?" Adrienne asked as I finally let her go after a three minute long embrace. "Sometimes all a man needs is a loving embrace from his woman." I said as we walked into the bedroom. As I sat down on the sofa, in the lounge area of Adrienne's bedroom, I said a quick prayer. "Lord I've been wrong due to my confusion. Grant me clarity so that I can do the right thing."

"Here honey." Adrienne said as she brought me some spring water. "What's the deal?" She asked looking so sweet. "I don't know exactly where to start but I'll just start. Baby I know that you are a good woman, this I know. After my relationship with Amerie, I thought I would never be able to love or know love like that again. I realize that God brought you along to save me. I was at a crossroads when you came into my life. I didn't know if I wanted to be the man I am now or remain the man that I was at the time. My lustful and macho ways are now behind me but I'm still not a perfect man baby. I still make mistakes and have a lot to learn about life and love." I was saying as Adrienne interrupted.

"Where are you going with all of this baby?" Adrienne asked sniffing through my bullshit. "Adrienne I need you to really listen and hear what I'm saying. Baby there are things that I do in life that I really don't want to do. The more I don't want to do certain things, the more I do them. Honey I've been sleeping with

207

Venus." I mustered out before I started sounding even more confused.

"You're sleeping with Venus?" Adrienne said then got quiet as she sat with her eyes closed. "I already knew that shit, Yes. I'm wise enough to see that one coming. By the way you talk about her, Venus sounds like a special woman. I knew it was only a matter of time before you two became sexually involved again. Sometimes we need to touch that hot pot before we understand that no matter how hungry we are that pot is not to be touched. I can appreciate the fact that you are man enough to willingly tell me the truth to my face, and not after you got caught. That shows me that you really do care about me. But I'm a woman who has her standards and principles. So I am not about to remain in a relationship with a man who is still struggling with whether or not he wants me and only me." Adrienne said as poised as she could be.

"So what are you saying baby?" I asked with a slight tremble in my voice, fearing the conclusion. "I'm saying that you need to take some time and work your shit out. Come back to me when you know that it's about me and only me." Adrienne said as she sat on the edge of her brass bed, looking at me seriously.

"Okay then baby, I guess that is what I'm gonna have to do." I said trying to leave the scene before it became too emotional between us. "Yes, but before you leave, I want you to make love to me." Adrienne said as she grabbed my hand pulling me into her chest. That move set off another passionate "not wanting to let go" love making session.

"Is this what you want to give up... Do you really want to give all of this up?" Adrienne asked as she rode me like a woman possessed. "No baby this is all your dick...It's all about me and you." I said as I picked Adrienne up and began stroking her slowly up and down, against the wall size window that stood tall in her bedroom. "All of this dick is yours" I continued.

"Don't leave me daddy... I don't want to be alone again." Adrienne said as she started moaning while I went deep in and out of her. "I'm not going anywhere... Here is where I want to be forever. I'm here for the long haul... I'm here until there ain't no mo...

SOLE`

"How did it go today?" I asked Akil as he came in the door grabbing me to slow dance with him, to the song that was playing in his head. "I guess it went well then." I added as he dipped me, like we were dancing in the Cotton Club. " Baby it went perfectly. Lee and Yes are in, plus I landed the Luster's soft sheen and Lincoln Mercury accounts today. They both want to run full page ads in the magazine." Akil said as he continued to dance with me.

"Well it was a good day for the both of us. I found out that my business has grossed a half of million dollars this quarter alone." I said sharing my good news with my man. "We fly... go baby... go baby... go baby." Akil sung as we continued to dance in the entertainment room.

After our celebration, Akil showered up and ate his dinner. Once he finished eating, he joined me and little Akil in the family room as we watched the Cosby show reruns on Nickelodeon. "Do you love your daddy?" Akil asked little Kil, as he held him high in his arms. Watching Akil interact with our son always makes my heart melt. Seeing a man be affectionate towards his son is so beautiful.

"Damn baby, look at this boy. He looks just like you." Akil said as he marveled at how much little Kil resembled me, especially as a baby. "He looks like the both of us baby." I said to Akil. But he does look just like me. While we sat there watching TV, I noticed just how tired Akil was from work. All it took was for him to put little Kil on his chest before they both fell asleep.

"Put him in his room and come on to bed daddy." I said to Akil as he carried little Kil off to his room, both looking like babies. When Akil came into our bedroom, I had lit a few candles and turned on some soft music for us to relax to.

"What's going on in here? Let me find out you trying to

get some of this tonight." Akil said as he kissed my cheek and snuggled up underneath the covers next to me like a big baby. "I see my baby is tired." I said as I softly stroked Akil's beard as he laid his head on my chest.

"Yea baby, I'm exhausted." Akil said as he closed his eyes and took a few deep breaths. It's funny, because for all the man that Akil is during the day, he is still my baby at nights…

INDIA

Who is this calling me at five fifteen in the morning, I thought as I answered the phone on its fourth ring.
"Good morning." I said answering the phone. "India, it's Paula. I have some great news girl, so wake up." She said all excited. "What is it?" I asked Paula, my excited manager. "The record label has pushed your album release date up by three weeks. They said the buzz and reviews on the album are better than anticipated. Therefore, the promo tour has been moved up by four weeks. We leave in three days girl. You are the next big thing in the industry honey. God is so good." Paula said enthusiastically.

Paula is a former R&B singer who lived the music business fast life of drugs, parties, and casual sex. She had three top selling and chart climbing R&B albums before she found God and made the transformation. Paula is the perfect manager and mentor for me. She always makes things happen for me and teaches me along the way.

"That sounds great Paula. So we leave in three days. How long will we be gone?" I asked thinking about how long it would keep me away from Denali. "If all goes according to plan, we'll be gone for two months. Don't worry, I've already made all of the arrangements so that Imani will be comfortable on the tour." Paula said. "Great, that's just great." I said still thinking about Denali.

"What's going on India? It's Denali isn't it? Look, I'll never tell another woman what she should do about her family and about her man. It's your life and your heart babygirl. I do however have a story that I would like to share with you." Paula said then continued.

"When I first signed to Motown, I was in a relationship for four years. My boyfriend at the time was struggling with whether or not he thought we should go to the next level or remain comfortable. I practically begged that man to marry me, but his mind and motivations were different at the time. My heart was literally broken after I told him that I would be on the road for six months and he didn't show any emotion at all. I mean, after four years of seeing me he didn't care if he wouldn't see me for the next six months. It was like he damned near pushed me out of the damn door." Paula said then continued.

"When I finally got out on that road, I met so many interesting men, that soon I began to care more and more about how I felt, more than about what my boyfriend at the time wanted. Although I was "out there" at the time, I would pray to God endlessly for him to lead my boyfriend into marriage. But for all of my desperate cries, there seemed to be no answer from God. Not only didn't Omar want to marry me, after he found out I had developed some new habits, he didn't want to have anything to do with me.

"So at the time, when things looked dark, I thought God didn't care about me. I then stopped praying and begging God to fix my boyfriend. Once I gave up on Omar, something crazy happened, I met Michael. When Michael and I first met, I thought he was a nice looking man, but I only saw him as a friend. At the time, I was heavily into drugs, partying, and the "life", while Michael was more spiritual and grounded.

"Michael didn't smoke. He did drink socially, but our worlds at the time where night and day. Yet for some strange reason we would talk, talk, and just talk for hours, that became days and for days that became months. Michael and I talked so much that through him I found God, and in him I found my husband. Michael and I have been married for seventeen years now and have two little daughters, that you know very well. As for my former boyfriend Omar, I ran into him a year back and he hasn't changed. He's still partying, has two kids by two different women, and also has a young "girlfriend". Now do you know the moral of that story?" Paula asked in a motherly type of way.

"What's the moral? That God works in mysterious ways?" I asked trying to stay awake. "It's not only that India. The moral is that what we want, wants us. But sometimes we have to let go of what we have, in order to get what we want, especially if what we have is holding us back. All of that time I was struggling with Omar, praying to God for help, he was preparing me to meet Michael. But we would have never met and gotten married if I would have kept holding on to Omar and my "dream". In order to see the answer to my prayers, I had to willfully accept God's Will in my social life. If Denali is for you, then you two will be together. Don't fear letting go of what you have, to get what you want." Paula added before hanging up with me.

Paula is always so timely and on point with her advice. Lately, I've been so frustrated with Denali's fear of commitment that I feel myself letting go. I don't know what I'm gonna have to do before Denali decides that he wants to be with me for the rest of his life. Well whatever it is that I need to do is gonna have to wait. It's now time that I give my all to my music career. I have given Denali more than enough opportunities to step to the plate. Now the team and game is leaving town. I just hope he understands that no woman can wait on a man forever. Sooner or later the show must go on with or without him…

DENALI

I've spoken to Donte` about what he saw that day in the living room. I tried to explain to him that what he saw was wrong, because daddy, Aunt Shawna, and Mrs. Success made a mistake. I've never been one to regret anything I ever did, but there's a first time for everything. I hope that image and experience is soon forgotten, and Donte` grows up knowing what love is.

Me and Shawna have kept the whole episode our little secret and vowed never to tell Veronica. It's just another little dirty secret that I have with some woman, about how we did the damn thing. The whole Veronica story was a lie. Shawna apologized for it. She said that she was high off of ecstasy. Shawna added that she wanted to sex me for the longest. So she figured that she had to do what she had to do, to make it happen.

Shawna told me that Success has also wanted some of me. That's why they teamed up and brought it to me like they did. After all of that drama and shock, I still somehow managed to get Success' number. Tonight, I'm supposed to hang out with her.

Since India has been playing those egotistical mind games with me, we haven't seen each other for the last week or so. She's been trippin` hard not wanting to talk on the phone, not wanting me to come to her studio sessions anymore. The last few times I was over at the house, she didn't want to give me any rhythm. So I figured I'll call Mrs. Success and kick it with her a bit, just to stay occupied.

That pussy Success is living with was too good, and I can't front like it wasn't. Being that Success is married, she won't be stressing a nigga out looking for a relationship or something.

"Hey baby, my husband Chris is out on business again so I'm free and ready to please." Success said as she hopped in my Lamborghini Diablo. This chick has got to have the fattest ass on the planet. Since I'm a butt bandit, I have to taste it just a few more times.

"You look good tonight love. I figure we'll go get a bite to eat then swing back over to my place." I said as I looked over at Success' lovely face. "That sounds good to me. Where are you taking me, to your house out in Jersey, or are we gonna stay in the city." She asked, revealing that she knew a little too much information about me. How did she know I lived out in New Jersey I thought? But I then realized, that Success is Shawna's friend and Shawna is Veronica's sister. So Success knew my whole profile.

"I figured we'll stay in the city tonight." I answered calmly. "This is a nice car honey. How much does something like this cost?" Success asked, commenting on my jet black Diablo that has a very mean look on the streets. "It cost a few pennies." I said

213

down playing the three hundred grand I dropped off at the lot, for the purchase. I have a rule to never ever tell anyone, except those who can afford it, how much I pay for the many luxury items I own. So I definitely wasn't gonna tell this chick…

YES

"Y'all niggas are always in here talkin` shit. Jennifer Lopez is not finer than Lisaraye." I said as I sat in the barbershop, on a late night getting my dice up. "If Jennifer Lopez didn't have a fat ass or if she didn't fuck with Puff, her ass would still be a nobody." Guy, my barber said as he shaped me up. The barbershop is always crazy like this. The fellas sit up in there for hours, talking shit about any and everything. "Yo y'all stay up. Guy, I'll see you on Friday playboy." I said as I walked out of the barbershop and jumped into the new CL600 that I had just upgraded to. After riding around in Denali's Diablo, I had to step my game up a bit. So I traded in the 500 and jumped into that 600.

As I'm coming down Broadway, leaning hard in my whip, bumping that old Keith Sweat "Make it last forever" CD, this black Navigator full of chicks roll up on me at the light. "Hey cutie." Shorty light skinned said from the passenger's side. "What's up ma, ma?" I said as I quickly took notice that there were four dams sitting pretty in the truck. "What are y'all getting into tonight? Where the party at?" I asked before the light changed. "Pull over and we'll tell you." Shorty with the long ponytail said from the backseat passenger side.

After I pulled over my six, the Navigator pulled in a couple a spaces behind me. "How are you doing? I'm Brooklyn" Shorty who was driving said, as she got out of the truck and introduced herself. "I'm Yes sweetheart. Where are you from? I notice an accent?" I asked because shorty was sounding country as hell. "I'm from Memphis, in fact we are all from Memphis. We are all up here vacationing and trying to get a record deal. Are you in the music business?" She asked, as she was giving up that groupies body english.

Now in my former days, I would have told shorty that I was Quincy Jones' son, or I would have ran my Christopher Williams game on her. But now I'm on something new and improved. I'm not gonna run game on shorty, just to freak off with her and her pretty friends. "Nah, I'm not in the industry. Why, what made you think something like that?" I asked sort of puzzled by her question.

"Look at this car you're driving. I figured that anyone as young as you look, pushing a CL600 Benz must be in the music industry." Brooklyn said, exposing just how much she thought in the box. "Well I'm sorry to disappoint you and your girls shorty but I'm not Damon Dash or one of those other music industry niggas." I said as I was walking off to get back into my car.

"Well that's okay, I'm still trying to get to know you. I will only be in town for another two days. So how about you show me a good time?" She said as she followed me a bit. "Damn shorty, I'm flattered but I'm practically married. So I have to respect that, you do know what I'm saying right?" I said as we stood with my car door open. "That's fine but take my number anyway. Like you said, you're practically married but practically doesn't count." She said as she slid me her number. She then walked off and jumped back into her truck with the rest of her clique, as they drove off smiling at me.

I liked honey's style and she was sexy as hell, but I'm good right now; I thought as I watched the truck make a right at the corner. Pushing a flamboyant and expensive car in the city, always causes crazy things to happen. As much as I know the dudes love a nice ride, the ladies are worst, when it really comes down to it.

I guess now that I've stepped my game up, the playing gets crazier. I wonder what Denali must be going through pushing all of that expensive "I'm rich", shit that he drives…

DENALI
"Yes, I'll have the steak." I said to the waiter as I

215

confirmed my order. Me and Success sat in the corner, at a candle lit table in the restaurant. Since I've taken a few moments and have had the opportunity to get to know Success, she turned out to be cool peoples. "Shawna told me that you take good care of Donte`, and even Veronica, with her expensive ass. I love Shawna and Veronica, but they are a little too expensive and glamorous for me. Now don't get me wrong, I love to look good. I just refuse to spend all of my money to do so." Success said.

"I hear you. I never understood why so many women will go broke spending their last on clothes and shoes." I said smiling at Success, while I was enjoying her conversation and company. As we sat there talking, I realized that me and Success shared a lot in common. Maybe we could end up being real cool friends? We both enjoy karate movies, we were both raised by loving grandmothers, and we both love to dance and party.

"So your husband, what is he like?" I asked all wrapped up in Success' pretty face. "He is an extremely driven businessman. He's one of those "the end justifies the means" businessmen. We used to spend a lot of time together but things changed after we got married." Success said as she sipped her water.

"Can you answer a question for me? How can a man chase a woman for three years, then when he finally gets her, he loses interest?" Success asked puzzled by the thought.

"Men are funny like that. We love a challenge and will do whatever it takes to get something we really want. The only thing is, many of us are not that good at maintaining what we catch. Do you know anything about fishing?" I asked Success as she sat there looking fascinated by my reasoning. "No I don't know anything about fishing." She answered giving me a pretty smile.

"Well I go fishing a lot and fishing is a good example of a man's nature. Some men will sit out there for hours waiting to catch a fish. I mean, I have been out in the water with niggas and they would sit patiently for six or seven hours before they catch something. The crazy thing is that after all of that waiting when

216

they finally catch something, would you believe they will throw it back into the water if it wasn't what they were looking for? Would you believe that after waiting seven hours a man would throw back a fish it took seven hours to catch?" I asked as she continued to look interested.

"What I'm saying is that sometimes a man will chase you until he catches you, then realize you are not what he was looking for." I said hipping Success to the man's psychology. "That is crazy but it does make sense. So what's the story with you and your second baby's mother India? Word is she is the only woman that has ever gotten your nose wide open. Is she the fish that you want?" Success asked perfectly playing off of what I had just said.

"Yea, that's my baby. I just don't know about marriage. I figure if I want to be with you and you want to be with me, why do we need all of that extra shit." I said sounding like a little punk.

"Come on Denali, you know better than that. You know that it's not that simple for us women. We need to feel secure and marriage is a strong symbol of security." Success said as we were deep in a good conversation.

"I hear India is about to be the next Shirley Caesar or Yolanda Adams. Now how is it that a woman so much into God would be in a relationship with a man like you?" Success said as she ate her ribs. "What's that suppose to mean. Shit, you sound like I'm a killer or something. I'm a good nigga girl, I'm a good catch." I said as I threw back at Success' verbal assault. "No, I didn't mean it like that silly, so don't get so defensive. I'm just saying, isn't there some conflict of interest there? She's a saint and you're a sinner. She's a woman of God and you're a child of God knows what. I know that she's not treating you right." Success said throwing more blows at me.

"Damn love, where is all of this coming from? You sound like you have a bone to pick with me." I said trying to figure out Success' angle. "Why are you so defensive baby, we're just talking? I'm just trying to figure out why would someone with their nose so wide open, jeopardize their situation as often as you do? If you love your woman, why don't you act like it…

SOLE`

"Let me turn that up, this is my song." I said as Shirley Murdock's "As we lay" played on Michelle's car radio. "How are things between you and Akil?" India asked me as I sat in the spacious back seat of Michelle's Audi. "We are doing well. I think Akil has finally woke up and smells the coffee of family. It's like he is now a happily married man instead of that struggling boyfriend he use to be our first eight years of marriage. He has grown so much as a man." I said turning to look back at India as I spoke to her.

"I'm happy for y'all. It's good to see you two making marriage look like a good thing. I just hope what has happened to Akil can happen to Denali. Denali is still content with the boyfriend and girlfriend thing. After a daughter and over five years of knowing me, he's still not sure." India said to us.

"You are not the only one girl. I have been with my man for close to three years and he still hasn't popped the question. That's why we still live in separate households. He wanted us to play house but I'm not going for that tricky shit." Michelle said to comfort India. "These brothers better step up, especially when they have a good woman on their side or we'll leave their tales." India added as she looked out of the window while we drove down the West Side Highway. "Y'all are not going anywhere. Denali and Lance have y'all exactly where they want y'all bitches. Trust me, they know that y'all love them and will do anything for their stink asses. Akil used to act the same way until he realized I was gone. I don't think a man really appreciates his woman until she ain't his woman anymore…

INDIA

"I'm surprised we found such a good parking spot." Michelle said as the three of us walked to the restaurant to have dinner. "Damn, can I roll with y'all?" Some young guy driving a

218

silver Durango said to us as we held up traffic. It always makes me laugh when men trip all over themselves, whenever they see a clique of attractive females. As we were getting closer to the restaurant I started to wonder, what was Denali doing and how is he going to handle the news I have for him?

"Yes sweetie, a table for three will be fine." Sole` said, flirting with the handsome young waiter with the bald head. "You better stop flirting with that man girl before he asks to marry you or something." Michelle said to Sole` playfully. Sole` is so beautiful, all she has to do is look at a man and he'll feel special. As we were taking our seats I noticed some dark skinned brother with a baldhead, that from the back looked just like Denali, sitting having dinner. But that couldn't be Denali all wrapped up in some other woman's face. Not when he's handling business.

For the next thirty seconds, I just stood there and analyzed this man's profile. Then it finally hit me like an earthquake… that is Denali. I knew he was still up to no good. Damn, why did I ever believe that he would change? I guess this is why he doesn't want to step up to the plate. He's still taking practice swings…

DENALI

"I think Chris Rock is the funniest comedian out right now." I said as me and Success moved our conversation to a less serious topic. "Yea, he's also my favorite comedian right now, along with Cedric the Entertainer. Martin Lawrence used to be my man, but he fell off." Success said before she continued.

"I need to go to the little girls room. I'll be right back sugar." Success said as she stood up, showing off her plump tail feather. As she walked to the ladies room, every nigga in the restaurant had their pupils glued to the back of her jeans. One chick slapped a chicken bone out her nigga's mouth for staring at Success' ass so hard.

While I was there waiting for Success to return, someone placed their soft hands over my eyes and said, "Guess who?" I recognized the scent immediately, it was that Jennifer Lopez fragrance that India wears. Even the soft texture of the hands were familiar to me. It's….as I turned around to see who it was, my heart stopped, balls busted, and my mouth dropped, all at the same time. "Hey…hey baby." I said trying to remain innocent and cool. Those hands and that smell.... it was India…

INDIA

"So is this how you handle your business." I asked Denali as I remained composed while he fell apart. "What … what...what are you doing here baby?" Denali said, as the sweat started to build up on his bald head. "I'm here having dinner with Sole` and Michelle. What are you doing here? Better yet, who is your lady friend?" I asked as the female with this huge butt was headed back to the table. "Success, this is India my girlfriend. Remember, the girlfriend, I was telling you all about. India this is my good friend, Success." Denali said introducing me to the mystery woman.

"It's nice to meet you Success, I'm Denali's ex girlfriend and the mother of his daughter Imani. I just stopped by the table because I didn't expect to see Denali here tonight. He told me that he had to handle business. That's why, I'm surprised to see him here with you having what appears to be a pleasurable evening. Well, I don't want to keep you two from enjoying your evening. Success it was nice to meet you. Denali it was nice knowing you, *asshole*." I said as I took the glass of wine that was sitting on the table and dumped it on Denali's shiny head.

For a second, I thought about taking the steak knife that was on the table and carving his dirty heart out. But I chose to handle this like a lady. I can't afford to have any negative publicity in my business. Remember, I'm saved and a Gospel singer. Once I got back to my table, I said to Michelle and Sole` who were looking on. "Ladies, I'm sorry but I have to get out of here. That asshole Denali just made me lose my appetite...

AKIL

"Hello." He picked up. "What the fuck is your problem dawg? What you think your shit don't stink?" I yelled at Denali over the phone. "Right now is not a good time Kil. Let me call you back." Denali said sounding rattled.

"Just tell me that India didn't catch your dirty ass in a restaurant with another woman. Just tell me that didn't happen Lee." I asked already knowing the answer. Sole` had already walked in the house breaking on me for what this nigga did. She went off on me like it was somehow my fault. This nigga Denali is getting other niggas in trouble for some shit he done did.

"Yea, I got caught out there tonight son. I would've never thought in a billion years, I would run into India's ass at ten thirty on a Tuesday night, in a restaurant in the city. Shit, she's usually sleep by ten." Denali said as he began to cop a plea. "Look you don't have to explain it all to me. But you better handle your business and get right with your woman, especially since she's leaving in three days." I said trying to wake Denali up.

"What the fuck are you talking about, she's leaving in three days? The promo tour doesn't start until the end of next month." Denali said sounding like he didn't have a clue. "Maybe you need to keep your eyes and ears on your woman and out of the next woman's ass. It's obvious that you don't know but India is going on tour sooner than you thought homey. Sole` told me that she is leaving on Friday. Damn Lee, what the fuck have you been doing? How come you don't know what's going on with your woman nigga?" I said purposely, hitting Denali with another dose of reality.

"Three days…she's leaving in three days? Yo Kil, I'll hit you back later. I have something to handle." Denali said to me in a panic. "Make sure you handle your business like a man and not a sucker. Get your shit together my nigga…

DENALI

I figured since I still had the keys to India's house I would show up before she changed the locks on me. When I pulled up to the house, I was so nervous that it started to bother me. If there is one emotion I hate it has to be fear. I'm afraid because I don't know what India is going to do.

"Baby I'm so, so, very sorry. I don't know why I did it but I did it. I just want you to know that we were having an innocent dinner. We were there only talking baby. In fact, I told her all about you and us." I said as India laid out crying on her bed. "India you know you mean the world to me. You're my queen baby, my earth. Those other women don't mean a thing to me." I said as I went to massage India's back.

"Don't you touch me! Don't you dare lay a fuckin' finger on me Denali." India said surprising me with her language. "What we stop having sex for two weeks, and you go out and find some new booty?" India said as the tears rolled down her face. "India you have to understand that I love you and want nothing more than for me, you, and Imani to be a family. I'm sorry baby. I'll leave you to yourself, just think about forgiving me. Can I call you tomorrow? Akil told me that you are leaving to go on tour on Friday. I would at least like to see you and my baby off. I'll miss y'all so much while y'all gone." I said as she continued to lay stretched out across her bed.

"Just leave my house and stay the fuck out of our lives. You ain't nothing but a lying, cheating, and undeserving dog. Denali get the fuck out of my house!" India yelled as she picked up the crystal vase that was on the night stand, and sent it in my direction.

It's funny because seeing India like that, put a little bit of fear in my stomach. I know that if I had to I could take her. But India has too much shit in here, she can throw and use as a weapon. So I took heed to India's order and got my black ass out of there while I could, before she tossed some more shit my way...

CHAPTER 25

<u>YES</u>

"Mr. Black you have a visitor out front" Denise my new temporary assistant, said to me as I sat in the office reviewing the numbers of this new IPO. "Who is it Denise? I'm busy right now." I said kinda irritated. "It's Ms. Waters. Should I let her in Mr. Black?" Denise asked nervously, fearing that if she upset me she would lose her job. "Sure send her in Denise." I said to Denise knowing who my surprise visitor was.

"I hope I'm not disturbing you. I just finished settling the biggest merger in our firm's history. And I want to celebrate." Adrienne said as she closed and locked my office door behind her.

"Congratulations baby, I know you worked so hard on that deal. Come here and let daddy kiss you." I said as I gave Adrienne a bear hug and a slow French kiss. " You know making money makes me horny baby. I just made our firm millions and myself a three hundred thousand dollars commission check. Feel how horny that makes me?" Adrienne said as she took my fingers and ran them along her warm and wet pussy.

"My Lord, it sure does make you horny. I'm glad you stopped by because I haven't had any lunch yet. And Daddy needs something to eat baby." I said as I cleared off my desk with a swift left hook. "So you're hungry huh? I might be able to help you satisfy that hunger." Adrienne said as she laid across my desk, lifted her skirt up, and served her loving to me on a platter.

"Yea baby, daddy likes it like that. Um um, this pussy tastes so fresh." I said as I sat down on my leather swivel lazy boy office chair and enjoyed the nutrients and minerals that Adrienne's excited pussy fed me. "Yes daddy just like that… work that tongue right there." Adrienne moaned in her usual expressive loud tone.

"Be quiet baby. I don't want the whole company to know how good it is to you boo." I said as I stood over Adrienne dropping my FUBU slacks. I then placed all I had to give inside of Adrienne's warm welcome spot. "Damn baby my pussy is warm just how I like it." I said as I eased in and out of Adrienne from the missionary position, while she laid spread out across my office desk. "I love having you all up in me... give it all to me just like that." Adrienne said as she somehow managed to grab my ass and control my rhythm and deep stroke.

I'm usually a man who can hold and control a nut but, Adrienne's pussy was feeling like three heavens. Even though I was only two minutes and twenty two seconds into it, my gun was ready to pop. "Oh shit, here I cum baby...oh shit here I cum." I said to Adrienne letting her know this fantastic voyage was about to end. "Here I cum baby." I repeated making it clear to the judges that I was throwing in the towel. Just as I was about to pull out and explode all over Adrienne's pelvic area, she grabbed my ass firmly.

Oh shit the fix is on… the muthafuckin` fix is on. I thought, as Adrienne trapped me, forcing me to release all of my baby makers into her. "Damn baby why did you do that? Why did you do that shit?" I asked Adrienne as I was feeling light on my feet. "Do what?" She answered all dumbfounded like she didn't know if she was coming or if she just left. "You do know that I just came inside of you right? You do know that shit right?" I asked looking at my office door as I pulled my black slacks up from off my ankles.

"You just did WHAT? Why in the world would you do something like that?" Adrienne asked like I just hit her with a news flash. "WHAT?" I thought. See this is some of that first grade class A bullshit right here. She knows what her ass just did. She knows it was her and not me that did that bullshit...

AKIL

It's official now For All Men (FAM) magazine will be hitting the stands in three short months. In our inaugural edition I have lined up a cover story with Jesse Jackson. We also have a feature story on the contradictions of manhood, a fashion lay out introducing some hot new African American designers, and a swimsuit layout, just a little eye candy for the fellas.

Today was the first official meeting I had with my staff of fifteen and it was great. I believe I have the best team that I could've possibly put together. I'm so excited about our product. I believe we will hold our own in this competitive magazine market.

"So here we are ladies and gentlemen, three months away from opening day. I want to thank you all for believing in me and the vision enough to commit your talents, energy, and expertise to making this happen. I believe that what we have created is something new to the marketplace. In the room now sits a team of innovators and you all should give yourselves a round of applause. I am humbled by the quality of work you all have produced. I can't thank you all enough." I was saying as the moment started to get a little too intense for me.

Having a dream come true and having people believe in you enough to follow, is one of the best feelings in the world. "It's alright boss, let it out." Matthew one of our photographers said as I struggled to fight off my tears. "I just want you all to know that I consider this company my extended family. So this weekend I will see y'all at the Kingdome." I said as I concluded our meeting, before I displayed any more emotion.

After another ten to twelve hour day at the office, I was ready to get home to my wife and son. But before I left my office, I was interrupted. "Akil do you have a minute?" Candice one of my senior editors asked as I was packing my bag to leave. Now Candice is a triple threat. She is beautiful, with brains, and has a lovely body. "Sure what can I do for you?" I said as I put my bag down. "I have a question but I don't think it's appropriate for me to ask my boss." Candice said as she started to bullshit. "Come on

225

Candy, you know we are one big family. So just talk to me." I said to make her feel more comfortable.

"Okay but this is a personal matter. I have a secret crush on someone in the office. This person has no idea how I feel about him and I have wanted to tell him. It kills me to be in the same room with this man and not be able to lick him from head to toe." Candice said as she was heating up. "I know that you don't want any office romances in here. But then again you encourage that we live a satisfying personal life. And nothing would satisfy me more personally and sexually than if you would allow me to just taste some of you Akil." Candice said as she made her move.

"Akil, I left my former employer not only because you offered me a better opportunity. Although that played a major role in my decision, I am here because I have always wanted you. Do you want me Akil? Do you want me boss?" Candice asked as she made her move, backing me up against my huge office window.

"Candice I'm flattered but it ain't gonna happen baby. I'm a faithfully married man. I love my wife more than anything you can give me. I'm sorry that you feel this way and there is nothing we can do about it. But now it's definitely time for us to head on home." I said as I put the brakes on Candice's sexual press.

That must have knocked the wind right out of her sail because she just stood there looking out of the window embarrassed. She was motionless, standing there looking out of my office's Empire State Building view. "And Candice, by the way, you're fired." I said as I left my office, turning the lights off on her ass. No way am I gonna get caught playing with fire again. That woman is way to fine for me to be dodging her sexual bullets on a day to day basis. Shit I know me, and ain't that much self control in the world. It wouldn't be long before she broke me down and we got up. I've been there and done that. I am now smart enough to know what to avoid and when to run. So Candice's sexy ass had to go...

DENALI

"So did she forgive you?" Success asked as we talked on the phone, at two thirty in the morning. "She didn't say anything to me but for me to get the fuck out of the house. I think that was the last straw. I know India and I have never seen that look in her eyes before. She is finished with my stupid ass. I doubt if she will take me back this time." I said to Success not realizing I was starting to sound lonely.

"Sounds like you need a hug baby. Why don't you come over here and spend the night with me? I really want to see you right now anyway." Success said inviting me over to her place.

"Are you sure that's a good idea?" I asked realizing, I left my gun in Jersey. Like I said earlier, I never go over to a married chicks house without my "bitch". "Yea baby there is no one here but me and my kitty cat." She answered jokingly. "Iight, then I'm on my way, now don't fall asleep on a nigga." I said before I hung up the phone.

As I drove out to Success' house in Queens, I began to think about just how scandalous this bitch really is. Here I am headed to honey's house while her husband is out of town on business.

When I got to the door, Success opened it up wearing nothing but a Brazilian thong. "Oh shit." I said as Success greeted me looking like she wanted to fuck. "So what's up Denali? It's already after three, let's get it on." She said to me as she held her titties together while licking them.

Damn, Success didn't even hit a nigga with a "come in, sit down, and relax yourself". It was straight get in here and fuck me. I knew that Success' husband wasn't serving her right because shorty is off the chain with her sexuality. Success wasted no time to handle her business Vanessa Del Rio style, spitting all over my dick as she sucked it.

I tried to fuck Success' brains out as we banged out in her bedroom, ruining the set up in the process. "Turn your ass over." I said to Success, as I had her laid out on her chest at the edge of her bed. With Success in that position, there was ass everywhere just how I like it. I then rode that donkey through the early morning like the black stallion that I be.

As I woke up and was leaving the next morning, I looked around the room, just to trace my steps. Damn, there were pictures of Success and her husband everywhere. Damn, this is one ugly looking muthafucka, I thought as I examined one of the many pictures in the room. This nigga looks like a guerilla or some shit. He has to be one of the ugliest niggas this side of the Mason Dixon. Oh hell nah, Success looks like she's hugging a damn monkey in this picture, I thought as I started laughing to myself, doing my best not to wake Success. But I was laughing my ass off.

You would think they have a loving marriage by their smiles in these pictures. But Success is dirty. I just hope dude knows that, with his ugly ass.

"Bye baby, I'll call you later." I said as I left her house with no draws on, with my balls smelling like budussy: Booty, dick, and pussy…

INDIA

I'm a whole lot stronger than I thought. I guess all of the times I caught Denali cheating on me in the past have prepared me for this. I'm thirty six hours away from entering another stage in my life and Denali is now a thing of my past. Seeing him look at another woman with such interest in his body language, just killed me.

I realize that I'm in a situation where I have to be professional and continue to focus on my career and daughter. I am not about to go crazy over some man who doesn't know what's good for him. If Denali isn't deserving to be with me, some other man is and will be. So Denali is a done deal. I'm finished.

"Hello India, it's Akil. What's up babygirl?" Akil asked, I guess to check up on me. "I'm okay Kil, just finishing up my packing. How are you sweetie?" I asked as I spoke into the phone. "I'm cool. Look I want to stop by and see you and Imani before y'all leave, is that okay?" Akil asked. "As long as you're by yourself and didn't forget the way, come on over, I'll be here." I said actually looking forward to Akil's visit.

"Hey Kil it's good to see you honey. You look wonderful baby." I said as I embraced him, noticing he put on some more muscle. "Where's my little diamond?" Akil asked looking for Imani. "She's spending some precious time with her grandparents before we leave. Kil are you hungry? There's some jerk chicken with rice and cabbage in there." I said as I went upstairs into my bedroom for a second.

"That sounds good as long as you join me. I want to talk to you baby sister." Akil yelled to me, as I was upstairs, to go through my dresser draw. When I came back down stairs, Akil had his shoes off, and was in the kitchen fixing the food, like he lived here. I have always loved Akil and Yes, they are both real good friends and positive men. It always amazes me to see how they act more like brothers than friends with each other. There have been many days and nights when I would just sit up and talk to either Yes or Akil, when Denali wasn't acting right. They are always there for me playing big brother.

"I know that Lee messed up and I understand if you don't want to have anything to do with him. Just know India, that Denali is a man that loves you and only you. When I was out there doing wrong, making my mistakes, it wasn't because I didn't love Sole`. It was because my definition of love didn't include faithfulness. I thought I could love Sole`, and still cheat on her. I didn't know what trust was, nor did I understand how important it is to say "no". But experience, regret, and pain taught me otherwise. I truly don't know why Denali did what he did, but as his friend and brother I want to apologize on his behalf. India we all make mistakes you and me included. If you can reconsider your position and give Denali another chance, then do so. But it's up to you to determine if he deserves another chance or not." Akil said as he ate his chicken.

After eating dinner, we then went into the living room to

watch some TV. "Hold on sis, let me give Sole` a call and let her know where I'm at." Akil said, as he picked up the phone to call his wife. While Kil was on the phone laughing and playing with Sole`, a part of me started to get jealous. It's amazing how God has changed their relationship and marriage. I just hope he will do the same for me. "Sole` said for you to give her a call when I leave. She said she has something funny to tell you." Akil said as he laid out on the floor, while we watched an episode of Soul Food.

After another two hours of hanging out with me, Akil decided to leave. "I'll call you before you leave. Think about what I said sis. I love you, be safe. Call me if you need anything." Akil said as he hugged and kissed me on the cheek, before he got into his stylish S500 Mercedes Benz. Akil has always been a good soul, but since his accident, Akil has become this great man. Akil coming over here was such a loving gesture on his part. I just hope Denali didn't put him up to it…

CHAPTER 26

<u>**YES**</u>

Venus hasn't seen her friend in weeks and we think she might be pregnant. "Here baby, go in the bathroom and take the test." I said as I passed Venus the EPT home pregnancy test. "Okay baby here I go." Venus said as she nervously closed the bathroom door.

Wow, Venus might be pregnant again, making me a father two times over. I can never understand why brothers don't embrace fatherhood. Nothing makes me feel better than seeing my daughter's eyes or having her little arms around me. If Venus is pregnant I hope it's a boy this time. I would love to have a little prince to go along with my little princess.

"Are you finished baby?" I asked as I impatiently opened the bathroom door. "Yes baby but it will take a minute before we get the results." Venus said as she hugged me wearing my oversized Addias tee shirt. "Damn, I can no longer take it. I'm going in the kitchen. I need a drink." I said to Venus as I went off to fix myself a homemade daiquiri. When I returned to the bedroom, all I had to do was just looked at Venus and I knew.

"Get ready for another one, I'm pregnant big poppa." Venus said causing me to smile and pick her up. "Wow Venus we did it again baby. I'm so happy I feel like running around the block butt naked, with this one sock on." I said as I started doing my silly man dance.

"How do you feel about the situation?" I asked Venus, as she looked a little concerned. For some reason she looked troubled. "I didn't plan on having another baby until I was finished with graduate school and married, honey. I'm happy because I know that our baby is a blessing. But I'm a little concerned about my goals." She answered, looking up at me as I hugged her.

"Sit down baby. Let me give you a foot massage." I said as I started to rub Venus' feet. "I just want you to relax and know that everything will work out perfectly. We are a team, baby. We do everything as a pair. You can still finish school and do the things you want to do. You do realize that I'm here by your side supporting you every step of the way right? Whatever it is that you want to do, we will work as a family and get it done, okay baby." I said to comfort my woman.

The more time I spend with Venus, the less time I want to spend with Adrienne. In fact, I haven't seen Adrienne's ass since the office incident, and amazingly I don't miss her. I guess Venus is the woman who has my heart. "I believe in us baby and I also know that things will work out. I'm happy that I'm pregnant. I'm happy that I could give you another baby." Venus said giving me that pretty smile and a happy kiss.

"Venus I want you to know something. I've been keeping a secret." I said as the spirit was moving me. "I haven't completely broken off all ties with Adrienne. Not until this moment. Baby as I sit here with you and my daughter in the other room, I realize that this is where I want to be. I don't want anyone but you Venus. I don't want to be anywhere but here with my family baby. I love you Venus…

DENALI

Tonight is business as usual in the Kingdome. It's elbow to elbow, jammed packed with fine ass women and handsome well dressed brothers everywhere. "Congratulations babyboy I see your ass is trying to keep up with me." I said congratulating Yes on his expected child. "Yes, yes, I'm so excited playboy. I'm so thankful that my kids will all have the same mother and father. No offense Lee." Yes said as we drank some Don P. in my special lounge area.

"No offense taken playa. So are you thinking about getting up with Venus and really doing the damn thing?" I asked Yes testing his level of commitment. "You know what Lee, I've been really thinking about it lately. Venus is the picture perfect wife. She is gorgeous, sexes me like crazy, can cook her ass off, and is independent and strong. She was a little worried about finishing grad school, and being married before she has another child. You know Venus is old fashion with her values. All of this "babymother", "babyfather" shit doesn't sit well with her.

"The other night it dawned on me, Venus is the woman that I want to be with. Adrienne is cool and she does have a part of me but it ain't my heart and soul. It's more like my balls or something. You know what I'm saying doggy?" Yes said as Akil and Sole` finally joined us looking like runway models. "What's up fellas?" Akil said as he joined us with his new joyful look on his face.

"Damn Sole`, you look good enough to eat girl." I said complimenting Sole` on how splendid she looked. "Word up Lee you ain't never lied. Could your jeans be any tighter? Sole` you got a fatty girl." Yes added as we all started laughing.

"Y'all thirsty ass niggas leave my wife alone." Akil said as he stood in front of Sole` covering her booty. "It's another packed night Lee. What you made another thirty thousand tonight?" Sole` asked, as she usually does with her business minded ass. "You know how I do. Money can't seem to get enough of me. I don't know what I'm gonna do with all of this damn money." I said arrogantly.

"So Lee, what are you gonna do about India?" Yes asked me as Akil and Sole` went downstairs to get their dance on, as usual.

"I need to step up and do something doggy. I ain't trying to have my baby hit the road, without her knowing how I really feel." I said to Yes as the alcohol started to kick in. "Lee you are my man and all, but I have to keep it real with you. You are full of shit my nigga." Yes said looking square at me.

"Now that you know India is on the next thing smoking,

233

you want to step up and get focused. I doubt if that's what you really want. I think it's something you are accepting. But I don't think it's something that you have chosen to have. I know you love India, Lee. But you really don't want all that she is willing to give you. India is on some "marriage, husband and wife, right before God" arrangement. Meanwhile, you still want a witey. You feel me?" Yes said as he got up and went to the bathroom.

Damn he has a point. I love India but maybe I'm not ready for all that India wants to give me. After Akil and Sole' returned to the table, we continued to party. "Damn every one from the magazine is down stairs, sweating their asses off on the dance floor." Akil said as he and Sole' returned looking like they were in a dance contest.

"That's what I like about this spot everybody comes to have a good time." Sole' added as she was leaning against Akil's right arm. For the remainder of the night we all had the best of time. We drank more champagne and told more jokes than our stomachs could handle.

"Y'all are gonna have to excuse me. I need to make a phone call." I said stumbling away from the table. "Hello" she answered. "Thank you baby for answering the phone. I've been calling you all day. What are you still doing up at two in the morning? You know you're an early bird." I said to ease the tension between us.

"What do you want Denali? I'm busy right now." India said sounding annoyed by my call. I also heard a deep baritone in the background saying something in her ear, as I was talking. "You're busy at two in the morning? Who is that I hear in the background? Yo what the fuck are you doing India?" I asked as I was getting hot and starting to feel sick to my stomach.

As I sat there putting two and two together I was about to lose it. "I know you're not fuckin` another nigga." I hollered into the receiver. "And if I was it's none of your business. You lost your right to question what I'm doing. So as you can hear I'm busy right now. Bye Denali…

INDIA

"Thanks for stopping by and seeing me before I leave. Take good care of yourself. Good luck with the engagement, your fiancé sounds like a real good woman." I said to Paul, my ex boyfriend, as I hugged and let him out of the door. So I've now seen everyone I wanted to see before I leave to go on tour. The nerve of Denali, to call over here at two in the morning, then accuse me of sleeping with another man. I guess he's so crooked he can't think nor see straight, but enough about him already. I need to get some sleep.

"Lord everything happens for a reason. All things are working towards perfection. I refuse to worry or feel sorry about what has happened between Denali and I. I know that my life is in your hands, so I can't lose or fail. Thank you Lord for correcting and perfecting my way. Amen…

SOLE`

"I really had a nice time tonight baby." I said to Akil as we jumped in the shower trying to sober up from the night's activity. "Sole` did I tell you that you looked so good tonight? You know you got it going on girl." Akil said as he started kissing my nipples while he held me. "Do you know what you're doing?" I asked as my nipples started to harden.

"Of course I know what I'm doing. I'm nice with this girly." Akil said as we started another baby making episode for us. As Akil was dicking me down, he started to talk. "Can I give you another baby?" Akil asked softly, while he loved me down. "Yes baby… yes baby…yes baby... give me what you want me to have." I answered as I started to lovingly kiss my husband. "Oh yes, daddy is almost there… I'm cumming baby. I'm about to give it all in you…booommm…

DENALI

If there is another nigga hitting my pussy, there is gonna be some muthafuckin` smoke in the city. I was heated on my way out to Mount Vernon, to find out what was going on. As I pulled up into India's garage, there were no signs of another dude, unless the nigga took a cab over. All that was parked outside were the CLK and Yukon I bought India, and the Escalade the record label gave her as a bonus.

When I opened the door, I didn't know what to expect. I was definitely prepared to tune a nigga up if I had to. I was walking through the house on edge, like I was the police or something. Fortunately, there was no one in the house but India, who was peacefully asleep.

India has the most peaceful look whenever she sleeps. It always looks as if she doesn't have a care or concern in the world. Wow, my baby looks so beautiful, I thought. I then just sat there watching her sleep so angelically for the next two hours.

As I sat there, I must've dozed off, because all I began to hear was a loud chant in my head, "He who findth a wife, findth a good thing... he who findth a wife findth a good thing." The chant wouldn't stop, even after I opened my eyes from my brief sleep. It was as if the spirits were telling me something. Telling me what I needed to do.

When I did open my eyes, they were immediately drawn to India as she slept. And at that moment, the moment that every man looks forward to had arrived for me. At thirty three years old, I was finally done playing games and was ready to be a man to a woman. At thirty three I was now ready to be a man to my woman.

At approximately five thirteen in the morning, it hit me like an epiphany. I was ready to be a husband and I wanted India to be my wife. Finally, I'm done bullshitting. I'm done running from the best thing that has ever happened to me. But there was one big problem for a nigga, India hates my guts right now. Well that's at least how she's acting. She did tell me to get the fuck out and to stay the fuck out. But maybe she didn't mean it.

Damn, I hope all that I'm hearing and feeling in my heart is for real. I'm not trying to make an ass out of myself.

Here I go. I'm stepping up and making my move like a

man. Damn this is some scary shit…

INDIA

The day is finally here. I'm going on tour, with the first show scheduled for tonight in New Jersey. As I woke up I spent some quality time with the Lord in prayer. I then headed to the bathroom before I started my daily workout.

How did this get here, I thought as I read the letter that was taped to the bathroom mirror.

"Baby I know that my word doesn't count for much right now. But please take these written words seriously. I can not apologize enough for what I did, nor can I undo what has already been done. All I have control over is what I do now and from this moment on. Baby I ask that you forgive me and give me the opportunity to do what I've never done. That is be faithful and true to you and only you. I'm talking the whole thing this time. India I ask that you give me another chance to be all the man you fell in love with baby. If you really believe in love, and if you truly believe in us, then meet me in the center of Grand Central Station this evening at five o'clock. I'll be standing there waiting for you to show. I love you India."

Is Denali crazy? I have to be in New Jersey by seven thirty. It's opening night tonight. Grand Central Station at five o' clock? That's the busiest place in the city at that time. What in the world is going on? What in God's name does Denali have up his sleeve…

CHAPTER 27

AKIL

     I have arranged for the magazines release party to be held at the Kingdome. We are expecting a major turn out and plan on pleasing every head that fills the building. "So it's a go we have Gerald Levert, Donell Jones, and Alicia Keys performing. We also added some adult entertainment for all the sexy people. If there are any kinks that need to be ironed out don't hesitate, call me ASAP. It's important that we make this event one of the city's biggest galas ever." I said to the event's promotion team on a conference call from my office.

     I am so excited about my life right now. I have a beautiful wife by my side, my son is growing everyday, my loving friends are supporting me, and I'm finally making my dreams come true. It may sound crazy, but the best and worst thing that could have ever happened to me was that car accident. It took me to almost lose my life to find a life.

     I now realize that God is the man. I now understand that I can not truly be the man and husband Sole` needs, the man and father my son needs, and man this world needs without God as my center. I now find myself thanking the Lord any and every time I have a reflective moment.

     The Lord was right. The life I have to live must be according to his plan. Especially since the life I was living before was killing and ruining me. So here I now stand with not only money, but with wealth. I have a loving relationship with my wife and not just a sex partner and roommate. I'm doing my heart's work and not just working a job. This is what life is all about. All that other shit I was into, was all bullshit that doesn't mean anything at the end of the day. Cars, clothes, a successful career, countless chicks, and all of the other things I let define and determine me, I'm now free of.

I am a husband, father, friend, and loving man today, because of all the shit I went through. But thank God I'm through. If life were perfect, maybe I wouldn't have had to go through all of the crazy shit I went through. But let me be the first to say, life isn't perfect. Therefore, I made bad decisions and foolish choices. Thank God there is forgiveness and correction in this life. Trust me, at one point or another we will all need to be forgiven and corrected. That's right, that goes for me and you too. So don't be afraid of failing or asking for forgiveness. That's the only way to turn a bad thing good. Trust me I know...

DENALI

Since I'm gonna do this, I'm gonna do it right, I thought as I arrived in Brooklyn and walked in to see my man Jermaine the jeweler. I figured why go give some Jewish cat named Jacob my money, when I can spread love to a brother who does the same thing. I've been coming to see my man Jermaine for years now. He always does his thing for me.

Jermaine tricked out my Cartier and Rolex for me. He always gives me a unique look. Jermaine is another older brother from the block that stepped his business game up, and I support that. Jermaine figured, why keep letting someone else profit off of the black dollar when that man really doesn't give a fuck about the black life.

"What it is old timer?" I asked as I walked into Jermaine's store doors. I immediately started getting the royal treatment that Jermaine gives to all of his customers. It doesn't matter if you are coming in to spend five dollars or fifty thousand, Jermaine treats all of his customers the same way. And I respect that.

"Man I'm here waiting for you." He said, which happens to be the line he tells to all of his customers. "So what can I do for

239

you today Denali?" Jermaine asked giving me his undivided attention.

"I'm here looking for the craziest engagement ring that you have in the store. I need the ring to say, "I love you more than money can buy." I said to Jermaine as we sat talking a bit, before he tried to get my money.

"Engagement ring, who's getting married? I know it isn't for your ass?" Jermaine said playfully tapping me on the shoulder. "Come on old man young dudes are still getting married." I answered as Jermaine lead me to the back of his shop. Jermaine has a nice classy and luxurious shop, right in the heart of downtown Brooklyn. "Nah seriously, you're getting married young blood. Trust, that's the best move any man can make, if he has a good woman. Let me tell you. If you think you're rich now, wait until you see all of the good marriage is gonna bring to you. I don't think I would have the shop today, if it wasn't for marriage and my wife Debbie." Jermaine said as he went into his special vault and brought out some one of a kind jewels for me to examine.

"Damn, that's beautiful Jermaine." I said admiring the red colored fifteen carat diamond engagement ring, he handed me. "That's right from the Motherland, just off of the boat." He said as he fell back and let me admire the ring in silence, which by the way is a sign of an excellent salesman. "This is it Jermaine. This is what I want my baby to have on her finger." I said ready to close the deal on the spot.

After dropping off ninety grand for the ring with Jermaine, I decided to call up the office, and just making sure everything was copasetic.

"Okay so Akil's magazine bash will be in two weeks. Remember I want him to have the best of the best. Did you call in the extra truck load of Cristal and Moet?" I asked Juanita my executive assistant. "Yes I have." She answered. "Listen, I won't be in the office today or for the next few days. And I need you to take extra care of things for me. Did you find anyone to replace

Damon yet?" I asked Juanita who is also my office manager.

Juanita is more than my office manager. She is actually the one who runs my empire for me. I just make sure Juanita is alright. "We've interviewed some quality candidates over the last three days. There is this one young lady that interviewed well. The only thing is she doesn't have a college degree." Juanita said.

"What exactly do you mean by she interviewed well?" I asked needing the bottom line. "She is exactly what we are looking for. She is everything Damon stopped being plus more." Juanita answered. "Well forget about the degree. Set her up for a private interview with me sometime early next week." I said. "Okay will do. I guess I'll see you next week. Enjoy your day Denali." Juanita said as we hung up.

Most people don't realize, nor do they understand, the extent of what I do. Most niggas just think my success and wealth is a stroke of luck. They see my cars and don't take into consideration the things I have to do and the choices I have to consistently make, to live how I do. Overseeing and running a business conglomerate causes me to wear many different hats. I have to be the leader, the asshole, the motivator, the big brother, and the philanthropist, sometimes all in the same day.

Now that I've checked in on my business affairs it's now time that I handle my business and make India my wife…

INDIA

After rehearsal, I decided to have a quick personal meeting with Paula before she headed off to handle some more business in Jersey. "Paula I have something to ask you. Now I need you to be painfully honest with me." I asked, knowing Paula would have it no other way. "Go ahead girl, you have my undivided attention." Paula said with care all in her gray eyes.

"Denali has asked me to meet him at Grand Central Station in less than two hours. I think he's up to something big. I think probably wants to take me away on a romantic getaway, even though he knows I have to go on tour. It's just his style to want

241

what he wants, when he wants it, with little regard for anything or anyone else. I know that he wants to make things right between us. But I don't know what I want anymore. For a long time, Denali was what I craved above anything else. But after I caught him in that restaurant with another woman things have changed. I'm excited about my career and the hype of the tour and album. However I'm still not at peace. Do you think, I should meet Denali and see what that may bring? Or do you think I should finish up here and head on to Jersey for the show later? Anyway you dice it, I know I need to make a decision. So what do you think?" I asked Paula, as she ran her fingers through her long thick black hair.

Paula actually was looking a bit surprised to see just how complex my situation had become. "Do what you would do if you wanted to make things right. Do what would bring you the most joy in doing. In other words, do the right thing babygirl. I'll see you later...

YES

Since I've told Adrienne that Venus is expecting, she dropped me like a bad habit. Funny thing is, she actually did me a favor with the move. Since I had the vision that revealed to me that Amerie and Adrienne were "good ones" but Venus is the "right one", it has only been about me and Venus. God knows I will miss Adrienne and all her goodness. But Venus is the right one and that means a world of difference.

I feel free and clean, now that I have officially cut off all ties with Adrienne. I'm now a one women man like my man Dave Hollister, and I'm cool with it.

"Talk to me." I said as I picked up my cell phone, noticing Akil's cell number. "Hold on dawg, I have Lee on the other line." Akil said as he clicked over. "This is some gay shit, three grown ass men on three way. I bet this was your idea Lee." I said as a joke, realizing that in all the years of our friendship, we had never spoke on three way before like this.

"You're a real funny faggot Yes. You're a funny guy."
Denali responded as he laughed into the phone. "So Mr. Romance,
did you cop that stone yet?" I asked Denali. "Yea I went ninety
thousand deep for it too." Denali responded. "Damn nigga, I see
that you're making sure that she says yes. Shit, for a ninety
thousand dollar piece of ice, I'll marry your bitch ass myself." Akil
said.

"Yo I just hope that she meets me in the station. I know her
tour begins tonight, and I'm inconveniencing her like a
muthafucka. She probably thinks I'm on some "I want what I
want" egotistical shit. If she shows up, that will finally prove to me
that she is the one. If a woman is willing to make that type of
sacrifice to be with me, I'm ready to die for her." Denali said then
continued.

"Speaking of which, I saw the craziest car accident today
on the FDR. This big ass Mac truck smashed into this little as Ford
Probe. The shit was crazy, it had me really thinking you never
know when it's time to go." Denali said sounding a little spooky.

"Well we don't have to worry about any of that. You just
make it your business to do right by my sister." Akil said to Denali.
"That's a guarantee." Denali responded. "Look I have a business
meeting in twenty minutes. I need to take a shit before I go in
there. That Mexican food I ate for lunch is kicking my
muthafuckin ass. So I'll have to get up with y'all sweethearts later
on." I said into the phone.

"Okay Mr. Shits, go bust your ass. I love y'all. I mean I
really do love y'all niggas." Denali said, all emotionally, causing
us all to get quiet for a moment. That wasn't the first time that we
have heard Denali tell us that he loved us. But something about the
way he said it, and the way it felt this time, was different. It felt
very crazy, almost like it was something we needed to know.

"Yo I love y'all too." Akil added. "Same here, now take
y'all loving asses on, I have to go take this shit...

DENALI

Here I stand, nervously, in the middle of Grand Central station with a ninety thousand dollar engagement ring in my pocket. A ring that I'm finally prepared to give India. As I'm looking at the giant size clock that stands in the center of the hall, I began to sweat underneath my Karl Kani sweat suit. It is five minutes to five and still no signs of India. Then again, there are a hundred thousand people hustling to make it home during these hours.

Will she show or has she gone off and started a new chapter in her life without me? This is so ironic that here I stand in Grand Central Station in the heart of New York City with beautiful women of all nationalities, colors, shapes, and sizes coming and going before my once lustful eyes. Yet now my heart and eyes are only looking for that one special woman.

"India where in the hell are you baby? I know you're not gonna leave me here hanging. Baby please show, baby please show up and be with me." I pleaded with India mentally.

Once the giant size clock struck 5:37pm, my hopes and expectations began to fade. So this is what India must've felt like each time she caught me out there fuckin` around. Damn, this shit hurts. This feeling of rejection and despair is making me sick. This shit is wack!

I will never ever…ever…ever cause another woman this amount of pain again. This shit hurts the soul.

Here it is six o` clock and India is still a no show. I can't take anymore of this. Let me get my ass out of here while I still have an ounce of dignity left. Just as I was about to step off and head on home, to probably cry a little bit, someone gently placed their soft hands over my eyes and said, "Guess who?".

The fragrance I recognized immediately. The soft texture of the hands, I could also detect. I knew my baby would show. She couldn't just leave her man hanging like a lost puppy. We have been through too much shit together for us not to know that our love is official. We won't allow anything to stop us.

As I turned around, excited by my surprise arrival, I had no idea it would happen to me like this. With all of the things I've done to women, I never thought this would happen to me. It just never crossed my mind. I hear stories and see the movies. But I would've never thought I was gonna go out like Willy Lump Lump. But when I turned, it wasn't India joyously awaiting me like I expected. It was that crazy bitch Alexus looking Devilish with a forty five pointed to my chest.

DAMN, her crazy ass was still stalking me. She did say that she wasn't finished with me, but damn. Alexus then gave me a hellish look and pulled the trigger to her forty five, sending a heat wave through my body. Oh shit, I'm hit. I'm shot right in the heart. I'm shot…I'm shot…I'm shot. Can you believe this shit?

I've been shot, at the hands of a vindictive woman that I didn't love much less care for. Here I am dying in Grand Central Station, in the heart of a city with some of the loveliest women in the world. I'm dying at the hands of a woman whose heart I broke and body I used, on my way to finding love. Can you believe this shit? I'm shot. What about getting married? What about getting it right? What about my son and daughter? What about growing old with India?

As my soul is watching my body lay there dead and the crime scene conclude, it becomes even harder for me to watch. As the cops were apprehending Alexus, the scene becomes even more and more surreal. People were running for their lives in fear because of the gunshot.

As I'm watching, I then see her running out of the cab, through Grand Central Station doors on her way to meet me. It was India, all dressed up, running with tears in her eyes to be with me. Running to be with her man, but not like this. Damn, I still couldn't do right by that woman, no matter how hard I tried. I still couldn't get my shit right, even when I wanted to.

"Don't cry India. I will always be with you, but now I will only live in your heart baby." I said to India as I realized my time on earth was being cut short. It was now time for me to leave this

245

world of power, money, and sex literally. It was now time for me to meet back up with my parents and grandparents. Time to live in that world, were none of this material and superficial shit matters. It was time for me to check out. But before I leave, I would like to say something.

"I'm sorry Sheila, Jackie, Carmen, Brenda, Lorraine, Toy, Cutina, Lashawn, Debbie, Davonna, Success, Meisha, Tanya, Kim, Shante, Candice, and to all the other three thousand women I slept with lustfully. But I'm really sorry to you India, who I slept with unlovingly."

If I could do it all over again, I would love before sex, because sex can produce a baby but love builds a family. I would love before sex, because sex can cause sickness and disease but love heals. I would love before sex, because love never fails. Now look at it me, I lost it all, my family, my friends, my money, my cars, my clothes, my jewelry, my homes, everything... even my chance at love because of empty sex. I guess I now know how much ass is enough for nigga...but now it's too late for me...but it's not too late for you...so now what are you gonna do......................

THE END

BONUS CHAPTER

SPECIAL MESSAGE FROM THE AUTHOR

I want to thank you for allowing me to share with you a story I felt I was inspired to give. It has been my pleasure and privilege to write this book and get it into your hands. This experience has brought me nothing but joy and excitement as a writer. I hope I have given you something entertaining as well as something enlighten to your soul. I pray that I have given you that which will make a positive difference in your world.

If I have made a positive difference Praise God for it's his blessings. If I haven't, then maybe next time. Once again thank you for helping to make it happen.

Now that I have expressed my gratitude, I would like to express some of the concerns, I may not have fully addressed in the story.

As I navigate through this world experiencing the elements of life that are common to all men, I have become increasingly concerned about a few things. For starters, I need to know what in the hell is going on between the man and the woman today? Has love become a bad thing? Have we traveled that far away from who we really are and what's important in life? I would hate to think that we are living in a society that doesn't give a *FUCK* (pardon my French) anymore.

Think about it for a second. Where has the love gone? Whatever happened to friendship and family? I know that some of us are afraid to love or feel unworthy of love, but did we kill it? I know we have all been hurt before whether by a parent, sibling, friend, foe, or lover. I'm saying though, is that it? Do we now just give up and become thugs and bitches, in our attempt at "keeping it real"?

Remember the days when we would leave our front door

open all day long? Remember the first time you noticed you had a crush on that cutie? Remember those house parties we used to have, with the red lights, where we would slow dance with that special someone? Remember those days when it was cool to get married and have a baby? Back when mothers and fathers were together. Back when you used to hear your parents getting right in the bedroom at night.

Remember when there was a sense of community among us? Of course you do. I remember most of that and I'm only twenty something. If you sit and really think about it, we have all experienced what a loving environment and community feels like. Regardless of how rich or how poor our environment may have been growing up, we have all experienced love.

I do recognize that times have changed. I know that we are now living in a new millennium, but I thought love never changes. I know that we are living in a technological society, but why have we stopped talking? I'm aware that we are all making more money, but why do so many of us still feel so poor? I walk the streets and see some of the most beautiful faces you will ever see, but why are we acting so ugly towards one another? I'll tell you why. We have stopped loving.

It seems like we care more about, Benz's and Bentley's, designer clothes, and how good we look; more than who we are becoming as men and women, and where we are going as a people. We all need to get our shit together, me, you, and mama and dem`.

I don't think there is anything wrong with wanting to wear designer clothes, rock nice jewelry, or drive a fancy car. My concern is when that becomes your life's focus and reason for being.

Now to my fellas, if your life's focus is just getting a nice ride and some rims so you can front for some materialistic chick, then you really need to get your mind right. It's time to make some mature adjustments. Homeboy, if your life's purpose is getting some ice, a throw back jersey or a stylish button up to wear, just to floss in the club on the weekend, you really need to get serious with it playboy. You're selling your manhood short. (For real, for real)

I understand that the music videos and the music we listen to will have us thinking its all about the "shiny" things. I'll admit it, I like to watch MTV cribs, and "How I'm living" myself. But be clear, that made for TV lifestyle isn't the sum reason of why we live. Anyone who has been thinking for themselves, realizes that there is more to life than accumulating material and luxurious things.

Our culture didn't originate with all of this material and "shallow" bullshit that we are allowing to drive us today. We come from a praying grandmother and a hardworking grandfather that gave their lives so that we could get an education, own homes, run businesses, and do all of the things we are doing today. So many of us need to fall back and respect that which came before us. Unfortunately, many of us have forgotten where we came from. Even in our church, it's about the house, the car, and the money. What in the hell is going on? Where did we go wrong my people?

There is definitely more to life than the bling bling, fat whips, money, clothes, and casual sex that we glamorize as the "life". I purposely used these characters the way I did to show you that it's cool to be educated, rich, powerful and successful. I wanted to show you with real life situations, what happens when our lust gets out of control and what happens when we allow love to take over.

I understand that everybody is trying to get their "freak on" today. And that's okay. My concern isn't sex because it's a beautiful thing. My concern is the HIV that is the number one leading cause of death amongst African Americans ages 24-45. A man and a woman having sex doesn't trouble me. I'm concerned about the unwanted pregnancies that have us running to the abortion clinics killing off our kids, like they aren't our kids. I am also very concerned about the pain and spiritual ramifications that we experience when we ignore certain principles that govern our sexual relations.

Now don't get me wrong, I'm all for having a satisfying sexual experience. I enjoy sex and love making just like the next man, probadly more. So don't think I'm on some "choir boy" shit. In fact, I enjoyed writing many of the sex scenes in this book (ha, ha). But don't get it twisted. Sex without love is half assed and won't satisfy your spirit and soul. You might call me "old fashion", but I like those days when a man and a woman got to know more than each other's first name before they took it there. I actually like the concept of "dating" and conducting ourselves as ladies and gentlemen. I think getting to know someone, finding the things you share in common, and seeing if you are going in the same direction with someone are important before you give them some of that thang.

If I would have lived by this motto from day one, I would've avoided a lot of the difficult situations I went through with females. Now I know all the fake thugs and wannabe "pimps" reading this might think I'm soft... but I'm cool. I know all the Little Kim wannabes might think I'm on some "loverboy" Kenny Latimore shit, for saying I think taking your time is a good thing. But regardless of what they may think, you would have to admit there are too many deadly elements in the "game" to be having casual sex with any and everybody. I don't care if you're using protection or not. You can lose it all out here messing around.

One of my life's objectives is to bring the love back to the forefront again. I want to inspire and see men being men, leaving all of this immature and sucker shit behind us. I want to inspire and see women being women, leaving all of the bitterness and disappointment behind. I think it's time that we all step up and get it together, myself included. If you're one that is tired of all this shallowness and the "bullshit", then take one step inward. Look at yourself and ask yourself three questions.

1. Have I been accepting the "bullshit" of society or have I chosen to live according to my heart's reason?

2. Am I the man/woman that God has made me to be or am I who they (media, history books, religion, culture) say I "should" be?

3. Do I want to take my life and relationships to a higher level?

For those of you that answered "yes" to the last question, I would like to challenge you to recite a short prayer with me...

"Lord show me who you truly are. I'm not asking for a religious dogma or affiliation but a relationship with your Truth and Spirit. I stand here willing to become all that you have created me to be. Make me into the man/█████that you created me to be. With your guidance I will become more than I ever thought possible. Without your guidance and Spirit I'm stuck at becoming what I see. Lord guide me gracefully." Amen

If you have just prayed that prayer, realize that things are changing right this minute. Trust me, you have just stepped into something powerful that will change your thinking and doing. So don't be surprise if you see what happened to the characters in this book (Akil, Yes, and Denali before he was murdered) happen to you.

You are now becoming "that" man and "that" woman. Remember, it's fly to drive a big car, to live in a luxurious house, having more money than you need. Remember it's cool to have a fulfilling sexual life. Just keep in mind that there is more to life. Learn to love yourself and the people around you in the process of getting money, flossin', and buying things.

To my fellas, love your woman and father your children...It will only make you a bigger and better man. To my ladies, respect yourself as a woman and know your true value in this world... It will only make you a bigger and better woman. Now I'm gone and y'all be good.

UNTIL THE NEXT TIME

LOVE YOURSELF & BE YOURSELF

I'LL HOLLA...

251

THANK YOU FOR READING

HERE'S MORE...

Real Book Series
Chapter II

Real Men

Do

Real Things

How Real Men Get Down...

RICH GILMORE

Real Men Do Real Things

- **What happens when the world judges a man by his cover but he's not what is advertised?**
- **What happens when people throw caution to the wind and follow their hearts in love?**
- **What really defines a man?**

…. Well here is an authentic story that answers those questions and tells the real to real about manhood, love, relationships, and life.

Real Men do Real Things is the first provocative tale of its kind. It tells the story of what happens when the "elements" of the "church" meets the reality of the "corner". It reveals the real side of what happens when the cameras and lights go off and a man has to be a man. It shows a woman's perspective in the "transition" of love. This story cuts no corners, it tells the truth about how it "really" is out here in the world and not how it "should" be.

"This story is for any and everyone from the church, to the club, to the street corner. The characters Newman, Cybil, and Isaiah are people who you'll know all too well. I promise that you'll laugh, think, and feel good because of this story"

$13.95

Author's Guarantee
Rich Gilmore

Diva Series Volume I

DIVAGIRL

HOW TO HAVE A GOOD MAN FIND YOU...

RICH GILMORE

DIVAGIRL

Here is a soulful revelation for today's woman dealing with today's man and the "BS" many bring with them. Read DivaGirl and Explore:

- Why men commit to marriage
- Why men need to be "The Man" in a relationship
- The myth of "Mr. Ideal"
- Why "D-Low Brothers" really ain't your problem
- Why "Bitches" and "Ho's" always finish last
  And so, so, so, much more... BELIEVE THAT!!!

No silly dating schemes, No 101 ways, No shallow advice, and absolutely No "GAME PLAYING" here...

"Divagirl will be one, if not the most insightful book you'll ever read about manhood, women, love, life, and relationships. I can assure you the reader that Divagirl will take you through a unique, entertaining, yet very empowering journey into love and life"

Author's Guarantee
RICH GILMORE

$14.95

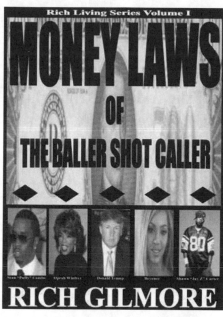

Rich Living Series Volume I

Money Laws

Of

The Baller Shot Caller

$7.95

☐ **Tired of the constant financial struggle?**
☐ **Trying to make a dollar out of fifteen cents?**
☐ **Have you been looking for some financial help?**
Well here it finally is…right in the palm of your hands!

Money Laws is the financial guide for all aspiring Baller Shot Callers. If you're looking to "get money" and take control of your financial destiny, then this is the book for you…GUARANTEED!!!

Read Money Laws and discover the five money laws of every Baller Shot Caller:

Law #1 - Be Money
Law #2 - See Money
Law #3 - Give Money
Law #4 - Expect Money
Law #5 - Associate With Money

LEARN WHAT THE BALLERS KNOW,
DO WHAT THE BALLERS DO

COMING SOON

RICH PUBLICATIONS is committed to being the #1 Urban Publishing Family in the industry. Bringing what's real and relevant to you the reader. We strongly encourage that you support our current & future projects because we are doing it all for YOU.

Upcoming Releases: By Rich Gilmore

Real Book Series Chapter III
"Sex, Money, Drugs, & Consequence" (2005)
The Realist Story Ever Told   *(Part I)*

Real Book Series Chapter IV
"Crazy & Deranged"

Manhood Enpowerment Series Volume I
"Certified Manhood"
Becoming The Man In The Game Of Life

Future Projects

Sex, Money, Drugs, & Consequence (The DVD Documentary)
A RICH FILMS PRODUCTION (2005)

Punaney Galore The Movie
A RICH FILMS PRODUCTION

For more info log onto: **www.richpublications.com**

About the Author

RICH GILMORE (27), Author & Entrepreneur.

Rich Gilmore is the Founder and President of
RICH ENTERPRISES Inc. which is the parent company of
Rich Publications LLC, Rich Films, and Rich Entertainment.

Rich was born and raised in New York City but currently resides in
the Northern New Jersey area with his wife Tanisha.

To contact Rich Gilmore for a book signing, speaking
engagement or special event: Or if you would like to ask
a question and/or make a comment, Email Rich at:

Rich@RichPublications.com

or mail to:
Rich Gilmore
P.O.Box 118
Lyndhurst, NJ 07071
Phone (888) 623-1800 Ext1
Fax (201) 842-0477

MORE

REAL BOOK PUBLISHING

COMING AT YOU SOON

STAY WITH US

WE'RE FOCUSED...

Punaney Galore - The Sexiest Story Ever Told

THE REALIST MAGAZINE FOR TEENS & YOUNG ADULTS

YOUNG Magazine

ISSUE #1 $2.00 U.S. $3.00 CAN.

YOUNG SEXY DANCERS

KOBE BRYANT
RICH...RAPE...REALLY?

IS HE CHEATING ON ME AGAIN?

AND1 Mix Tape:
Real Basketball?

www.richpublications.com

ARE YOU A TRUE PLAYA?

WHAT THE YOUNG PLAYAS & DIVAS ARE READING

www.RICHPUBLICATIONS.com

COME HOLLA AT US

WE ARE DOING IT BIG!